Praise for Shelli Stevens's
Foreign Affair

"Intriguing story, a whirlwind romance that keeps you guessing to the very end... Shelli Stevens has a way of writing that makes you feel as if you are part of the scenery. Wonderfully written."

~ *Sensual Reads*

"*Foreign Affair* is a great story that had me wondering if Lena and Travis could ever get over the overabundance of misunderstandings and get their HEA."

~ *Guilty Pleasures Book Reviews*

"*Foreign Affair* was a delicious story..."

~ *Joyfully Reviewed*

Look for these titles by
Shelli Stevens

Now Available:

Trust and Dare
Theirs to Capture
Four Play

Savage
Savage Hunger
Savage Betrayal

Seattle Steam
Dangerous Grounds
Tempting Adam
Seducing Allie

Chances Are
Anybody but Justin
Luck be Delanie
Protecting Phoebe

Holding Out for a Hero
Going Down
Command and Control
Flash Point

Print Collections
Chances Are
Holding Out for a Hero

Foreign Affair

Shelli Stevens

SAMHAIN
PUBLISHING

Samhain Publishing, Ltd.
11821 Mason Montgomery Road, 4B
Cincinnati, OH 45249
www.samhainpublishing.com

Foreign Affair
Copyright © 2013 by Shelli Stevens
Print ISBN: 978-1-60928-885-3
Digital ISBN: 978-1-60928-557-9

Editing by Tera Kleinfelter
Cover by Scott Carpenter

This book has been previously published and has been revised from its original release.

First Samhain Publishing, Ltd. electronic publication: February 2012
First Samhain Publishing, Ltd. print publication: January 2013

Dedication

Foreign Affair was the very first book I ever wrote, and I'm so thrilled Samhain Publishing has given it a new home. Thank you to all my readers, my family and friends, and anyone who's helped let me live my dream of writing and call it a career.

Chapter One

Lena Richards kept a bright smile pasted on her face as she listened to her obnoxious client ramble on about Aspen. *Be cheerful. Don't let her know you'd like to take a butter knife to those plastic breasts.*

"I want the most exclusive lodge. Not some Travel Channel knockoff deal of the week." Her client tossed her head, but the platinum curls didn't budge. "This is my honeymoon, for Christ's sake."

"Of course." Lena gave an understanding nod. The woman wore enough dead animals to open a postmortem zoo. Beyond her clothing and accessories, nothing about the woman looked real, and she hadn't shut up since she'd entered the travel agency. She was like one of those yakking dolls with a pull string. Only this doll had a rack like a porn star and the personality of a pit bull.

"I don't care what the cost is. I'll make my fiancé put it on his credit card."

"A honeymoon is special. You deserve nothing but the best. Let me find some brochures and information on Aspen for you." Lena's mouth curved into a smile as she opened the file cabinet to her right. "I'm actually getting married mysel—"

"I don't give a damn if it's my honeymoon or my weekend off. There's nothing more appalling than middle-class lodgings." The woman crossed her legs, and her gaze moved over Lena. Her lips thinned in obvious distaste.

What a bitch. Lena's mouth tightened as she searched for

the Aspen folder.

No doubt, she was being written off as some Walmart-shopping Pollyanna from Hicksville.

All right, maybe she didn't own a Louis Vuitton purse, and she didn't own some jacket made up of a dead, skinned animal—not that she'd want to. She worked at an upscale travel boutique. It brought in enough to pay the bills and keep her dressed well, but in no way did it give her an allowance to support a Hollywood wardrobe.

Lena forced her warmest smile. "Give me just a moment, Miss Monroe."

Carolyn Monroe. Fifty bucks said the woman had her name changed legally so she could thrive on a dead woman's fame.

"Ah, here we are." Lena placed the folder on the oak desk that separated them.

As she sifted through for a particular brochure, she noticed Miss Monroe eyeing a box of imported French truffles sitting on Lena's desk.

"Another client brought those in. Please, have one." Lena slid the box toward her.

The woman looked horrified. "I couldn't. Do you realize how much *fat* is in just *one*?"

Yes, have five. Lena smiled and murmured, "I try not to look at the nutrition label on those things."

"Well, you should."

Lena drew in a deep, calming breath and kept the smile on her face. This woman just begged to be slapped. She found the brochure she needed and set it aside, then took out a couple more.

"These are the more exclusive lodges. I might also add that the one on top is famous for celebrity sightings."

As she'd predicted, Miss Monroe's eyes lit up with pleasure, and she snatched the paper from her hand. "I'll look these over and get back to you."

"When is the wedding, if I might ask?"

The woman's lips thinned. Interesting. Had it been because of the question? Or perhaps a little turbulence in the engagement?

"Early summer, I imagine. My fiancé is an architect in New York. We're still working out the relocating bit." Miss Monroe stood, slipping a purse that cost more than Lena made in a week over her shoulder. "Thank you for your help, Leah."

"It's Lena," Lena corrected, but the woman had one foot out the door already.

"Lord, am I sorry you got that one."

Lena glanced up as her coworker, Lakisha, approached.

"Funny, I didn't get that impression when you took off toward the break room when she came in." Lena smiled and then asked, "You think her boobs were real?"

"About as real as my hair." Lakisha pointed to her braided extensions. "Wanna go get some lunch?"

"Thanks, but I'm not hungry. I had one of those drinkable yogurts on the way over."

"Okay, gross." Lakisha shuddered. "That's like drinking curdled milk or something."

Lena winced. "Thank you for that image. I probably won't be having another one anytime soon. I just started on them because Keith is encouraging me to get down to a size six before the wedding."

"Encouraging you?" Lakisha put her hands on her own wide hips and glowered. "Sometimes I think that fiancé of yours has got a few screws loose in his head. You ain't got nothing to be ashamed of, girl. You got curves on that tiny little body of yours."

"Mmm hmm." Lena wasn't about to argue that she had curves. Being five-three and eating fast food once a week did that. Keith had been trying to convert her to rabbit food for years. It wasn't as if she hated it. She just didn't want to eat it *all the time.* She didn't tell him about the occasional fast food she downed, so he had the impression she lived as a devoted health nut.

Lena glanced at the clock. Lord, it was barely noon. Still five hours to go. Pushing down an errant strand of her short, blonde hair, she sighed.

The movement must've drawn Lakisha's gaze, because she frowned and grabbed Lena's hand.

"Where's your ring? Seeing as you two finally set a date and all, you think you'd be flaunting it like crazy now. Is he upgrading to a new one?"

"I'm getting it resized." The engagement had been announced almost three years ago. With all the time that had lapsed, the ring had gotten a little snugger. *Or I've gotten a little fatter.* "I don't think I'd want anything too flashy on my hand anyway. Keith bought it with practicality in mind."

"Now that just sounds like more romance than a gal can handle." Lakisha's tone went dry.

Lena shoved the Aspen file back into the cabinet and frowned. "Romance is overrated. It won't secure your retirement or your kid's college education."

Lakisha stared at her a moment, blinked, and then threw her head back and laughed.

"Good thing you don't believe in romance, Lena, seeing who you're marrying and all."

That comment resonated in her head long after she went

home that night.

"Man, what a day." Lena kicked the door shut and tossed her scarf onto the couch.

When there was no response, she frowned and walked down the hall toward the bedroom. "Keith?"

"In here, babe."

She cringed, tempted to remind him there were better endearments than *babe*. She followed the sound of his voice and wound up in the bathroom. "What in the...uh, what are you doing?"

Keith glanced at her reflection in the mirror and paused, the tweezers frozen midway back to his nose. "What does it look like I'm doing?"

"Well..." She shook her head and averted her eyes, biting her lip to avoid laughing. "Never mind. What did you want to do for dinner?"

"Oh, I already ate. Don't worry about cooking anything." He jerked another hair from his nostril.

She crossed her arms, her irritation level kicking up a notch. "Actually, I wasn't offering to cook. I'll just run down to Dave's Deli and get a salad."

As she turned to leave, Keith dropped the tweezers and reached for her hand, pulling her back into the bathroom.

"That came out all wrong." He wrapped his arms around her waist and pulled her to him, dropping a small kiss on her lips. "I appreciate the offer, and you know I love you."

Lena pried his hands off her and took a step back. Had he always been this dense?

"Of course I do, Keith. I'm sorry I interrupted you."

She snatched her scarf back off the couch and left the

house, shutting the door with as much restraint as she could manage. After climbing back into her car, she sat for a moment, glancing up at the lights of the house.

Keith had balanced himself pretty precariously on her emotional tightrope lately. She'd found herself wondering, more than once, just how she'd ended up here. Going on ten years in an unmarried relationship with a man she'd dated since high school. Who would put up with that? Most women would have ditched him long ago.

With a growl of frustration, she started the engine of her Volkswagen Beetle and backed out of the driveway.

I don't want to ditch him because I'm comfortable with him. There is nothing wrong with our relationship.

There isn't much right with it either, another voice argued. She shook her head to be rid of the contrasting voices and turned her focus on her driving.

The road was deserted, which wasn't unusual for the cozy neighborhood they'd chosen to live in. They'd bought the house a year ago because the buyer's market had been so hot.

Technically they weren't married, but legal documents or not, they might as well have already said the two sealing words.

Despite how perfect things should've been, they seemed to be going through some kind of slump. More sex happened in retirement homes than in her house.

The last time they'd had sex had been terrible. Keith had come home a little frisky one night after having a few beers with the boys from the firm. He'd been the instigator, crawling into bed still dressed and more than a little drunk.

She'd awoken from a deep sleep to feel his tongue ramming into her mouth and his hands pushing up her nightshirt. It had lasted all of two minutes.

Lena shuddered and pushed away the somewhat

distasteful memory. *You can't have it both ways. You can't have passion and fire, and still have a stable, functional relationship.*

Besides, not all the sex between her and Keith was that bad. For the most part it had a nice, pleasant feel. *And predictable*, the challenging voice piped up again.

"Lord, what is wrong with you, Lena?" she snapped aloud to herself. "You are in a mood tonight. You *like* predictable."

Even as she insisted it, she felt the rebellious seeds of denial shouting out in protest.

Keith was the only sexual partner she'd ever had, and sometimes she wondered if that was such a good thing. It hadn't started out the best. They'd begun dating during their senior Homecoming in high school, and she'd lost her virginity to him on their prom night not even six months later.

They hadn't planned to have sex, had thought it better to wait, so there had never been the anticipation of making it a special occasion, perhaps even renting a hotel room or something.

Nope, nothing so grand for her. She—the good girl who had every intention of holding out until marriage—had been deflowered in the back seat of a Toyota in the parking lot at Sears. With Megadeth playing on the CD player and the torn plastic backseat as a makeshift bed, what could have been more romantic?

Lena's head whipped to the right, and she gazed in dismay as she passed Dave's Deli. Damn, she'd intended to stop there. She debated turning around, but then her gaze landed on those familiar golden arches.

Lifting her chin in defiance, she sped the car up. Screw being healthy.

When she returned a half hour later, Keith sat at the

15

kitchen table going over some files. He didn't even glance up.

"I'm sorry if I upset you," he murmured.

Lena, feeling full and greased up from her fast food binge, gave a sweet smile and shrugged as she slipped onto the chair near him. "It's all right. I was a little grumpy from the lack of food."

"Well, I'm glad you got something." He looked up and tapped her nose with his pen. "And you're such a health nut. Just like me. You'll be a size six in no time."

She was not *even* about to go there. "Did anybody call for me today?"

"I don't think so. Wait, no, Stephanie called."

"Steph?" Lena clapped her hands together and lurched to her feet. "She promised to take me to lunch before the wedding plans got too serious."

Keith's lips twisted. "Ah, yes. Lunch with the trust fund baby." Lena ignored the familiar jab at Stephanie's rather large inheritance, grabbed the phone and dialed her best friend's cell number.

"Talk to me."

Lena laughed. "Good Lord, where have you been? You haven't called in at least three weeks."

"Don't be so dramatic, that's *my* job. You know I've been working on that film in the Caribbean."

Lena collapsed onto the plush couch and pulled off her shoes, curling her feet underneath her bottom. "Okay, maybe I did, and I was so insanely jealous that I blocked it out."

The laughter on the other end rang through familiar and sweet. "Yeah, be jealous of me and my lifestyle as a struggling actress. No time off, and only offers for sleazy B movies. What an absolutely thrilling life. Which is why I'm coming to take you to lunch in two days."

"Two days? You'll be back by then?"

"I got back to Seattle last night. I'm exhausted." Stephanie's tone supported her statement. "But I'll take tomorrow to rest, and then on Saturday I'll drive down and we can go."

"Are you sure you don't mind?" Lena massaged her stomach, which had begun to seriously protest its latest meal. *Fast food was the devil.*

"Mind?" Stephanie's voice rose incredulously. "I cannot tell you how much I'm looking forward to this."

"To lunch? With me?" Lena's eyebrows rose. "You must've eaten some bad shrimp down there."

"I'm a vegetarian, you moron. And trust me, this is going to be the best lunch you've ever had. Just think French and dress cute. Anyways, I've gotta do some last minute laundry. Be ready to go on Saturday at noon."

"All right, Steph. Take care of yourself, and, damn it, go get some rest." Lena hung up and turned back to Keith, who appeared to be focusing on his files.

"You look tired." She walked over to him and kneaded his shoulders. "How's work going?"

"It's fine, though far more hours than I'd care to spend defending abusive husbands and drug addicts." He gave an offhanded shrug.

"And flirting with the female clients, I suppose?" she teased and ruffled his hair.

He scowled and gave her a look of disbelief. "Are you kidding? You'd run screaming if you met half my clients."

She'd never cared for the clients whom Keith chose to represent but had supported him as she knew she should.

She kneaded his shoulders harder and was rewarded with

his grunt of approval.

"Mmm, promise you won't stop." His eyelids drooped, and he leaned back against her, resting his head against her breasts.

Encouraged by the sudden attention, and knowing they needed to try and work on the intimacy factor, she leaned forward and let her breath tickle his ear. "I don't have to stop. But why don't we continue this in the bedroom? It'd be a lot more comfortable."

His body tensed, and the breath left his body in a heavy sigh. He leaned forward, and her hands slid off his back and down to her sides.

"I'm sorry," she replied, stung. "I didn't realize the offer was that unappealing."

"It's not like that, Lena." He averted his eyes as he spoke.

"No? What *is* it like, then?" she asked, taking a step back from him and folding her arms across her chest.

"I'm tired. I've had a helluva week." He raised his gaze to her, but she couldn't gauge his emotions.

"Funny, you had a helluva week last week too." She didn't try to hide the sarcasm, just shrugged. "Never mind. I'm going to sleep."

She headed toward their bedroom, wondering if it was possible for one more person to make her feel like an idiot today.

"I'm not sure you should wear that."

Lena glanced up from fastening a black heel strap around her ankle and frowned.

"Wear what?"

"That."

"This? You gave me this sweater for Christmas, Keith." She glanced down at the red cashmere sweater. "What did you want me to do with it? Use it to wash my car?"

"The sweater is fine, Lena." He stepped forward, grabbing the hem of her skirt and pulling it downward. "This shows off too much of your legs."

"You're kidding, right?" Lena blinked. "Jesus, you're not. Did you attend some kind of *make your woman submissive and wear tents* seminar?"

"Of course not." He apparently failed to share her humor. "It's not appropriate to travel in."

"We're driving into Portland, not flying around the world."

"Yes, we are." Stephanie popped through the door with a huge grin. "And don't you look absolutely perfect."

"What?" Lena tilted her head. *What had Stephanie just said?* "I must've heard you wrong."

Keith turned to Stephanie and shook his head. "Of course she can't travel in that outfit. It's almost an eleven-hour flight. There's no way she'll be comfortable."

"Flight?" Lena blurted.

Stephanie rolled her eyes. "Keith, don't be so damn uptight. She looks hot, and you're just worried about some other guy snagging her. Relax, turbo, you've got to trust your woman."

"Uptight?" He jerked backward and snarled, "I am not uptight, and I'll have you know I have all the trust in the world in my fiancée."

"Okay, stop it." Lena threw her arms up between them. "Will somebody please tell me what the hell is going on? Aren't we going to lunch at a French restaurant?"

Stephanie paused and glanced at her, almost in surprise.

"Of course we are. It's in Paris. I thought you figured it out, Lena. I'm taking you to Europe as a pre-wedding gift. The last vacation you'll ever take as a single woman."

Lena's jaw dropped, the word Paris spinning around in her head. "You're taking me to France? Is this a joke?"

"No." Stephanie shook her head. "I asked for some time off from this project. So I want to take a vacation."

Lena stared at her in amazement. "But I can't go to Paris."

"What? You have to," Keith snapped.

"I—I have to work, for one reason...."

"I rearranged your schedule," Keith intervened. "I've known about this for about a month. You've got the next two weeks off. Your work arranged to cover for you."

"You did what?" Lena's eyes widened. "But how? This is so sudden. I'm not even packed."

"Well you'd better hurry up and do it before the limo gets here."

"Limo?"

Stephanie grinned. "I hired one. But we're going to miss our flight if you don't hurry your butt up, so let me help you."

"I can't believe this," she muttered as they finished packing. "Is this really happening?"

"Oh yeah." Stephanie nudged her in the side after tossing another shirt in the case. "This is happening."

Once Lena snapped her suitcase shut, Keith pulled her in for another hug and gave her a quick kiss.

"I wasn't too keen on this whole trip, babe. But we're not married yet, so it's kind of hard for me to say no."

Stephanie rolled her eyes. "You know, you're kind of a control freak, Keith."

"Yeah, and you're kind of a bitch." Keith gave her a hard

smile.

Lena, refusing to get sucked in by their usual bickering, instead grabbed her jacket. "Can you guys at least *try* to get along?"

"Yeah, sure. I'll work on that. Right after we get back from Europe." Stephanie grabbed her arm and ushered her out the door.

A second later Lena found herself stuffed into the back of a shiny limo. And then, as she waved good-bye to Keith and the limo pulled away, it all began to sink in.

"I'm actually going to Paris."

"Yes, you are." Stephanie gave a wicked smile and pulled out a bottle of Dom Perignon. "This is your *get out of jail free* card, Lena. So you'd better get ready. We're celebrating."

"Apparently." Lena accepted the glass of champagne and watched Keith walk back into the house as the limo pulled away.

"And since I'm using my money to fund this trip, I have one condition for you."

"And that is?" Lena would have agreed to anything at this point. *She was going to freaking Europe!*

"There is to be no talk whatsoever about Keith. You are a single woman these next two weeks. Flirt. Have fun. It'll be like a two-week, European bachelorette party."

Lena hesitated. Hell, all she had to do was agree, it didn't mean she'd actually flirt with anyone.

She raised her glass and clinked it into Stephanie's. "You've got a deal."

"Good." Stephanie winked. "And, by the way, speaking of party? We're going to Amsterdam first."

Chapter Two

"Will you please get up? You're sleeping the entire day away."

Lena groaned and pulled the pillow over her head. She may as well have had a hangover for how awful she felt. What a long flight that had been.

"It's not daytime, Steph. It's the middle of the freaking night."

Stephanie spun from the mirror and pounced on her, dragging the blankets off Lena's curled up body. "It is the middle of the night in Portland. We, in case you haven't noticed, are in Amsterdam. *Amsterdam, Lena*. It's ten in the morning here. Now get your ass out of bed before I drag you out."

Lena answered with her face still buried against the pillow. "Can't we just take a couple more hours to sleep?"

"No, we can't sleep. I want to go eat Dutch pancakes and drink wonderful coffee." Stephanie grabbed Lena's leg and jerked her toward the edge of the bed. "Once you have your coffee, you'll feel fine."

Lena pulled her leg back from Stephanie and then sat up on her own.

"Jesus." Stephanie sat back on her heels, her face settling into an expression of wonder. "What did you do to your hair?"

"Don't make me hit you. You know I'm not exactly Mary Poppins in the morning." Lena yawned and patted down the hairs on her head that were sticking straight up. "I'll go shower."

An hour later they strolled down the streets of Amsterdam, careful to avoid the astonishing amount of bicyclists. Cars rarely passed by.

Lena had traded in her pajamas for jeans and a black sweater, with a heavy wool coat to combat the cold. She nursed a latté as they walked the streets of the city. The weather must've been just above freezing. It almost hurt to breathe. Not that she cared. She was in Amsterdam.

Amsterdam.

"This is too amazing. Saying thank you seems somewhat inadequate." Lena glanced at her friend, giving her a big grin. "So where do we go now?"

"This great café." Stephanie stepped to the right and allowed a bicyclist to pass on the left. He smiled, waved, and pedaled on by. Stephanie's gaze followed him down the road. "People are so friendly here. Not to mention hot."

"I don't really look anymore." Lena shrugged and paused to lean over the rail of the bridge they were on. "But this *view* is gorgeous."

The canal shimmered in the muted winter sunlight. Tour boats glided through the icy water. Beyond the canal lay buildings that had probably been around longer than America had been a country.

Lena inhaled the cool air and watched her breath drift upward as she exhaled. "Do you smell that? It smells like aged Gouda..." Her nose scrunched. "And cigarettes."

"Hmm, speaking of..." Stephanie dug into her purse. She emerged a moment later with a pack.

"When did you start smoking?"

"Last film I worked on," Stephanie replied. "I planned on quitting, but then I realized that we were going to Europe, and everybody over here smokes. So I figured, what the hell. I'll quit when I get back."

Lena narrowed her eyes, watching her friend. Stephanie was stunning. Her mother was half-Japanese and half-Caucasian, her father German. Her long, black hair swung halfway down her tall, slender frame while blue, almond-shaped eyes and olive skin made her appear exotic.

"I was here once when the temperature hit below freezing." Stephanie waved her cigarette toward the canal. "That was frozen, and there were kids skating on it. Totally fantastic."

Lena turned her gaze back to the canal and sighed. "Oh, how fun. You know, we should try to go to the Van Gogh museum."

Stephanie crushed out her cigarette. "Sure, but first, let's eat." When they entered the café, Lena gave it a dubious look. Thick smoke hung in the air, and soft music played from a stereo behind the bar. They found a booth near the back and settled in.

Lena removed her sunglasses and grabbed the paper menu off the table, relieved to see it also offered the English translation of the food. "I'm starving. Do you think they're serving lunch yet?"

"Hello, hot guy at the bar," Stephanie whispered, ignoring her question. "And he was showing strong signs of interest when we walked in."

"Now that's a surprise," Lena murmured. "You could draw looks from the blind."

Stephanie raised her eyebrows and smiled at the man, making Lena glad that she had her back to him.

"Okay, he's coming over."

"What?" Lena dropped the menu, her pulse quickening. "Are you nuts? He could be a complete wacko."

"Well, hello, my fellow Americans." The voice, a deep and

sensuous baritone, lifted the minuscule hairs on the back of Lena's neck.

I will not turn and look.

"Oh, now that's too bad." Stephanie pouted. "I was hoping you'd be foreign and not another boring American. Accents are so delicious."

"I'm sorry to disappoint you." He didn't sound apologetic in the least. "Was that an invitation to sit down a second ago?"

"You're a quick one." Stephanie slid over in the booth and made room for him.

Lena saw his backside first as he walked past her. Okay, so he looked good from behind. His hair was brown and cut short, but it had some curl to it. A hunter green crew neck sweater covered thick, broad shoulders and muscular back. Hmm. A possible swimmer? Her gaze traveled down to the solid looking butt tucked into faded jeans.

The front of him would be a big mess. No man could look that good on both sides. He probably had yellow teeth, acne scars and crossed eyes.

He turned around.

Sweet Jesus. This icon of a man could make the statue of David appear to be an overweight nobody. It shouldn't be legal for a man to look this good. Lena's defenses went on red alert, a common reaction when she was confronted with an impossibly good-looking man.

His brown eyes met hers across the table, and he gave her a broad smile, displaying perfect, white teeth. She gave an inaudible harrumph. What, did he promote toothpaste too?

"So where are you from, Mr....?" Stephanie asked as she trailed a manicured nail up his sleeve. She didn't seem near as bothered as Lena by their new friend.

"Bentz," the man replied. "But formality is wasted in a

place like Amsterdam. Call me Tyler. I'm from New York."

"New York?" Stephanie replied. "I love New York. Great shopping. The name's Stephanie, and this is my best friend Lena."

Tyler shook Stephanie's outstretched hand and then turned to Lena, who'd tucked hers back into her lap.

"Nice to meet you, Mr. Bentz." Lena gave an inward groan, wishing she didn't sound so damn stiff.

Tyler cocked an eyebrow and pulled his hand back, keeping his gaze locked on her.

She shifted uncomfortably in her seat, turning her gaze away from the amusement in his brown eyes. The hot body she could ignore, but the steady intensity in him struck a chord in her.

Stephanie grabbed another cigarette and lit up.

"So, where did you say you girls were from?"

"Portland, Oregon. Well, she is. I'm from Seattle." Stephanie blew a stream of smoke into the air and declared, "I think I want a beer. Do you think they sell joints in here?"

Lena's stomach flipped, and she jerked her gaze to her friend. "You're not really going to smoke marijuana, are you?"

"Don't be a prude, Lena." Stephanie rolled her eyes. "I know you took a hit on a joint in high school. And besides, we're in Amsterdam. It's practically expected of you."

"You just had to bring that up," Lena muttered, her cheeks warming. She glanced at Tyler. "I never inhaled."

"Mmm hmm." Stephanie laughed. "You wouldn't believe how defensive she gets about that."

Tyler smiled, glancing down at his menu. "Well, I'm just going to have a Hoegaarden."

"A what?" Lena asked, curious despite herself.

"It's a white beer," he explained. "It's great over here. Make sure you ask for a lemon though."

"Oh. Like a hefeweizen? That's my favorite." *Easy girl, it's just a beer.* She forced a casual shrug. "It's too early for beer, though. I'll just have water."

Stephanie gave her a pensive look. "No beer? What's gotten into you?"

"Nothing. I just don't want to drink some hole garden, or whatever you call it. I'm just here to grab something to eat."

As if on cue, the waitress appeared and took their orders. After she left, Tyler turned back to the women. "So, what brings you two to Amsterdam? Business or pleasure?"

"Hopefully pleasure." Stephanie's voice turned husky. "I've been searching for a way to unwind for the last couple months. And I think I may have found it."

"Oh, Jesus," Lena mumbled under her breath. Stephanie sure didn't waste any time. She'd baited the hook and was trolling the waters.

"And you?" Tyler turned to her. "Pleasure as well?"

"What?" Lena gave him a sharp glance. "I'll have you know I'm en—"

"Lena." Stephanie interrupted her, stopping her before Lena could declare her engagement.

Lena scowled, remembering their deal that they were just two single women on this trip.

"I'm *enjoying* myself on this vacation. Nothing but hotels, tourist traps and lots of pictures. In fact, Steph, remind me to pick up one of those snow globes, will you?"

The other two stared at her, their expressions twisted to show their puzzlement. *Could I sound like more of an idiot?*

Before turning back to Tyler, Stephanie nodded as though

she were beginning to understand what was going on in Lena's head.

"And why are you here? You look too well dressed to be backpacking."

"I did the backpacking scene in college. I'm just here for a few days on business."

"Well, that's too bad." Stephanie pouted. "Although, what a place to mix business with pleasure."

Overkill, Steph. Overkill. Lena's jaw clenched as she slid out of the booth. "I'll be back in a few."

Tyler watched Lena scurry away, noting her perfect backside. *Well, well. Maybe Amsterdam did have its perks.*

He'd begun to regret his decision to take the assignment here. He was bored out of his mind, and it had only been two days. Most of the work had been completed in the first day, and he hated doing the tourist thing by himself. He still had until Tuesday before he was due to fly back to New York.

Maybe, if he could convince her, Lena could help pass some of the time by. She intrigued him. He wanted to spend more time with her. Get her to come out of her shell a bit. Lord knew what he'd find underneath that protective demeanor, but he knew it would be worthwhile to find out.

Stephanie had just finished saying something, and he had no idea what. She didn't seem to be waiting for a response, so he smiled and then asked, "Hey, how long will you two be in Amsterdam?"

Stephanie gave him a suggestive smile. "A week. Why, Mr. New York, you got something in mind?"

Lena returned five minutes later to find her food on the

table and Stephanie sitting all too close to Tyler, laughing at something he'd just said.

"Tyler just invited us both to go out to a bar tonight, and I've said yes," Stephanie informed her. "I know you wanted to check out the nightlife."

"Oh, well, of course I do." Lena's laugh sounded shrill even to her own ears. She couldn't believe this. All she wanted to do was avoid this man, and now Stephanie had set up an entire night out with him?

Stephanie paused with her fork halfway to her lips. "You know there's a reason I went into drama, and you didn't."

"You're an actress?" Tyler asked.

Lena smiled at Stephanie, but inquired her question to Tyler. "Have you ever heard of the movie *Delicate Dreaming*?"

Tyler shrugged, shaking his head no.

"Ah, it was one of her first movies. Indie film." Lena turned back to her sandwich.

Stephanie giggled and set down her fork. "I'm an unknown, struggling actress, and Lena likes to give me a lot of crap about it."

Lena gave a reluctant smile. "No, you give yourself far more crap than I do."

Tyler glanced across the table at her. "You should smile more often."

Lena focused on chewing the bite of food in her mouth before replying, "I'm not sure if that was a compliment or an insult."

His eyes flashed with humor. "You can take it however you want, but I meant it as a compliment."

Lena clenched her teeth as her thumbnail pierced the bread of her sandwich. She refused to let him bait her. She would just shut up and ignore him as they finished their lunch.

"So, what hotel are you staying at?" Stephanie asked Tyler later as they walked out of the café.

He told her the name of a four-star hotel, and Stephanie whistled in approval. Lena remained silent. She knew of the hotel, and knew it to be a very pricey and posh place to stay. The lucky bastard.

"Well then, Tyler..." Stephanie stepped toward him. "We'll see you at nine."

"Sounds good." He didn't avoid the kiss Stephanie planted on his lips. After she pulled away, he turned to Lena as if to see what she might do.

Surprised at his boldness, Lena gave him her best *are-you-kidding-me* look and took a step back from him, folding her arms across her chest.

He laughed and pulled a card out of his pocket. "Here's my card. I wrote my hotel number on the back if you need to get a hold of me before then."

Stephanie took the card from him, and they watched him walk away.

"Well, he could be a lot of fun."

"Fun?" Lena inquired. "Is he just for fun, or is he someone you're really interested in?"

"Interested in?" Stephanie burst out laughing. "Lena, we're in Amsterdam on vacation. I'm not thinking long-term. And I don't have time to be interested in anyone, anyway. I'm just looking for some good, casual sex. Besides, didn't you see the ass on him?"

"Unfortunately," Lena mumbled under her breath and followed her friend across the street.

Lena yawned as she applied mascara to her thin lashes, an unlucky genetic trait from her mother. She blinked at her reflection to help them dry and then set down the wand, turning to where Stephanie was lathering lotion onto her bare legs.

"Do you really think it's a good idea to get involved with Tyler?"

Stephanie shrugged. "Will you drop it already? We're on vacation. I look at it like another thing to indulge in. You have the rich European foods, and I'll have the rich European men."

"Tyler doesn't seem rich, and he isn't European," Lena pointed out.

"I never said it had to be Tyler." Stephanie gave her a curious glance. "Not that I'm vetoing him as a potential."

Lena accepted the response with a mild laugh. "Wow, I wish I could look at sex like that."

"No, you don't." Stephanie straightened and tossed the bottle of lotion onto the bed. "Because you're the good girl, happily engaged to the one man you've ever been to bed with."

Lena shrugged, her stomach tightening at her friend's words because they were a pretty good assessment. "And you think there's something wrong with that?"

"Nothing." Stephanie shrugged. "If that's what you want. I just could never settle for only having experienced one man. I mean, do you have any idea how much good sex you're missing out on?"

"Hey." Lena raised a finger at her friend as she came to sit down beside her. "I have good sex."

"Do you now? That's not the impression I've reached after talking to you in the past few months."

Lena sighed and looked away. "All right. Maybe it hasn't been the best lately. But what do you expect after eight years?"

"I'd expect more than one orgasm a year."

"Well, some women just aren't as prone to orgasms as others."

"Like being prone to allergies? This is an orgasm, Lena. Everyone has the potential to have one. Though, some men need to be handed a map of a woman's body and be given a clue with a capital C." Stephanie went to the closet and browsed through the clothes she'd hung earlier.

Lena didn't respond, a little annoyed because Stephanie's comments had been more than slightly accurate. She went to search her own still-unpacked suitcase for something to wear.

Stephanie plucked a dress off a hanger and turned around. "This will do."

"Wow." Lena shook her head and turned away from the small piece of fabric some might call a dress.

"What should I do with my hair?" Stephanie lifted the heavy weight of it off her shoulders. "Should I put it up?"

"Yeah, that would look good," Lena agreed. "I think I'll leave mine down."

"Cute." Stephanie glanced up, clearly amused. "When did you cut it, anyway?"

"A few months ago. It's actually grown out a lot."

"It's nice, but I like it better long."

"Gotta love your brutal honesty, Steph." She glanced back into the suitcase. "But, for now, why don't you help me decide what articles of clothing to throw on my body?"

"I swear to God, this thong is cutting me in half." Lena resisted the urge to reach down her pants to adjust it.

While Lena had showered, Stephanie had run down to a local boutique to pick up the scrap of black lace.

"You will never, ever convince me to wear one again."

"Hey, in those pants there's no way you could've gotten away with granny panties." Stephanie pushed her shoulder bag higher onto her arm.

"Hmm. And speaking of... I don't know how I even got into these pants." She looked down at the clingy, black pants and the pink V-neck sweater that exposed her expansive cleavage.

"Lena, you look hot. If I swung that way, I'd be all over you." Stephanie's heels clicked in a rhythmic staccato through the darkened streets.

"Thanks, Steph. It means the world to hear you say that."

Stephanie adjusted her breasts inside her bra and gave a broad grin. "You know I'd kill for tits like yours. Mine are barely there, and what you can see are due to a bra that makes you wonder where they went when you take it off." She shrugged. "I just want us to stand out tonight."

Lena once again looked at her friend's outfit, and a shudder ran through her. "I'm sure that won't be a problem."

She wouldn't be caught dead in an animal print dress that stopped just below each butt cheek. Stephanie had taste in clothes that could make a hooker jealous.

Lena spotted Tyler the moment they stepped inside the lobby of his hotel. He waved to them and then made his way over.

He looked good. Even better than at lunch. Lena just about smacked herself when she realized the sensation pulsing through her body could only be described as lust. *So not going to go there.*

"Don't you look nice?" Stephanie purred when they met in the middle of the lobby.

"Thanks." Tyler's eyes were appreciative as he took them in. "You two look fantastic."

Sure, he smiled when he looked at me, but it was Stephanie who got the longer look. Could it be more obvious which one he would rather get into bed?

She ran that thought through her head again and gave a small gag of self-disgust. Who cared if he wanted to get it on with Stephanie? *You are engaged, woman.*

They left the hotel and set off for the walk into town. Tyler told them about a little jazz café he wanted to take them to. They arrived to find the place flooded with locals.

Lena ordered her dinner, surprised to find that Tyler ordered the same thing. They'd picked the Gouda cheese croquet to start and stewed shank of lamb for their entrée.

Stephanie, being the vegetarian, had the terrine with mozzarella, tomato, eggplant and spinach.

"Let me try a bite?" Lena gestured to Stephanie's plate after their food was set in front of them.

Stephanie slid her plate over, and Lena stabbed a bite with her fork, lifting the piece to her lips. She moaned in appreciation and closed her eyes. When she opened them, Tyler's gaze rested on her.

"What? It's good." Her cheeks heated under his amused stare.

He nodded, and his smile widened. "I could tell."

Her stomach flipped again. She tightened her grip on her fork and turned back to her own food. A half hour later they were done with their food and enjoying a beer.

"Who wants dessert?" Tyler asked, taking another sip of beer. "They have a great hot pudding here—"

"Ugh, please no." Lena grimaced, placing a hand against her stomach. "I couldn't eat another bite. This beer is pushing it."

"All right." Tyler glanced out at the dance floor where couples were moving to a fast jazz song. "Well, do you know how to swing dance?"

Lena shrugged and followed his gaze. "I took some lessons on a whim once."

"Really? Maybe we should burn off that food." He raised an eyebrow and stood, offering his hand. "Dance with me, Lena."

He wanted to dance with her? Seriously? Lena's stomach was doing all kinds of aerobics now.

"Dance with you?"

"Yeah go for it. Dance with him." Stephanie nudged her, eyes shining a little too bright.

"I'm really not that good..." Lena protested, but broke off when he pulled her onto the floor.

Any relaxation that had occurred over dinner wiped away the second he touched her. His arm snaked around her waist, and he pulled her entirely too close to his solid chest.

Lena took a deep, steadying breath, trying to calm herself. Instead, she inhaled his spicy, male scent. *If this was temptation, then Tyler must've bathed in it.*

He clasped one of her hands while keeping the other about her waist, leading her as they danced to "In the Mood".

They moved around the dance floor, laughing and weaving between all the couples. The tension eased from her body, and she started to have fun. And the shocker? Tyler could dance.

"You're not bad." She had to raise her voice above the music.

"You were hoping I would be?" His gaze lowered to meet hers. Damn, those eyes again. They were just brown. Why did they have the ability to reduce her to the level of an intimidated, babbling teenager in heat?

35

"No, it's not that. It's just not too often that you find a guy who can dance." She drew a sharp breath in as he dipped her.

"Right." His lips twitched, and his arm tightened around her waist, pulling her upright as the music shifted into a slow ballad.

"I'm really not very comfortable with the slow songs." Lena's voice cracked as his hips pressed tight into hers.

"Relax, Lena. I'll help you through it." His hand traveled down to the small of her back.

His words and voice were hypnotic, and Lena closed her eyes. Every nerve in her body tingled when his fingertips started a light massage at the base of her spine. She caught herself just as she started to press herself against him.

Dear God. She had to get away from this man before she made a complete idiot of herself.

She glanced over at the table and noticed Stephanie speaking somewhat anxiously into her cell phone. She looked up at that moment and gave a tight smile and a thumbs-up sign, gesturing at Tyler.

All right, this little moment with Tyler had to end and now. She'd just have to catch him off guard.

"Okay, here's the deal." She took a deep breath in and then glanced at a point beyond his shoulder. "You're incredibly sexy, and you know it. But I don't feel too great monopolizing you all night. Steph's been lusting after you since this afternoon."

He glanced down at her, his lips twitched in amusement. "Are you saying you're not lusting after me?"

She froze, the air stranded in her lungs. Her plans at shocking him into letting her go backfired, and she couldn't have formed a word if she wanted to.

"Because that really hurts a guy's ego, Lena. Come on. Tell me you haven't thought about me ripping off that pink silk sweater—"

"It's cashmere, and I am *not* interested in you..." Her face burned with a blush. "You're hell-bent on embarrassing me, aren't you? I don't see why you're even making the effort. Go find Stephanie. She wants you, and you want her."

"No, I don't."

"Well, of course you do," she argued in exasperation. "Why wouldn't you want her? She's beautiful. You couldn't take your eyes off her when she walked in."

"Yes, she is beautiful. And I couldn't take my eyes off her *dress*. It's hideous." He laughed and shook his head. "But I'm not interested in her. She's not what I want."

"Oh, really?" Irritation pricked at her, and she tried to step away, but his arms tightened. "And just what is it you want, Tyler?"

"Someone a little less flashy. Subtly attractive, with sexy brown eyes."

"Sexy eyes? Please," she scoffed. "And you sure are particular. Where is this woman? Back in your hotel?"

"Not yet." His hand trailed up her back and closed around the nape of her neck. "But you're welcome to join me later."

Chapter Three

Lena's pulse went into double time, and she watched his gaze lower to her mouth. *Oh, no. He's going to kiss me.* She tried to jerk away, alarmed as his fingers increased their pressure and held her still. His head dipped.

"Lena, we've got a problem." Stephanie swept in like a cyclone, just in time to stop the kiss.

Thank heavens.

Lena succeeded in jerking out of his arms. "I'm so sorry. It's not how it looks."

"She's lying. It's exactly how it looks." Tyler sighed, pushing a hand through his hair.

"What?" Stephanie glanced at them both. "No, not with Tyler. I mean with my work."

"Your work?" Lena blinked away some of the haziness in her head. She folded her arms across her chest. "What about it?"

"Apparently there's an issue with the last few scenes we shot." Stephanie shook her head and groaned. "We need to reshoot."

"Reshoot? Seriously?" Tyler's brows rose.

"Yes. And unfortunately, I have to leave."

"Like the restaurant? Or the country?" Lena blurted in shock.

"The country."

Lena's heart sank. "Oh, God... When? We just got here."

"Tomorrow night." Stephanie raised a hand to her forehead. "This is *so* frustrating. I have to go. I don't have a choice. It's just such crappy timing."

Not wanting to be insensitive to her friend's distress, Lena put a hand on her arm and shook off her own disappointment. "Look, these things happen. We can reschedule this whole trip." Even as she said it, she knew it wouldn't happen.

"What?" Stephanie appeared taken aback. "Of course not. I wouldn't make you do that. You'll stay, of course."

"Stay?" Lena's eyes widened. "No, I can't stay. Not without you."

"Of course you can. Have Tyler show you around while he's not working."

"That's the most insane suggestion I've ever heard." Lena's voice had dropped to almost a whisper. All that time together alone? Such a bad idea.

"Is it really so insane?" Tyler spoke up. "I think it could be fun. I'm only here a few more days, and have a small amount of work left. And I've been bored out of my mind until you ladies showed up."

"It's a bad idea." Lena gave Tyler a pointed look. What the hell was he trying to pull? "If you go, I go, Steph."

Stephanie's stare said she obviously thought Lena had lost it. "We'll discuss this back at the hotel. I need to make some phone calls, and my urge to party is dead." She turned to Tyler. "Thanks for dinner. I hope we'll get to see you again before I leave."

"*We* leave." Lena held her ground.

"Well, hold on." Tyler raised a hand, stalling them. "Why don't we do breakfast and maybe check out a little more of the Red Light District before you guys leave? If you have time, that is."

Stephanie shrugged, looking dejected. "That sounds fine. We've got to eat anyway, might as well have fun doing it."

"Great, meet me at my hotel around ten tomorrow?"

"Fine," Stephanie agreed. "They scheduled me on a red-eye flight tomorrow."

Lena swallowed a groan and gave Tyler a glowering look. Maybe he'd take the clue that she was really not pleased. Lifting her chin, she turned and followed Stephanie.

Tyler skimmed the headlines of the *New York Times*, sitting in one of the plush lobby chairs. He glanced at his watch, checking to see how much longer it would be before the girls arrived. Any time now.

He turned his attention back to the paper, but his thoughts weren't focused entirely on the articles in front of him. They centered on Lena and the feelings that had encompassed him while dancing with her last night.

Maybe he had come on a little strong at the end, but he hadn't been able to stop himself. She was just the sexiest little thing, emphasis on the little. At least a foot shorter than him, and he was six-foot-two.

Maybe it was because she could go from so smart-mouthed to so completely innocent within seconds. She'd nearly fainted when he'd asked her if she lusted after him. He knew they were leaving today, and so he also knew he had to take a chance. Do something to convince her to stay.

He spotted them the moment they entered the lobby, and his gaze trained on Lena. Sexy didn't even begin to describe the outfit she wore, and she probably had no clue of the effect it would have on men. A short, plaid skirt and demure, buttoned-up blouse with that wool coat left open over it.

She must be cold, he thought, as he noted her nipples pressing tight against the shirt. The many ways to warm her up flitted through his head, and he smiled.

Lena watched him watch her. Her heart pounded harder with every step closer to him. Lord, she wished she hadn't worn this outrageous outfit, but something inside her had wanted to look good for him this morning.

How hormonal-college-girl is that? You are such an idiot. You're engaged.

Her legs felt rubbery as she and Stephanie stopped in front of him. She would change the moment they got back to the hotel.

"Good morning, ladies." Tyler folded the paper and stood up with a smile.

"Hi, Tyler." Stephanie glanced past him, her interest obviously lacking from what it had first been when they'd met.

I guess I picked up where Stephanie left off. Lena fidgeted with her hands. She could deny it all she wanted, but this morning she was all too aware of him.

His scent hit her again, as hard as it had last night. For the first time in her life, she found herself wishing for a cold. A cold that would stuff up her nose and take away her sense of smell.

He wore reading glasses, which he tucked away as she watched. And then there was the Cornell University sweatshirt he sported. She averted her gaze from him, willing this short gathering to end as soon as possible.

Tyler set the paper on the table beside him. "Have you ladies thought about where you want to go?"

"I want to have some more fun before I leave," Stephanie replied. "There is a mind-bending little brownie out there with my name on it."

Perfect, now they could separate. Lena forced a regretful smile. "Oh, you know, I won't really enjoy that. Maybe I'll just meet you back at the hotel."

"No, don't do that," Tyler interjected. "If it's really going to be your last day in Amsterdam, you shouldn't spend it in the hotel. Stephanie can go hit her hash bar, and I'll take you around town for an hour or so."

Damn. Couldn't he take a hint? "Oh, that's really not necessary."

Lena shot Stephanie a warning look, which her friend apparently ignored.

"Sounds great. How about I meet you guys in an hour at that café we had lunch at yesterday?"

"It's a plan." Tyler's response cut off any further protests Lena could make.

Lena let out a breath from between her teeth as Stephanie walked away. Fantastic. As if walking around Amsterdam didn't have enough temptation to offer, she'd be strolling along with Mr. Sex on a Stick.

"You look cute." Tyler gave her a quick look.

"Thanks." Lena gave an inward cringe.

Always the cute one. Why couldn't she be the *damn that chick is hot* girl? She made a little groan. Did it matter, at any rate? *You are engaged, Lena. Try to remember that tiny little, massively significant fact.* Somehow it seemed to become harder every minute she was around this guy.

"You weren't thrilled about meeting up for breakfast this morning, were you?"

"I don't know what you mean," she lied. "I'm all right with it. We all gotta eat somewhere."

"You just seem like you're a little...uncomfortable around

me." He guided them toward the river.

"I'm not...it's not..." Lena's cheeks grew hotter from his confrontation, and she cleared her throat. Damn, he was doing it *again*. "That's ridiculous. Why would I feel that way?"

"I don't know. Maybe you're not used to people hitting on you?"

Her head swiveled toward him in surprise. He might have a point, but she had to intention of acknowledging it. "Or maybe I'm not used to people being so vulgar about it."

Tyler laughed. "Vulgar? Oh, sweetheart, if you think that's vulgar, you ought to see—"

"I'd rather not," she interrupted. "And please, lose the sweetheart part. It makes you sound like a redneck or something."

"Right. But I have to warn you, I go by Billy-Bob back home," he drawled with a poor attempt at a southern accent. He smiled when she gave a reluctant laugh. "In any case, I'm glad we get to be alone."

She made to follow him as he crossed the street toward the bridge. "Oh really? Why is that?"

"Because I never got to kiss you last night."

Before she realized what his intention was, he'd grabbed her around the waist and had dragged her body against his.

"Wait." She slammed her hands against his shoulders in panic. "Okay, listen. It's not that I don't want you to kiss me, because I do. Okay? I confess. It's just that there's things you don't know, things that make this whole situation—"

"Do you ever stop talking?" His mouth came down on hers, and she gasped, bringing her hands down to push him away. The moment her palms touched his chest, she got distracted. Damn. Talk about hard.

Her thoughts scattered and her resistance melted on a soft sigh. Lena fell into the light kiss, which was as teasing and addictive as any drug Amsterdam had to offer.

Tyler gave a murmur of approval as she wound her arms around his neck and pressed herself closer to him.

His hand buried into her hair, and he deepened the kiss. Lena moaned and opened her mouth to let his tongue take control of hers. Obviously more than willing, he tightened his grip around her waist and let his other hand reach down to stroke her neck with his strong fingers.

When he let her go, she couldn't catch her breath. She stared at him with wide eyes and touched her fingers to her lips.

"You kiss like the men in the movies."

Tyler gave her a small smile and ran his glance over her again. "I don't think you should fly home tonight. We could have a great time in Amsterdam together."

"Fly home..." The blood drained from her head. "Oh, my God. I'm flying home tonight. Jeez." Guilt sliced through her. Sharp. Heavy. "What am I doing? What am I *doing*? Don't kiss me, okay? We can't do that again."

"Okay. What just happened?" Wariness flickered in his gaze. "Did I miss something? Unless I'm mistaken, that kiss had you as turned on as it did me."

No, he was totally right. Which terrified her.

She sighed and bit her lip. "Don't get me wrong, Tyler. I liked that kiss. I liked it a lot, but I can't do it again."

"I've always felt self-deprivation to be a complete shame. But whatever makes you tick, lady." His stiff shrug revealed some of his irritation as they resumed walking again.

Another twinge of guilt made its way down her spine. She couldn't really blame him. She had become that irritating *yes-I-*

mean-no girl. But jeez, she couldn't afford to be kissing men when she was engaged. Did that count as cheating? Lena gnawed on her lip. Wasn't there that whole out-of-zip-code exception? And surely out of the country must count for something. Should she tell Keith when she got home?

Her guilt grew, eating away in her belly. What was the right thing to do?

The next hour passed in near silence, with only the occasional small talk being made about a tourist attraction they would pass. When the time for them to meet up with Stephanie arrived, she just about wept with relief.

"How's it going, Steph?" Lena gave her friend a strained smile.

Stephanie gave a relaxed nod and a thumbs-up. "It's going very, very well. Can we get some food? I just got really hungry."

Lena readily agreed and gave a silent prayer of thanks that she wasn't alone with Tyler anymore.

"I hope I don't miss my flight." Stephanie threw her clothes into the suitcase at an insane pace. "You shouldn't have let me take that nap."

Lena shrugged. The truth was she'd lost track of time thinking about what had happened between her and Tyler.

"You were tired."

Stephanie scowled. "I still can't believe my shitty luck."

"Yeah, it's a pretty bum deal."

Lena pulled out her own bag. It was a bad turn of events, but it would also be a relief to be put, say, an ocean between herself and Tyler.

"Look, I'm going to take a quick shower. My flight is in

three hours." Stephanie grabbed a clean pair of panties and a more comfortable outfit.

"All right. I'll give Keith a call and let him know I'm going to try and catch a flight out tonight."

"I wish you'd stay." Stephanie stopped at the bathroom door and turned to face her.

Me too. But she couldn't risk a repeat incident with Tyler, and the temptation around him was too great. *Take yourself out of the equation.*

Lena gave her friend a slight smile and shrugged. "Don't worry about it, Steph. Go get your shower."

Stephanie sighed and disappeared into the bathroom, and Lena reached for the phone.

She used her phone card and then waited to be connected. The phone rang and rang, until the voicemail picked up. She scowled and hung up. After a moment's hesitation, she picked it up again and dialed Keith's parents' phone number. A moment later the gentle voice of her future mother-in-law answered.

"Hi, Maggie, it's Lena."

"Oh, hello, Lena." The voice on the other line chirped with animation. "How are you two doing?"

"Great. But I was hoping to talk to Keith. Is he around by any chance?"

Maggie paused. "Lena, have you been drinking?"

Lena gave a short laugh and flipped through the magazine on the table. "Not recently, Maggie. Why do you ask?"

"Well, did you two get in a fight? What's this all about?"

Lena felt the first sense of unease and closed the magazine. "What do you mean?"

"Lena," Maggie hesitated. "Keith told us you two were going to spend a couple weeks in Maui. You left yesterday."

Lena shook her head and frowned. "What? That doesn't make any sense. Maui?"

"Lena, I'm not sure what this is about. Are you two playing a joke on me?" Her future mother-in-law went quiet for a moment. "I saw him off yesterday. He came to say good-bye."

Lena swallowed with a little more difficulty. She reached behind her to sit down on the bed, her knees going weak. "He went to your house before he left for Maui?" *Ask the next question. Ask it.* "Was he alone?"

"No, of course not. You were in the car," Maggie said, clearly exasperated. "You had a headache and didn't want to come in."

Lena closed her eyes against the roar in her head, and it took moment before she could speak again. "I wasn't in the car, Maggie."

"Of course you were, Lena. I saw you."

Lena's hand closed over her mouth. She wasn't hearing this. This just couldn't happening. Damn it, they were *engaged.*

"You saw me? *Me*, Maggie? Or could it have been another woman?"

Another long, awkward silence.

"But I saw blonde hair...and he said it was you." Maggie hesitated, and then almost in a panic she asked, "What are you saying, Lena?"

"Maggie, I'm in Amsterdam. I can't be in Maui and Amsterdam at the same time. So what am I saying? I'll let you figure it out."

Chapter Four

When Stephanie came out of the bathroom, Lena had curled up on her side on the bed.

"Ummm, Lena? What's going on?" Stephanie sat down next to her and touched her shoulder.

Lena didn't look up, her face smashed against the pillow, eyes unblinking as she stared across the room. The anger grew thick in her throat, and she had to force the words out. "Keith is cheating on me."

Stephanie stayed silent for a second and then a short burst of laughter. "What? Of course he's not. Keith? That boy is as straight and narrow as they come."

Lena rolled onto her back. "Well, Mr. Straight-and-Narrow is in Maui right now screwing some other woman."

Stephanie shook her head. "How did you figure that out?"

"His mom told me." Lena sat up and hugged her knees, a harsh laugh escaping her. "His mom had a complete breakdown when she realized she'd unintentionally informed me that her son was cheating on me."

"I can't believe it," Stephanie repeated, her voice growing with rage. "What an ass. What a dumb-ass prick."

"I can think of better things to call him." Memories of this afternoon floated through her head. "I don't know...maybe its karma. I cheated on him too."

"Excuse me?" Stephanie's head swiveled back to her, and her eyebrows rose. "You cheated on Keith? Bullshit. When?"

"Earlier today."

"What? But you were with Tyler and me all morning." Her eyes widened. "*Shut up.* What happened in that hour alone together? Did you guys have sex?"

"*Sex*? Are you kidding me? Of course we didn't." Lena paused to bite her lip. "But we did kiss."

"You kissed." Stephanie's expression dimmed and her lips curled downward. "That's it?"

"Yeah." Lena touched her mouth, which started to tingle as she remembered the kiss. "And it was absolutely amazing. So romance novel cliché. I say no, and he still kisses me, and damned if I didn't enjoy it." She shook her head. "But it was *wrong*. It shouldn't have happened."

"And you consider that cheating?"

"Well, yeah, I suppose."

"It doesn't even compare. Kissing a guy is like breaking a nail to me." Stephanie flung her hands up in the air. "It happens all the time. And for the record, you know I've always thought Keith was a complete idiot."

Lena pulled herself off the bed and walked to the mirror hanging above the dresser. She stared at her reflection—her pale appearance. What the hell was Keith *thinking*?

The fury that had been simmering inside her boiled over. She closed her hands around a hairbrush on the dresser and threw it across the room.

"You know what, Steph? Besides that kiss, I've never once cheated on him. And I've wanted to. I've had opportunities, but did I? No. Because we were in a *committed* relationship. Doesn't that mean anything to anyone anymore?"

Stephanie stood up and walked over to her. "Of course you didn't cheat on him. You're too good for him. I've been telling you this all along, but you just didn't get it."

Lena moved to the sink to splash some cold water on her face. She wanted to slam her fist through the mirror.

"Look...something's bothering me here, Lena." Stephanie began in a cautious tone. "You're very angry, and have every right to be, but you're not crying. You don't seem very...heartbroken."

Of course she was. Wasn't she? Lena braced her palms on the sink and stared down the drain. Or maybe Stephanie was onto something. Why wasn't her heart cracking into a billion little pieces? She didn't want to acknowledge the possibility out loud.

She shook her head and averted her gaze. "The tears will come later, I'm sure." But would they?

"So what are you going to do? Do you want to go back home?"

"Not with Mr. Happy Pants away getting laid in Hawaii." Lena dragged a damp towel down her face and then met Stephanie's gaze in the mirror. "So what *am* I going to do? Besides get really drunk, because, *hello,* that's a given."

Stephanie came up behind her and placed comforting hands on her shoulders. They stared at each other in the mirror. "You're going to go to Paris and stay at the apartment I've rented."

"I couldn't do that." Could she? The idea of retreating to Paris to lick her wounds had appeal.

"Of course you can. And you will."

"Will I now?" Though it would be good to get away and think. Or *not* think about a certain bastard fiancé.

"Yes, you are." Stephanie suddenly grinned. "And you're going to have Tyler take you all over Amsterdam for the next few days before you leave."

"Tyler is going to show me around? You think I should have

Tyler show me around?" Lena started to laugh and then faltered. *Oh. Now there was an idea...* "I think I just made up my mind what I'm going to do."

Stephanie nodded. "Oh, now see, there you go. That sounds positive. What are you going to do?"

"Maybe I shouldn't say what I'm going to do, but *who* I'm going to do." Lena folded her arms across her chest. "Tyler."

Stephanie choked, and her eyes widened. "I don't think I heard you right. Did you just tell me you're going to *do* Tyler?"

Lena turned around, determination pumping through her blood. "If my fiancé thinks he's the only one who's going to have a last-minute fling before the wedding, then he's an idiot. I'm going out, and I'm getting laid."

"What are you already drunk?" Stephanie exploded. "Lena, don't tell me you're still going to marry him."

Lena blinked, taken aback. Cancel the wedding? The thought hadn't even occurred to her. "I don't know. Maybe we could go to counseling. This could be our seven-year itch thing. We're way too invested to just call it off, don't you think? But first..." She gave a slight smile. "Maybe I should have some fun. If he can do it, so can I."

"I don't think you have the slightest idea how fucked up that sounds. But let's focus on the other point for now. Tyler." Stephanie shook her head, seeming to choose her words with consideration. "Hon, you're not exactly the type to just go in for casual sex. I mean, you've only ever been with one person."

"And, hey, maybe that's my mistake. I've been sheltered my entire life by trusting the only man I've been intimate with. Maybe this is my opportunity to try someone else on for size. Sure, the circumstances aren't exactly ideal—"

"You want to try Tyler on for size?"

"Yes. No, that's not what I mean. Crap, can we not overanalyze this? Please, Stephanie..." Lena's determination wavered a bit with her best friend showing such disapproval. "Okay, I get that you're not going to give me the thumbs-up on this decision, but could you at least pretend it's a good idea?"

"I just don't want you to get hurt."

Lena gave a slight smile. "That's pretty much the trade phrase for the best friend. So let me answer that with another familiar line. I'm a big girl, Steph. I think this is something I need to do. Besides, you're not the only one who's been fantasizing about riding the Tyler-go-round."

Stephanie's lips twitched, and then she smiled. "Well, then have a good time. Go get a piece, and don't think about Keith for the rest of the week. I know you're on the pill, but you'd better use a condom too."

"I will, I promise. I'm only going to stay in Europe a couple more days. I don't want to go to Paris alone. I just want to experience a little more Amsterdam, and a little more Tyler." She knew her next words were a total lie. "And please, don't worry about me. I know what I'm doing."

Lena walked through the streets of Amsterdam, her mind fighting a fierce battle on whether to stick to her morals or trash them in the nearest dumpster. Sure, she'd talked the talk with Stephanie, but now, with her fury fizzling, and currently on her way over to Tyler's hotel room...

Yes, Keith was cheating on her, but did that make it acceptable to go out and do the same to him? An eye for an eye. A lover for a lover. She shivered and wished she'd remembered to grab her jacket.

Kissing Tyler had been like peeking behind a door that had always been locked. The one with the big *Keep Out* sign hanging outside. She'd opened the door and, damn it, why shouldn't she go in?

It had been amazing, that kiss. It had made her think things she'd never thought. Feel things she'd never felt. He'd made her want to rip off both of their clothes and go at it like porn stars. And Lena Richards never had porn-star-like thoughts. More like Mary Poppins and Mr. Rogers getting it on thoughts. This feeling with Tyler was pure, unfiltered lust.

And if used with caution it should cause no long-term damage and therefore wouldn't be such a bad thing, Lena added her own silent disclaimer.

Her resolution came back full force. She would do this, but she wouldn't tell Tyler about Keith. As far as Tyler, he would just believe her to be a woman taking a vacation who decided to have some fun. Knowing about Keith would be immaterial to him and to their situation.

Besides, if she told him and he got all weird about it, then it would just be embarrassing.

This is a good idea. She took a deep breath and quickened her stride, trying to recall the last time she'd shaved her legs.

Tyler flipped open his laptop and logged into his email. His interest in Lena had hit a roadblock, seeing as she was on a flight over the Atlantic right now. Disappointment clawed at his belly, but he swallowed it, not wanting to linger on the emotion. It didn't do an ounce of good to wallow in what might have been.

He adjusted the hotel robe and tried to focus on work stuff, but his thoughts were still on the kiss from this afternoon. The way her body had melted into his while his mouth had explored hers. Damn, she'd tasted sweet.

He shook his head to clear the image. "You're a fucking

sap, Tyler. It didn't happen, so get over it."

As he opened an email from his boss, a knock sounded on the door.

Who the hell...? His brows drew together, and he shut the laptop. He slid off the bed and made his way toward the door.

He took a deep breath and peeked through the peephole. The blood in his head rushed south, and he blinked. Well, would you look at that? His lips curved into a smile as he opened the door.

She stood before him in that same sexy, schoolgirl-like outfit she'd worn this morning. He couldn't read her expression, but she twisted her hands in front of her, looking adorably nervous.

Tyler took a breath in, restraining the urge to rip open all the buttons on that demure white blouse.

"Hi," she said softly.

"I thought for sure you'd be on a plane tonight." He smiled, leaning against the doorframe and hoping his instincts were right. "What changed your mind?"

Lena stared at him, her gaze boring into his. For a moment she could have sworn she heard the music to "Let's Get It On" in her head.

She'd done it. She was actually here in Tyler's hotel room. And, damn, he looked good. Even though her wore a fluffy hotel robe, she could see the hard muscles of his chest and smattering of hair.

"Lena?" He straightened up a bit, and his brows drew together. "Hang on. You don't look so good. Are you okay? Why don't you come in?"

She stepped through the door and past him, but didn't

trust herself to speak. She kept her back to him and went outside on the balcony, taking a moment to look down at the city below. The air hit cold against her lungs, but she didn't mind too much.

"Answer me. What's wrong?" He came up behind her and placed a gentle hand on her shoulder.

His touch ignited her already simmering desire for him. If she didn't do this now, she'd chicken out. She took a deep breath and spun around, grabbing his robe and jerking him to her.

"Easy—" He broke off when she grabbed his head and stood on her tiptoes, pulling his mouth down to hers.

Her tongue plowed between his lips and came up against his. His body went rigid, and for a moment she wondered if he'd push her away. Then his hands settled against her waist, and he backed her up against the guardrail.

She stroked her tongue over his, pulling open his robe and running her fingers through his chest hair.

He gave an approving laugh and pulled his mouth away from hers. Lena groaned as his lips settled against the wild pulse in the curve of her neck.

Keep the control. If he takes control, you'll be emotionally vulnerable.

She squirmed away and pushed him back from her, moving forward so he had no choice but to back up into the room.

"I'm sorry." He frowned. "If this is moving too fast for you—"

When the back of his knees encountered the bed, she tackled him, knocking him backward onto the mattress. She reached out a hand and slid it into his boxers, wrapping it around a—*oh my*—pretty damn big erection.

Tyler's eyes closed, and his loud groan sent a tremble of excitement through her. Keith had never given such an intense reaction to her touch.

"Hang on, Lena." He shook his head as he held her away from him, giving her a suspicious glance. "This morning you were pretty adamant that we shouldn't even have kissed. Now... What's going on?"

Lena froze, and heat flooded her cheeks. "What's going on? I would think it's pretty obvious—"

"Well, yeah, it is." He moved away from her. "But I just don't want you to rush into anything you're going to regret."

Nearly two feet of space separated them now, and his gaze roamed over her, but she saw wariness in his eyes as well.

"Lena, I like you. Enough that I don't want to feel like an asshole in the morning for taking advantage of you. Are you sure you want to do this?"

Argh. Could he make this fling thing any more complex?

"I'll be blunt. I am *trying* to seduce you here. I am a woman who is blatantly throwing herself at you. There shouldn't even be an issue. So are you going to sleep with me, or do I have to find someone else who will?"

He blinked. "Are you drunk?"

Oh for the love of... "Why does everyone keep asking me that?" All the doubts came rushing back. *Bad idea, Lena. You should have known it from the start.*

"You know, forget it. I wanted you and had the crazy notion you wouldn't mind getting me into bed, but apparently I was wrong."

She'd almost made it to the door when he grabbed her by the waist and spun her around.

"Oh, I want you all right," he said, his voice low and thick. He lifted her so her legs wrapped around his waist. "I just had to make sure you knew what you were doing."

Chapter Five

Tyler's mouth came down on hers again as he pushed her back against the door. He gripped the edges of her shirt and ripped it from her body, sending buttons flying. The bra he struggled with for a second before successfully unclasping it in the back.

His mouth closed over one nipple, and she cried out, the sensation so intense it sent her senses spinning. He squeezed her ass and continued to suck on the sensitive tip of her breast while moving them toward the bed. At one point he tripped over his suitcase in the journey.

Lena laughed and wove her fingers into his hair when he cursed. She pulled his head back up and pressed her lips to his, opening her mouth to him. His tongue entered, and she groaned as the heat building inside her turned up another notch.

A moment later the air rushed from her lungs as he dropped her onto the bed. She stared up at him, blood pumping through her body and moisture pooling between her thighs.

His lips curved into a sexy little smile as he unfastened her skirt while holding her gaze. He pulled the fabric down her hips and over her legs, then drew his hand down her belly to cup the mound of her sex. Pleasure shot through every nerve in her body, and she lifted her hips with a stunned cry.

She'd been deprived of pleasure—of passion—for too long. Maybe she'd never had it.

This was crazy. Wonderful. Crazy wonderful.

He released her, and she groaned in protest at the loss of his touch. He gave a soft laugh and removed her nylons and shoes.

When he had both shoes off, his mouth closed over her big toe.

Lena giggled, exhilarated, and tried to pull her foot away. "Hey, no toe sucking."

Tyler glanced up at her and raised his eyebrows as his tongue slid over the arch of her foot.

"Oh, well, I suppose that's not too bad." she murmured, a bit breathless now.

He set her foot down and kissed his way up her leg.

Her breath locked in her throat. Dizziness assailed her as she realized where his mouth headed. *Oh, wow.* Keith didn't do oral sex. Didn't consider it *sanitary*. Unless, of course, he was on the receiving end.

Her thoughts trailed off when she realized he'd stopped. He seemed to be analyzing something. She glanced down to look at him.

Shit. She'd forgotten all about *that*.

Tyler paused and looked up at her, his eyebrows raised in question. Lena blushed, knowing what he would ask.

"I tried to shave it into a heart last week, but I guess it didn't turn out so well. I know. It sort of looks like a freakish bunny thing, but I... God, I'm just going to shut up now."

"You're adorable." His smile grew, and he leaned down to kiss her artistic attempt.

She started to argue, but then his mouth moved south of the distorted heart, and she lost all ability to think.

His tongue slid into the folds of her sex, and she gasped, clutching the pillow above her. He moved upward to flick against her clit, his hot breath and moist tongue drawing a ragged moan from her.

"Tyler." She gasped and tried to move away, the pleasure growing almost too intense.

He gripped her hips and held her still, continuing to circle her clit. Again and again, until the pleasure spiraled through her and exploded.

The orgasm shook her, robbed her of the ability to breathe, and made every inch of her body shake.

Her pulse slowed again, even as he continued to rain kisses over her thighs. She shook her head and let out an unsteady exhale. *And I thought oral sex wasn't necessary?*

"Damn," she mumbled, staring at the ceiling. "I've never... Wow..."

"We're not done." He pulled himself back up and grabbed a condom from his wallet on the nightstand. Lena let her fingers glide through his hair as he rolled it on.

A moment later, he tried to move over her, but she resisted and pushed him back onto the bed. His surprise and pleasure was evident as she straddled his thighs.

"Please," she murmured. "Let me try it this way."

She pushed herself down onto him nice and slow, letting his thickness stretch her out, even as he kept sinking into her. The man was huge.

"Lena. God, woman, you're tight." He groaned, and his hips lifted, bringing him deeper inside her.

She closed her eyes and bit her lip to avoid saying, *lack of sex does that to you.* Oh, it felt so good to have a man inside her. The knowledge that he wanted to be there, that he desired her, was all the more thrilling.

"Ride me," he murmured and lifted his hands to her

breasts, squeezing them and brushing his thumbs over the tips.

Lena rocked her hips, getting a feel for the movement. Top wasn't a position she'd often been allowed, and damn it if she didn't intend to make up for lost time.

She quickened her movements, circling her hips and moving up and down on his shaft.

"Yes." The word hissed out of his mouth. His eyes closed, and he pinched her nipples.

Her breath came out in short gasps the harder and faster she moved on him. With his hands working her breasts, the pleasure built again, only faster this time.

She bit her lip and ground down on him, her hands flat against his chest as her body trembled through a second orgasm. Her nipples tightened against his hands, and the walls of her sex clenched around him.

"*Tyler.*" She cried out his name, riding the waves that ripped through her body.

He took over, sliding his hands to her hips and thrusting upward into her. Faster and harder until he groaned. His own body went rigid beneath her, and his eyes squeezed tight.

The room went quiet. Only the sounds of their heavy breathing. She slid off him, a silly little smile on her face. *So that's what good sex is about?*

A yawn popped her jaw, and she rolled onto her back. Should she leave? Maybe he didn't like a woman to spend the night. Hell, she had no idea of the norm.

"Come here." He slid an arm around her waist and tugged her down next to him. "Let's get some sleep."

What a relief. The idea of hiking back to her own hotel in the middle of the night sounded like a rotten plan.

She yawned again and snuggled into his embrace. This part

was nice too. Really nice...

Lena groaned and turned her face away from the glaring light. She rolled over and encountered a solid chest, and then an arm slid around her body.

Her eyelids flittered open, and she looked up into Tyler's face.

"Hey there," he murmured, a drowsy half smile on his face.

The first sense of embarrassment washed over her. She lowered her gaze. "Good morning."

This must be the hard part. How in the hell had she forgotten to consider the morning after?

"Don't do that." He reached out and touched her face. "Don't get shy on me. Last night was incredible."

She tucked her head against his chest and slid an arm around his waist.

"I'm not shy." She hoped she sounded more confident than she felt. "I just...I just have never really done something like this."

He tilted her chin up and pressed a soft kiss against her lips.

Tingles raced through her body, and a shiver moved down her spine. Lifting his head, he murmured, "It's Monday morning. I have some work to do today, but it should only take a few hours. Will you spend the day with me?"

Her pulse kicked up a notch at his words. He wanted to spend more time with her. "That would be great."

"Good." He brushed the hair off her face and dropped a kiss on her forehead. "I need to take a shower."

He lifted himself out of bed, and disappointment settled in her stomach. *He doesn't have time for morning sex. Get over it.*

"All right. Have fun in there." She gave him a small smile. Should she just leave now?

"I plan on it." His gaze ran over her, lingering on her lips. "Because you're joining me."

Or maybe he does have time.

"You didn't think I was going to shower alone, did you?" He raised his arms over his head and stretched.

Her gaze drifted over his hard abdomen and broad shoulders. The image of that body wet in the shower sent heat straight between her legs. She swallowed hard.

"Hmm. I guess showering together could be fun."

"Lena, you have no idea." He scooped her up and carried her into the bathroom.

Lena languished around the hotel room, spending the alone time watching television shows in a language she couldn't understand. At one point she called the airlines to change her plane ticket so she could fly out in the morning.

Two hours passed before Tyler returned as promised and took them out for a late breakfast.

They sat in a café and drank espresso, looking out at the rain falling soft on the quiet streets of Amsterdam. The only other people in the café were a couple speaking in soft tones who would, every once in a while, give a burst of laughter.

Tyler turned his gaze to her. "I'm so glad you didn't get on that plane. I hate sightseeing alone."

"You're glad I stayed for the sightseeing?" she teased.

"Well, and other reasons." He grinned. "Is this your first time to Europe?"

Lena nodded and stabbed another bite of pancake before

lifting it to her mouth. Keith hadn't been into traveling, thought it a waste of money. Which was the reason she lived vicariously through the travel boutique.

Tyler leaned forward and traced the pad of his thumb over her lip. "You had some powdered sugar on your mouth."

Feeling bold, she raised an eyebrow and then used her tongue to draw his thumb into her mouth. His eyes darkened, and she met his heated glance with an open invitation. After a moment he pulled his hand away and cleared his throat.

"So you never did say what made you change your mind."

"About?"

"About sleeping with me."

Her sultry smile faded and reality rushed back to meet her.

Don't tell him about Keith. Remember your vow. Not to mention it could just make things a little uncomfortable.

She took a deep breath and shrugged. "Does it really matter? The point is that I did. And now we're here."

"I was just curious." He took a bite of his own breakfast. "You made it pretty clear yesterday that you had no intention of hooking up with me."

"Well, I changed my mind." Her throat tightened. "But I mean, you got laid. Isn't that what every guy wants? Especially on vacation?"

His brows drew together, and she winced. *Maybe that had been a little harsh.*

"I'm on business, not vacation. Who turned you into such a cynic?" He took another sip of coffee. "And did it ever occur to you that I'm not like every other guy?"

"Okay, fine." She shrugged. "So, you're going to tell me you weren't thinking about how to get into my pants the other night?"

He faltered, and a flush of red appeared at his neck. "Well...I—"

"And there's my point." She sighed. She didn't want to do this, but it had to be done. Time to lay down the law.

Putting her hands on his, she leaned forward and met his gaze. "Tyler, maybe I should just let you know exactly what I'm looking for."

He shrugged. "Fair enough."

"I want to have a great time seeing Amsterdam. I want to spend this time with someone I'm going to have fun with. And I want to keep having some mind-blowing sex."

Tyler's lips curved into a cocky smile. "Mind-blowing, huh?"

"Yes. And don't get a big head over that." She rolled her eyes. "Now let me tell you what I *don't* want. I don't want this to get too personal. Don't bother telling me what your sign is or if you have a massive family back home, or how many kids you want some day."

Tyler's stare turned thoughtful as she laid out the rules. His lips pursed, and she found her gaze drawn to them. *Jeez, he has the sexiest mouth.*

She cleared her throat. "I realize this may sound a bit cold, but I figure the less I know about you, the easier it will be to keep my emotions out of this."

He gave a slow nod. "Women do get attached quicker. It's a valid point."

"I thought so."

"So you want sex?" He leaned back in his chair.

"Yes."

"Nothing but good, hard sex?"

"I didn't say it has to be hard."

"Okay."

"Was that a yes?" She held her breath. Part of her had been convinced he would tell her to shove her rules where the sun didn't shine.

"It wasn't no."

"So, yes?"

He took her hand and flipped it, raised it to his lips, and kissed her palm. "As you said, I'm an average guy. I think a little vacation fling could mean a good time for both of us."

Lena's stomach twisted into knots at the brush of his lips, and she bit back a groan. "Fantastic. Are you ready to go back to the hotel?"

"No." He stood up, his hand still clasping hers. "We're in Amsterdam. We're going to do a little more than have good sex."

Damn it. "Okay. What are we going to do?"

"Go sightseeing."

They rented bikes and spent the day touring the city. Lena ended up lagging behind him many times, which only compounded her theory that he must be some kind of athlete. Though, she didn't mind bringing up the rear. It gave her plenty of opportunity to stare at Tyler's.

They went to the Waterlooplein Market, an open-air flea market, where she had to resist the urge to buy everything and anything. Then they visited a clog shop, where she did relax with her money enough to buy a pair of the trademark wooden shoes.

During a tour of Anne Frank's house, their mood turned somber while they reflected on the girl who'd written the diary that touched so many hearts. Tyler held her hand, keeping silent when her eyes filled with tears.

Later, they spent sunset walking the streets and talking to

people, really just getting a feel for the city. When early evening arrived, they stopped to find a restaurant for dinner. They settled on a little Italian place after seeing the candles flickering through the windows of the restaurant.

"Amsterdam isn't famous for their wine, more so the beer," Tyler murmured after the waitress left.

Lena grinned. "I don't mind wine every now and then, but I'm much more of a beer girl."

"Really?" His gaze turned pensive. "It's a good thing we've only got two days together. Otherwise I could fall for you."

She bit her lip, ignoring the flutters his comment caused in her stomach. It was all just flattery of course.

She grabbed one of the warm breadsticks that had just been delivered to their table. "Two days. So you got all your work done in only three days?"

"No, I was here before you and Stephanie arrived. I've been working my butt off to get a branch of our office set up here. I basically attended a bunch of meetings and did a lot of paperwork—which I finished the last of this morning."

"Sounds fun." She nibbled on the parmesan-covered bread. "What kind of work do you do?"

His gaze didn't leave her mouth as he answered, "I can't answer that, remember? Too personal."

Crap. She winced and gave a small shake of her head. "Am I a hypocrite or what? I'm sorry. I forgot."

He winked. "Just don't let it happen again."

The dinner arrived then, and the conversation went quiet as they dug into their food.

Tyler twirled his fork through his pasta and lifted it to her mouth. After a slight hesitation, she parted her lips and closed her teeth around the fork. A second later she closed her eyes and groaned in satisfaction.

After swallowing the bite she murmured, "Wow. That is delicious."

Keith never indulged in such romantic notions like feeding her food and, wow, had she missed out. Sort of like *Lady and the Tramp*, only a whole lot sexier.

"Did Stephanie catch a flight out last night?"

"She did. And she wasn't very happy either. Especially after she heard I would be going after you."

"Jealous?" His mouth curled into a smile.

"No, I wouldn't say that. She was worried about me." Lena grimaced. "Sorry, Tyler, but in Stephanie's world you would have just been a tally in her diary."

"Ouch."

She laughed. "So, do you want dessert?"

"Yes. Lena *a la* mode."

His words made her hand jerk, and a loosely anchored tortellini flew off her fork and across the table. Tyler raised an eyebrow at her as he retrieved the lone pasta.

Her cheeks warmed. She was more than a little excited by his sensual teasing.

She licked her lips and met his gaze. "Then you'd better hurry up and finish your dinner."

Tyler opened his eyes, the sleep in his body ebbing away. The memory of last night and the passionate sex after their dinner still lingered. He smiled, rolling over and reaching for Lena. The bed was empty.

He jerked upright and looked around the room. Empty. Had she left? The thought had just crossed his mind when he heard the shower running.

He leaned back against the pillows, annoyed at the sense of relief. She would leave today. He'd known that. His sexy little fling was leaving, and soon their time together would become just a memory.

He'd understood what she'd wanted, had been more than happy to comply with her demands. But, damn it, he hadn't expected the time to go by so fast. He scowled. Funny how she'd been the one worried about getting attached.

The shower stopped and a moment later the bathroom door opened as she emerged with the cloud of steam.

Her hair was slick against her head, a towel tucked around her tempting curves. She gave him a tentative smile, as if she might be sharing some of the same emotions.

"Hi. You woke up."

"Yeah. So what time do you have to leave?"

"My flight is at three." She adjusted her towel and went to pull a pair of panties from her suitcase.

"That gives us just enough time to go for a boat ride in the canal. You up for one?" He surprised himself by the suggestion, but he couldn't send her away just yet. Everything within him told him to delay it for as long as possible.

She gave a quick nod, her relief obvious. "Right. I can't leave Amsterdam without a ride on the canal. Let me just dry my hair and get dressed."

He climbed out of the bed. "I'll just grab a quick shower first."

They walked along the river but didn't touch each other. Lena sighed, wondering if he had the same motives she did for keeping their distance. She thought it would be less painful if they eased their way into letting go.

Winter being the off-season in Amsterdam, the boat they climbed into was empty, save for the driver. Lena settled into her seat and found herself tucked up next to Tyler.

The man who piloted the boat glanced back at them with a grin before pulling it into the middle of the river.

"I am Hans. You are Americans, no?"

Lena smiled. "Yes, we are. I'm Lena, and this is Tyler."

"I am pleased to meet you both." Hans guided the boat under a bridge and nodded. "You are beautiful lovers. You will be married soon?"

Lena choked, and Tyler gave her an amused glance, taking her hand into his.

"No marriage plans yet," he said.

Lena gave him a sharp glance, relieved when he winked. "I've been trying to talk her into it for months now, but she's a stubborn girl."

The tension eased from her body. To indulge the romantic guide, she'd play along.

"I'd marry him, but he snores terribly, and his feet smell like dead fish."

The guide laughed and muttered something in Dutch.

Tyler turned to her. "Do my feet really smell?"

"Well, you haven't seen me licking *your* feet, have you?" she teased.

He scowled. "I'm calling bullshit. And I do *not* snore."

She giggled and relaxed a little more. She leaned her head against his shoulder, and he slipped his arm around her. Why not? How many times would she be in Amsterdam, sitting by a sexy guy who gave her the best orgasms of her life?

Okay, and why did just thinking that make her a little sad?

Conversation dwindled as they took in the scenery and enjoyed the ride.

The whole thing just seemed so romantic. Maybe because they were in Europe, but still...somehow she got the impression even if it had been Keith beside her—and he hadn't been a cheating bastard—the romance factor would have been non-existent.

She rested her hand on Tyler's thigh and tried to smother out the unhappiness seeping in. Not to mention the anxiety.

She was going home today. Home to her *normal* life. Then again, define normal. Was being betrayed by the man who you supposedly loved normal?

Not that you're any better now. The thought ran through her head, making her uneasy. But she didn't regret it. Not for a moment. And she would walk away with a wonderful memory.

Tyler stroked the back of her neck, and she turned, lifting her face toward him and giving a brief smile.

"Thank you for the past couple nights, Tyler. I'll never forget them."

He glanced down at her, his expression unreadable. "They were for you. I wanted to give you everything you wanted out of these couple days. Mind-blowing sex and more."

A sad smile curled her lips. "You did."

His fingers tightened, and she wondered if he wanted to say more, but instead he leaned forward and dropped a kiss on the top of her head.

She bit her lip as it trembled, and blinked back the sudden tears in her eyes. What on earth was wrong with her? Strictly sex. That's what she'd wanted. She needed to get her ass on the plane as soon as possible.

"*Ja.*" Hans nodded from where he sat. "I think you two will last many years together."

Neither of them answered. Tyler's hand withdrew from her neck, and Lena shifted so she could put a small amount of space between them. Suddenly she needed it. Might not want it, but she knew she needed it.

She sighed and mentally geared herself up to go home.

They arrived at the airport not long before her flight. Lena checked in, knowing she was already late, and turned to Tyler.

"What do I say?" *Keep it light, Lena.* "You're nice on the eyes, great in bed, and a fabulous tour guide." She forced out a laugh. "Thank you, Tyler. I had a fantastic time."

Tyler nodded, his mouth twitching as he shoved his hands in his pockets. "Ditto on all of that."

"Except for the tour guide part. I would have been lost without you."

She realized the double meaning in the statement the moment the words left her mouth. Heat stole into her cheeks. "That came out kind of intense. I meant...I only wanted—"

He grabbed her shoulders and pulled her against him, then brought his mouth down on hers, fierce and possessive.

She parted her lips and let his tongue take control of hers. She groaned, wanting to savor this final taste of him.

How was this possible? Despite her own efforts, she'd still gotten a little attached to him.

He pulled back after a moment and took a deep breath. "There. Now that was a proper good-bye." His smile seemed tight. "Now, go or you'll miss your flight."

And then he left her. Lena sat down in one of the plastic chairs, not quite ready to check in for her flight. She buried her face in her hands, trying not to think about going back to reality. Back to everything as it had been before—in all its appalling glory.

Her stomach churned.

Keith was still in Maui and wouldn't be back for another week. At least that was the impression Keith's mom had given her. One week of analyzing their relationship. To decide whether they should get counseling and continue with the marriage plans, or call off the whole thing.

Stephanie had all the luck to be in the Caribbean. Why hadn't she considered taking up Steph's offer to use the apartment in Paris?

Maybe it wasn't too late...

"Ma'am? Did you need to check in?"

Lena blinked and looked up at the airline employee behind the counter.

"Check in?"

"Yes, check in," he repeated with obvious patience. "Where are you flying to?"

She paused and then gave a slow shake of her head. "No where, at the moment."

"I'm sorry?"

"No. *I'm* sorry." She turned on her heel and ran through the airport.

Her legs pumped hard, and her breath came out ragged. She caught him just as he was climbing into a taxi.

"Tyler!"

He paused and glanced around, a frown marring his face.

"Tyler," she screamed again, running toward him.

He caught her just before she slammed into him like a tornado and held her a couple inches away.

"Lena?" His eyes narrowed with concern and another

emotion she couldn't name. "Is something wrong, what happened?"

"I...I need to ask you something." She struggled to get a breath in, still winded from the run.

"What? What do you need to ask me?" He glanced over her shoulder into the airport. "Lena, you're going to miss your plane. What are you thinking?"

"I'm not. I'm not thinking at all." She gave an uneven laugh as she looked up into his eyes. "I'm going to Paris, and I want you to come with me."

Chapter Six

Tyler's grip on her elbows tightened. "You didn't get on your plane?"

"No, I didn't."

"Lena, you just missed your plane home."

"Deliberately missed it," she emphasized. "Look, I'm not *going* home right now. That's why I didn't get on that flight. Did you hear the question I asked you?"

"Yes, I did." He turned to the taxi driver and waved him on to another waiting customer.

"And?" Trying to think about how nuts she had to be right now, she waited, her breath locked in her chest.

"Lena, it's an amazing offer." He hesitated. "I would love to go to Paris—especially with you. But I'm scheduled to be back at work in a couple days. Back at work in New York."

"Oh. Right. I-I didn't even think of that. I'm such an idiot."

Turning away from him, she walked over to a bench by the windows and sat down, pressing her trembling fingers against her knees.

"You're not an idiot." He came and sat beside her. "The timing is just a little off."

"Of course." She shook her head. *Try and salvage a little pride here, girl.* "I know it was a real last-minute decision. Completely spontaneous."

"I think it's great. Spontaneity makes life more exciting." His words seemed to be a poor attempt to comfort her.

"Okay. But I still come out looking like a moron." *So much for pride.*

"You're not a moron. So, what are you going to do now?"

"What am I going to do?" Lena frowned. "Well, I'm going to go to Paris, of course."

"Alone?" His eyebrows shot up.

"Well, *you* can't come with me, and unless I happen to meet *another* hot guy that I want to take to Paris... Then I guess it's just me."

He made a quiet harrumph, not looking thrilled. "Don't pick up a strange guy. You might get into trouble."

"Hey, you were a strange guy."

"Point taken, but still, I don't like that visual of you picking up a stranger. Have you got a place to stay?"

"I do. Stephanie rented an apartment in the city, and she's given me free use of it for the next week and a half." Here tone lightened. With or without Tyler, she still planned on going to Paris. "You know what? This is going to be wonderful."

"I'm jealous."

"And you should be. You need a real vacation where you don't have to work all the time."

"Yeah, that'll be the day," he admitted and thrust a hand through his hair. "Well, Lena, have a good time in Paris. Maybe I'll see you around some time."

No, he wouldn't. And they both knew it. She sighed and gave him another searching look.

"Hey. I, umm, hope I didn't just make things weird with this whole running after you bit."

Tyler laughed and pushed a strand of her hair behind her ear. "No, you didn't make anything weird. You made me lose my taxi, but nothing's weird. Actually, I'm flattered."

"Good. You should be." Her pulse skipped at his touch. "Well, take care of yourself, Tyler."

"You too." He stood and gave a small salute, and then turned to wave down another taxi.

Go get your luggage, you idiot. She stood up and headed back into the airport, hoping her luggage was where she'd abandoned it.

She pressed the back of her hand against her forehead, trying to ignore the lump of disappointment in her throat. A few minutes later she found her luggage in the same spot, but with a security official glowering at her and waiting to give her sharp reprimand.

She debated getting on a flight to Paris, but decided to take a train there tomorrow. That would be cheaper. Which meant she'd be spending another night here, and she didn't have a room. Visions of showing up at Tyler's hotel room weaved through her head, but she quickly dismissed them. There was no way she would embarrass herself in front of him again today.

She'd just check into the small hotel that she and Stephanie had used before.

Lifting the suitcase off the ground, she turned to head toward the exit and rammed into somebody.

"Oh, I'm sorry." Lena glanced up, then stepped back, her mouth open in shock.

"You know, I don't really *remember* Paris." Tyler plucked her suitcase from her hand. "I partied too much and wasted my time trying to pick up cute French girls."

"Is that so?" Her heart pounded, and her smile felt big enough to leave cracks on her face.

"Yeah. Come to think of it, I don't remember the last real vacation I took. I'll call my office in New York and let them know

I'll be staying for some vacation time."

"And you can just do that?" Lena raised an eyebrow.

"Of course."

"You're that powerful?"

"I make people tremble with fear."

"You make me tremble," she admitted. "Although not with fear."

Tyler paused, whatever he'd been about to say apparently forgotten. He laughed and shifted his weight to his other foot.

"When are you leaving for Paris? Tonight?"

"No, I want to take a train and see the countryside. It leaves tomorrow." Her smile turned wry. "I'd offer to buy your ticket, but then I'd have little left to shop with."

"I can buy my own ticket, sweetheart." He steered them outside to where a taxi waited. "And if you're good, maybe I'll buy *you* something in Paris."

"Hmm, how good?" She glanced at the protective hand that he'd settled on her hip. "That must be some job back in New York."

He gave her a brief glance. "I guess you'll never know. That is, if you want the same rules to apply in Paris as in Amsterdam."

"Oh. Right." Did she still want that? No...but yes. It'd have to be that way to be safe. To protect her heart. "Silly me. What on earth was I thinking?"

"I don't want to know anything about you." He quoted her earlier words.

The taxi pulled away from the curb and sped off toward the city.

"You're just using me for sex?"

He leaned over and kissed her hard, his fingers threading

into her hair. "Does that answer your question?"

She glanced up at him through her lashes and managed to whisper, "I can't wait, stranger."

Tyler came out of the bathroom and paused in front of the mirror, rubbing his hand over the stubble on his cheek. He stifled a yawn and splashed some water on his face to wake himself up.

They'd stayed up almost all night eating Chinese food, chatting and watching a movie on the hotel television. Not to mention more amazing sex.

He shook his head, unable to believe he'd at first turned down her invitation to go to Paris. How much more of an idiot could he be?

Lena's sexual response to him was a constant surprise. Her passionate intensity made him curious about her sexual history and love life in general. But he knew better than to delve into those waters. If she decided to open up, she'd share when she wanted to.

Her voice traveled from the bed. "Come and have some of this almond chicken."

When he came out of the bathroom, she sat up, the shirt he'd loaned her falling around her knees. Even in his shirt, she looked damn sexy.

"I can't believe I'm eating cold, leftover Chinese food for breakfast in Amsterdam." She giggled and took another bite.

Tyler smiled and walked over to the bed. After sitting down, he allowed her to feed him a good-sized bite of the greasy food.

He swallowed and then groaned, rolling over onto his back. "I need real food. Steak and potatoes or something. I haven't eaten this much crap since college."

"I know," she said after swallowing a mouthful of rice. "It's fantastic. I'm sure I'll gain twenty pounds and die of a heart attack before I turn thirty."

He rolled onto his side and propped a hand under his head. "What are you, twenty-two?"

She shook her head and then raised her chopsticks in warning.

"It's just your age." He realized his error but couldn't prevent the irritation that picked at him. "It's really not that much information. I'll tell you mine. I'm thirty-two."

"Well. Stop the presses. I'm sleeping with an older man."

"I suppose I am old." He raised an eyebrow. "To someone who's probably never heard of The Rolling Stones."

She wrinkled her nose at him. "I've heard of them. Isn't the singer that guy with the big lips?"

Tyler laughed and sat down on the bed. "Twenty-three?"

"Twenty-six."

"You look young. I had you pinned for a sorority girl. At least now I don't feel like a total cradle robber."

"Ah, come on, Tyler," she said with a playful grin. "I thought every guy wanted them young and wild."

"Sorry? What magazines have you been reading?"

Lena's lips twitched, which turned into a giggle. "Sorry, I just had to give you crap."

"Give you crap," he mimicked and grabbed her ankle, pulling her toward him.

She lost her balance and fell onto her side, shrieking as the container of Chinese food spilled over her and the bed.

Tyler bolted up and off the bed, choking back a laugh. "Oh, jeez. I swear, that wasn't supposed to happen."

79

"Wasn't supposed to happen?" Lena glared up at him as sauce oozed over her body and the bed sheets.

His shoulders shook from laughing. "Wow, you look hilarious. But really, I'm sorry about that."

Lena pulled a piece of chicken out of her hair and flung it at him. It smacked onto his forehead before rolling off his face and nestling in the collar of his shirt.

He cocked his head and took a step back toward her. "Well, I'll be damned if that wasn't an invitation for a food fight."

She yelped and made a grab for the rest of the food, but he dove onto the bed and sent the food flying. His sudden weight on the bed had her rolling into the middle, straight toward the growing mound of almond chicken. Her body arched over it, and she swiped a handful of the mess, launching it into his face.

He swore and lurched at her, pinning her against the bed as he scraped the food off himself.

"Beg for mercy," he commanded, holding the glob over her head.

"I will not." She writhed under him. "Get off me."

His dripping hand lowered closer to her. "Beg."

Lena groaned and eyed the handful of dripping food. "Oh, all right. *Please*, Tyler."

"Now, Lena, that didn't sound from the heart." He clucked his tongue.

"Ugh." She thrust her hips under him, trying to buck him off. "What do you want me to say?"

"I want you to say, 'I'm sorry, Tyler. You are a powerful, hot, well-endowed man'."

"Now, Tyler, I don't know if I could lie so blatantly." She gave him an innocent look and then glanced down at his jeans.

When his nostrils flared, she squeaked and started to recite his phrase. "I'm sorry, Tyler. You are a powerful—"

"Too late." He smashed the food into her hair, ignoring her shrieks.

"Oh, you suck." She struggled to sit up as the sauce dripped down the back of her neck.

Tyler wiped the sauce off her face and kissed her forehead. "You should have just admitted that my dick is big."

He ducked her fist as it flailed toward him. When her other hand shot out, he grabbed it and pushed it between them, holding them to his chest.

"I am so disgusting right now," she cried. "And how am I going to get you back?"

"You don't need to get me back, and I'll make it up to you."

She didn't respond as his mouth closed over the small area where her neck and shoulder connected, but she gave a small shudder. He eased her onto her back, his tongue reaching out to lap up any remaining sauce. His fingers smoothed the pieces of food out of her hair.

"This is so not seductive."

"Liar." His hand slid down to cup a breast. "Just pretend it's massage oil."

"It's not massage oil, it's vegetable oil." She pushed her hands against his chest. "No, really. Look at us. We're swimming in Chinese food."

Tyler grasped her wrists again with one hand and pinned them above her head. "Yes, I've noticed this. It's kind of erotic, isn't it?"

"You think pulling chunks of food out of my hair is erotic?"

"Damn right." Then he lowered his lips to hers.

She refused to open her mouth, her body still rigid beneath

him.

Changing techniques, he slowly outlined her mouth with his tongue before plunging past her compressed lips into her mouth.

She gasped, her shock obvious, but a moment later her body softened against his. She opened her mouth to him, and her tongue came out to spar with his. He gave a sound of triumph and released her hands so he could massage the back of her neck.

Lena came up for air, panting. "You are a dirty, dirty man, Tyler."

He laughed and sat up, grabbing her hand. "Well then, let's do something about it."

"What are we doing?"

He led her to the bathroom, grabbing a condom off the dresser first. "You're a mess. We need to get you a shower."

"Oh, so now you agree? You get me all wound up and then tell me to jump in the shower?"

He reached into the shower and turned it on. "Yes. And I intend to help you out with both dilemmas. I'm coming in with you."

Her mouth curled upward, and she reached out to pull off his shirt as he removed hers. Once they were both naked, he pulled her into the roomy shower stall.

She stepped under the spray, and the water washed away any lingering sauce and food.

Tyler ran his gaze over the curve of her breasts, all slick with water. His dick hardened further, and he distracted himself by pouring some shampoo into his hand.

She glanced over her shoulder at him. "That's an awful lot of shampoo, don't you think? I mean, my hair is almost as short as yours.

"I was never very good at rationing." He pushed her head under the water before pulling her back out. "There we go."

She sputtered, blinking the droplets of water from her eyes as he massaged the shampoo into her hair. She relaxed as his fingers moved over her scalp.

"Mmm, that feels good." She let her head loll against him, her eyes shutting.

He rinsed the suds out of her hair and picked up a loofah and the bottle of body wash.

"You actually use a loofah?" She reached out to look at the bottle of body wash. "Citrus Sunshine?"

"It came with the hotel." He took the bottle back from her. "And why not? A lot of people do."

"A lot of chicks do."

Tyler squeezed a healthy amount of soap onto the loofah. "You are just full of stereotypes about men, aren't you?"

"Mmm hmm."

He moved the loofah over her body, watching the slippery film of scented suds it created. His breathing became heavier, and he tossed the loofah to the floor to use his hands instead, molding the slippery weight of her breasts. Her nipples hardened into his palms.

"You have the sexiest body," he muttered into her ear, pressing his rock-hard cock against her back.

She moaned and pushed her butt back against him. His dick jerked against her, and he swiftly inhaled. He slid one hand down the curve of her belly and into the hot folds between her legs.

She was already wet for him. He pushed two fingers inside her slick heat, and she cried out. He smiled, continuing to squeeze one breast while sliding his finger up to rub her clit.

Her breathless cries encouraged him, and he kissed the back of her neck and pressed harder on her swollen nub.

"*Tyler,*" she screamed, her body tensing.

He turned her around and lifted her, pushing her down as he thrust up into her hot sheath. The walls of her sex clenched and unclenched around him as she cried out through her orgasm.

He pounded up into her, faster and harder. The water sprayed down on them, and his nails dug into her ass cheeks to keep her from slipping.

His sac tightened, and he gasped, empting himself with a groan. He sank to his knees, gasping for breath as she nuzzled his neck.

Tyler leaned back against the wall with Lena draped half on top of him. He stroked her back as they caught their breaths.

"God, Lena. I am so glad you didn't get on the plane."

She sighed and kissed his shoulder. "Me too. I swear, I wasn't even certain what an orgasm was before I met you."

He froze, his brows drawing together. She couldn't be serious.

"I mean, I've had them," she said in a rush. "Just...not that often."

"Have you just not had much experience with men?" Tyler winced the moment the words left his mouth.

The entire idea seemed ludicrous anyway. Lena was sexy, not to mention that she had one hell of a personality, and she was spontaneous and fun.

Most women would have run crying if they found themselves in the middle of a food fight using Chinese food, but not Lena. She'd rolled up her sleeves, so to speak, and dove right in. Even getting a couple cheap shots in herself.

He knew his question had hit a mark when she stiffened against him. Her fingers ceased in their absent tracings on his stomach.

"Why does it matter how many partners I've had?"

"It *doesn't* matter. I'm sorry, that just came out wrong." He paused. "You know, if we're going to be spending another week holed up together, then we might wanna compromise on this whole secrecy thing. Conversation is going to run dry pretty quick."

Lena sighed, and she relaxed against him again. "Oh, Tyler. I'm sorry. And you're right. I guess...some things aren't so bad. But honestly, I just want this to be a fun little vacation fling. Is that so wrong?"

"No, not wrong." He shook his head, but inside couldn't quite grasp why she wanted it that way. "A little bit surprising, maybe. I guess I'm just not used to women who are only looking for a booty call."

"A booty call." She gave a slight frown, as if not appreciating the label. "Hmm...yeah, I suppose that's what this is. It just sounds a little tawdry."

At least she agreed on that aspect. She could emotionally push him away all she wanted, but this woman obviously did not engage in casual sex on a regular basis.

"Don't worry about it, sweetheart." He dropped another kiss on her mouth. "As long as you're enjoying yourself."

"Oh, you have no idea. I'm having a *fabulous* time. Especially, but not limited to, the bedroom."

He pulled them both up, and his legs shook. Damn, that orgasm had taken a lot out of him.

He laughed and stepped out of the shower. "Yes, I gathered that part."

She rolled her eyes, following after him. "Well, I could have been faking that part."

"I'd be able to tell if you were." He wrapped her body in a soft cotton towel. "There are obvious things that happen during an orgasm, slightly more than just moaning and a precision-placed scream."

She looked almost annoyed at something. What he wouldn't give to know what went on in her head.

She shook her head and looked away. "You're awfully cocky, but you're right. I wasn't faking."

"Did I call it or what?" Tyler opened the bathroom door, letting the steam rush out.

"Well, maybe I *will* fake one, one of these times, to see if you can tell."

"Don't waste your energy when you can have the real thing. Go get dressed." She was so adorable in her defiance. "We've got to be on the train in the next couple hours."

"I'll be ready to go in about ten minutes." She gave him an impish look. "But after seeing you with that loofah, I'm thinking you'll be a bit longer. Maybe you need to exfoliate or something."

Tyler reached out to snap her with his towel, but she'd already ducked back into the room. He smiled and turned back to the sink to brush his teeth.

Chapter Seven

"My first ride on the Eurorail." Lena just barely bit back a squeal as she claimed her seat next to the window. "How long is the ride from Amsterdam to Paris, do you know?"

"No clue. It's been a while since I've been over here." Tyler settled down across from her.

She twisted off the lid to her Diet Coke she'd picked up before they left and took a sip. "Did you get a chance to go on the trains when you were here before?"

"I did." Tyler glanced at her as he pulled a copy of the *New York Times* out of his bag. "We went to Germany, Spain and Paris."

"I would love to go to Germany." She gave a wistful smile and stared out the window. "You know, I've been in Europe for five days, and I have yet to see a castle. Can you believe it? Isn't that horrible?"

"Castles are overrated."

She jerked her gaze back to him, her eyes wide with shock. He continued to read the paper, oblivious to her stare. How was it possible that anyone could be so immune to the charm of a castle?

"How can you say that? It's not like there's a castle on every corner in America."

He shrugged. "Castles aren't at all as fascinating as they're made out to be."

"And how is that?"

Tyler glanced up at her, as if to ensure she really wanted to have this conversation. He sighed and set the paper down.

"You've been raised with these marshmallow-coated ideals of what a castle is, derived from fairytales like Cinderella and Sleeping Beauty. You've turned a castle into what boils down to a romantic Barbie Dream House." He made a sharp gesture with his hand. "In reality a castle was just a very common living facility built strictly as a means of survival."

Lena gaped at him. "I've never heard so much crap in my life. How can you reduce a castle to some kind of boring practical architecture?"

"Because it is," he insisted. "Castles weren't designed to be turned into glorified, romanticized structures. They were built to provide residency and a means of protection. Sure, some of it dealt with vanity. It was a sign of wealth. Power."

"I refuse to have this conversation." Lena quelled any annoyance that might have risen but, in truth, his reasoning almost amused her. "I refuse to have you distort my vision of what a castle is."

"All right then. Keep your Barbie Dream House." His lips twitched.

"I will, thank you very much."

He chuckled before turning his attention back to his paper.

Lena turned and stared out the window to where the scenery had just begun to change. She watched the endless fields of green and the occasional hillside speckled with brick houses and churches.

"It is *so* beautiful here."

Tyler didn't respond, but she didn't expect him to. He was once again engrossed in his reading.

"I'm getting kind of hungry again." Lena turned back from the window. "I think I might make my way down to the area with the food. Did you want to come, or do you want anything?"

Tyler glanced up at her. "If you want to grab me something then that would be great."

"Sure." She stood up. "Anything in particular?"

"Doesn't matter. I'll eat whatever."

"Okay, I'll find you something." She slid her purse over her shoulder and made to slip past him. "I'm going to walk around the train, so if I don't return right away don't worry too much."

"I'll try not to." He caught her hand and pulled her back down to him, holding her still for a moment to drop a light kiss on her lips. "Thank you for offering to grab food, that's very sweet. I appreciate it."

Lena's cheeks warmed, and she gave a small smile. "You're welcome. I'll be back later."

Walking through each compartment she realized just how few people were actually on the train. After going through many separate cars, she got dizzy from the motion and arrived with relief in the dining car.

She grabbed a couple pre-made sandwich-type things, paid for them, but wanted to sit a moment before heading back to let the dizziness subside. She glanced around at the tables and her gaze landed on the only other person in the car.

The woman had been watching her and gave a friendly smile.

Lena smiled in response and went to sit down at one of the tables and stared out at the scenery. Then she saw it. A soft gasp escaped her as she stared at the jagged remains of what appeared to be a castle.

"It is very beautiful, no?"

Lena turned to the other women who had been watching her and nodded. "Yes, they're incredible. I'm glad *you* agree."

"You are an American, no?" The woman questioned, raising an eyebrow.

"Yes, I am." Lena moved to sit across from the woman. "My name is Lena. I'm from a city just outside of Portland, Oregon."

"Wonderful to meet you, Lena. I am Claire Ames. I live in Paris." Claire offered a delicate hand for Lena to shake.

"That's where I'm headed. I've never actually been there, but I send my clients all the time."

"You will love Paris." Claire touched her immaculate, black, pinned hair. "Have you been traveling since you arrived in Europe? Where are you coming from now?"

"I've been in Amsterdam."

"Amsterdam? I love Amsterdam." Claire gave a wistful smile. "It really is such a charming place to visit. Are you traveling alone?"

"No." How did she explain Tyler? Hmm. Ambiguous would work. "I'm traveling with a friend."

"And you are married?" Claire's gaze dropped to Lena's hand in question.

Keith. The blood drained from her face. God, she'd almost forgotten about him altogether.

She shook her head and then glanced toward the doorway, checking to see that Tyler hadn't decided to follow her, but she and Claire were the only two occupants.

"Engaged. We just set a date."

"Ah, true love."

Ha. If she only knew.

"You are very young still, no? To marry someone you have a deep love for is a beautiful thing." Claire gave her a knowing look.

"Yes, I suppose it is."

Claire's statement had put a spotlight on her ever-changing feelings toward her fiancé.

"I am sure you both will have a wonderful life together." Claire's expression became curious, as if she sensed Lena's lack of conviction.

"Yes, I am sure we will." Lena cleared her throat, desperate to change the subject. "What about you? Are you married?"

"Yes, I am. I have been married for twenty years now."

"That's wonderful. And how did you two meet?"

"It is a bit shocking." Claire gave an awkward laugh. "At the time we first met, I was introduced to him through my husband."

Lena blinked. *Whoa, didn't see that coming.*

"I know what you are thinking. It is not as romantic as you would expect, nor very ethical. And I have been judged my entire life by my decision." Claire gave a soft sigh. "Maybe I should explain to you. My first marriage was not a bad one. My husband did not mistreat me. But I did not *love* him."

Lena attempted an understanding nod.

"You see, I married very young, at eighteen. My husband traveled frequently, always I was so lonely." Claire's expression grew distant. "I met Luc when my husband was away at a weekend seminar. My husband had arranged to have us attend a dinner party together. Luc would go in his place to represent the company."

Lena stared at her. *Wow, the poor husband must have been pissed when he found out his coworker moved in on the wifey.*

"Sometimes I wonder if he wanted me to meet someone else." Claire fidgeted with an out-of-place hair that didn't exist. "When I knew I was in love with Luc, I told my husband I wanted to divorce. And he let me go. He kissed my cheek, and told me to be happy."

Lena stared at the other woman in amazement. *Maybe the ex wasn't all there in the head.*

"That must have been a hard decision for you to make."

"It was very difficult." Claire's voice cracked for the first time. "Being raised in a devout Catholic home, divorce was not even a word to be spoken. And when I fell in love, real love, I knew I would sacrifice almost anything to be with Luc. In the end, I did. My parents and siblings no longer speak with me."

"I can't even imagine," Lena whispered. "And you feel you made the right decision?"

"But of course. I have never once regretted my decision. I put my own happiness before what other people wanted for me." She smiled, her expression softening. "I have been married for twenty amazing years to a wonderful man. I gave my heart to him, and he gave his to me. We have three children together, one who I just sent away to college."

Warmth stirred in Lena's heart from those words and an ache in the same place that she couldn't explain. "Do you think your ex-husband ever got over you?"

Claire burst into laughter. "I would guess it took a few months at the most. He is now married and happy. No children, however. He never wanted children. But we still send cards to each other on occasion."

Lena smiled. "That's amazing. It's just so great to hear that something so painful could turn out so good."

"Sometimes the most difficult choice is also the most obvious." Claire gave a shy smile. "I am sorry. I am a very open person. I hope I have not made you uncomfortable with my tirade."

"Not at all," Lena replied honestly. "I'm so glad I met you. I know I'll always remember this moment. Sitting on a train on my way to Paris, talking to a very fascinating woman who's made me..."

"Made you...?"

Question my own life. Lena smiled. "Think. You've made me think."

"That is so very sweet of you, Lena." The older woman gave her a brief smile. "I hope you will be happy in your own life."

"Hmm. Me too." Easier said than done.

"Just make sure you do what you want, and not what everybody else expects you to do. Go with your heart, and you will be fine."

Lena stood up and scooped her food off the table. "Claire, it's been lovely chatting with you, but I should probably get back to my friend now."

"Have a wonderful time in Europe, Lena. I wish you the best." Claire gave a small wave, and Lena waved back before returning to her car.

When Lena arrived, she spotted Tyler right away. He had his back against the window, one knee drawn up into his chin. His lips parted a bit and, as she sat across from him, she listened to the sound of his heavy breathing.

Now this man could tempt her to give up everything. More than just a nice guy, he was also so damn good looking. His long lashes veiled those rich, brown eyes. Why should a man have such long lashes? She scowled. It was enough to make a woman jealous as all hell.

"What are you finding so interesting to look at?" he drawled without opening his eyes.

"You've got the prettiest eyelashes."

His eyelids snapped opened. "Tell me you didn't just call my eyelashes pretty."

"Well, they are. They're so long and curved. Do you have

any idea how long we women stand in front of a mirror, stabbing ourselves with hazardous mascara wands?"

"Please."

"Makeup is a dangerous thing. If you saw an eyelash curler, I'm sure you'd run screaming."

Tyler sat up and swung his feet onto the floor, shaking his head. "That's why I'm glad I'm a man."

Lena tossed him a sandwich and leaned back against the window on the seats across from him. "That's not why you're glad you're a man. But that is an entirely different argument, and we don't *even* want to get into that."

"I'd be curious to hear your point of view." Tyler unwrapped his sandwich while she did the same, and then he glanced up her.

"No, you wouldn't." She took a healthy bite and gestured toward his food. "It's not exactly a conversation that goes well with eating."

"Try me. I was raised with two sisters." He mirrored her by taking a huge bite of his sandwich.

"Okay, you asked for it. The way I see it..." She paused to take a sip of water. "Men get all the money and all the respect, while we women are stuck fighting it out just to get somewhere in this world."

"And you really believe that? You don't think things have changed?"

"Oh, sure, we've come farther than the days where women sat at home popping out kids and scrubbing the floors all day, but there's still things women have to deal with that men can't even begin to understand." She licked her fingers and set down the other half of her sandwich.

Tyler watched her in amusement. "And that would be?"

"Here's my theory. There's at least three Ps that women endure, and they all boil down to the big P."

He cocked his head. "You've lost me. Please elaborate."

"Period, pantyhose and pregnancy. Three Ps. And they all come out to the motherlode P of them all. Pain." She lifted her hands and grimaced. "It's just something you men will never understand."

"What, is that written in the latest *Cosmo* or something?" Tyler's laugh was a bit fearful. "The three Ps?"

"Of course not, but it doesn't take a genius to realize this. I mean, look at pantyhose. You have this piece of nylon that would barely cover a zucchini, and you expect it to slide over a woman's leg?"

"It's a challenge." He nodded in agreement, then his eyes brightened. "But think about all the extra support."

She snorted. "Support, my butt. I walk around just trying to breathe for the next hour. But I will admit that it helps smooth out all the little imperfections."

Tyler gave her a slow smile. "You don't have any imperfections, sweetheart."

"Don't try and charm me. Every woman has imperfections. We've just gotten great at disguising them. So, beyond the nylons and onto the other two Ps."

"The other two," he interrupted quickly, "I'm guessing are not something we want to delve into."

"I thought you were up for it? What happened? Oh, is your stomach getting a little queasy?"

He held up his sandwich and made a wry face. "Well, I'm just not quite finished eating."

"Hmm, yeah. Sorry about that." Lena gave him a thoughtful look, picked up her sandwich, and took another bite. "I just think it's funny that men can't handle words like blood and menstruating."

The sandwich paused halfway to his lips, and his eyes narrowed as he looked back at her. "Okay, you need to stop."

"Wait, wait. I just thought of another P word. You're going to love this one. Placenta. Come on, Tyler, say it with me. Placenta."

Tyler's face contorted into a mask of disgust, and he thrust his sandwich into his backpack. "Excuse me while I go puke."

"Have fun," she called after him and cheerfully polished off the last bite of her sandwich. "Raised with two sisters, my ass."

When he'd disappeared out of their car, she let out the stream of laughter that had been building up. Sitting back on the seat, she propped her feet up on his side and glanced out the windows.

The lush, green land sprawled out for miles, and she stared out, one hundred percent enchanted. Everything was so foreign.

At home there were large evergreen trees for miles around, and mountains. Both of which were extremely beautiful, but there was something charming about the simplicity of the countryside she looked at now.

Her thoughts strayed toward Keith again, and guilt stabbed at her.

Hey, he's still banging some chick in Maui. Have your own fun and worry about tomorrow when it comes.

Lena nodded, more inclined to listen to the little devil on her shoulder.

She sighed and squeezed her eyes closed, resting her head against the cool glass of the window.

One thing had become all too clear, though. There would be no going back. No matter how much she tried to convince herself she could go home to Oregon and try and work things out, nothing would ever be the same. Not after Tyler.

Chapter Eight

When Tyler returned to their car, Lena's attention was too focused on the view outside the window to notice him.

She was so passionate in everything she believed in. That aspect of her personality drew him to her almost more than the physical attraction. Things were so comfortable with her he had no problem just being himself. And neither did she, apparently.

He winced, remembering their mini talk on females. Then again, he couldn't remember the last time a woman had amused him so much.

Lena must have seen his reflection in the window because she turned to him with a sheepish grin. "I hope I didn't *really* make you sick." The apology came in her tone rather than in words.

"Nah, you're okay. I lost my appetite a bit." He rubbed a hand across his stomach. "Your shock factor test made a little dent, but my appetite will return full throttle in a bit."

"Just a little dent?" She shook her head and grinned. "I'll have to do better next time."

"Please don't." He came and settled next to her, laying his head in her lap and stretching his legs out across the other seat.

She reached out to play with his hair. "You have two sisters, hmm?"

Tyler's lips twitched. He wouldn't call her on the "no information" rule. This time. "I have two sisters. One younger, she's twenty-five, and one older, she's thirty-six."

"Ah, you had *those* kind of parents." Lena gave him a knowing nod. "The ones that just kept going like the Energizer bunny and have kids that are ten years apart."

"Yeah, well, those days are over." Tyler grimaced. "Fortunately they're a bit too old to be getting it on."

"Oh, you are *so* wrong. It's not like you hit fifty and give up having sex. I mean, come on. It's *sex.*"

"Okay, even if you're right, I'd rather not sit around and discuss my parents' sex life," he drawled. "How about you? Do you have a parade of brothers at home ready to kick the ass of any guy who touches you?"

"Absolutely not." Lena let out a loud laugh. "I am an only child. I always beg my parents to tell me if I was an accident, and they insist I wasn't. But I'm pretty sure Mom got knocked up and they lived together for a few years before actually getting married."

"You really believe that?"

"I don't know. My parents both went through the hippie phase after the hippie phase had already ended. My mom was only seventeen when she had me."

"That's pretty young. Hippies, huh? So, you were raised in a relatively modern, relaxed environment then?"

"Oh, just a bit." She rolled her eyes. "I remember one time I came home from a school dance and found my parents smoking pot. It was a total role reversal. I swear, I must have lectured them for at least a half hour."

Tyler laughed and shook his head. "I can't even imagine. My family is your classic, cookie-cutter, sitcom family. I have two sisters, and they both were homecoming queen. My mom is a motivational speaker, and my dad teaches middle school band. The combination is just about as Brady Bunch as you can get."

"And you?" Lena glanced down at him with a teasing glance. "Were you the quarterback scoring all the women as well as the points? Do you have an old homecoming king crown floating around somewhere back in New York?"

"Me? Nope. I would have been hanging out with your parents."

"You've got to be kidding me." She tugged playfully on his hair. "You were the black sheep of the family?"

"Baaah."

"It sounds like you would fit in well with my parents."

"I've changed a lot, though. I was a rebel in school, skipping class to get high and play my acoustic guitar, but I gave it up once I got out of college. Started my grown-up job."

"Ah." She went quiet for a moment. "And I still have no clue of what you do."

"By your choice," he pointed out.

"This is true."

"Even though we've gone slightly beyond the rules in the past hour."

He waited, knowing she was thinking about all the boundaries they'd crossed.

"Do you *want* to know what I do as a career?" he prompted when she didn't reply.

She tilted her head as if taking a moment to consider it. Then she looked down at him with a sly grin. "No, I don't. You see, right now I can pretend you're a linebacker for a pro football team. Or I can imagine you're on vacation from the Secret Service. I mean, I do have to wonder where you got that really tight...ahem." She cleared her throat. "Shall I say...behind?"

"You like my *derriere*?"

"I *love* your derriere." She gave him a light pat on the forehead.

He chuckled. "I will inform you that my tight, oh-so-enticing behind comes from playing soccer. And as for the career, I'll keep that part about myself quiet as you wish."

"Soccer? Hmm, I took you for a swimmer."

"No thanks. Too wet of a sport." He grinned. "Lena..."

"Yes?"

"Nothing. That's just not a name you hear every day." He yawned. "What is it short for? Thumbelina or something?"

"No, and if that's a joke on my height, I'm going to deck you." She shifted in her seat. "My parents are huge jazz fans. They named me after Lena Horne, the jazz singer."

"I've never really listened to her."

"That's okay. A guy from New York who grew up in an overly functional family wouldn't be listening to jazz anyway." She nudged his shoulder.

"Hey, you'd be surprised. And I don't recall calling them overly functional. I said they were perfect." He scowled. "And you know, I like jazz. Miles Davis is a staple for anybody's CD collection."

"I like Miles Davis. More points for you."

"Am I being scored?"

"Of course not. I was just teasing."

"Gotcha. All right. I'm going to try and take a nap here." Tyler closed his eyes.

"And why is it that you get the comfortable position and I end up with a stiff neck?"

"Because women are meant to suffer, remember?" he murmured, feeling a little drowsy.

"Yes, I think we established that. Hey, I met the most

fascinating woman when I went to the dining car."

He gave a grunt of acknowledgment.

"You know how sometimes you meet someone and you just know that they've somehow made an impact on your life? Like you will never forget them, no matter how insignificant they seem at the time."

He knew exactly what she meant. It struck a chord. He didn't answer, though. His energy had been sapped. She didn't seem to expect an answer, because she grew silent. A few minutes later, he was asleep.

"*Bonjour*, Lena." Lips brushed in a soft caress across her forehead.

"Time to wake up. We're here. The City of Light."

Lena blinked her eyes open and then came fully awake. She sat up, and pain shot down her spine.

"Ouch. I knew this would happen. I can't even move my neck." She sighed as Tyler reached around to massage the back of her neck. "Next time, I get to sleep in your lap."

"Now, if you're expecting me to argue with that, then you'd better think again." Tyler raised a suggestive eyebrow.

Her mouth twitched, and she swung her bag over her shoulder. "Pervert."

"And you love it." He gave her hip a light squeeze as he followed her toward the exit.

Lena sighed and didn't bother to deny it. "You're right, I do."

He gave a soft laugh in her ear as they stepped off the train. They moved through the station side by side. Lena adjusted her jacket, feeling like a lump next to many of the sleek women they passed. Jeez, what a bad day to throw on sweats.

"Wow, I don't know why I didn't pay more attention to this place last time I was here."

"What?" Lena looked around. "The train station?"

"Yes, *Gare du Nord*." He stopped and glanced around.

Lena took a moment to view her surroundings. "Actually, I love all kinds of old buildings. Wasn't this rebuilt though? In the mid 1800s?"

Tyler turned to her with a look of admiration. "Very good for someone who's never been to Europe."

"We travel agents pick up all kinds of tidbits over time."

"A travel agent? Somebody just let the cat out of the bag." He winked and then kept walking.

"*Shit.*" Lena groaned. This had gotten so out of hand, and all by her insistence. *Enough already.* She bounded after him. "Okay, look. I don't care anymore. It's too annoying trying to remember that I can't talk to you like a normal person."

"So, you're saying you don't care?" he asked as they hailed a cab. "I just don't want to have to screen my conversations with you."

"Talk about whatever you want, and if it gets too personal, I'll let you know."

"Okay, Miss Indecisive. You've got a deal." Tyler helped her into the taxi and then sat down beside her. "Do you have the address of the place we're staying?"

"Yes, I should." Lena dug into her purse and pulled out the slip of paper that had the apartment address. She handed it up to the driver, and he took it from her and then swung into traffic.

"Do you know anything about this place we're staying?" Tyler asked as he pulled her hand onto his knee.

She entwined her fingers through his and shook her head. "I really don't. Steph just said it was supposed to be nice." She looked out the window and sighed. "I can't believe I'm actually in Paris. I've wanted to come here for so long."

"Why haven't you?" Tyler asked as he massaged her fingers. "I'm more curious now, knowing you're a travel agent."

Lena shrugged. Because Keith had always insisted they wait until after they were married in order to save money. Yet, he had no problem going to Maui with some bimbo.

"I just never had the time," Lena replied noncommittally.

"Make the time," Tyler urged. "What kind of travel agent doesn't travel? It's like working at a chocolate shop and not eating candy. Besides, if you were to settle down before you saw the world, you'd regret it later."

"What do you mean?" Her body tensed as she glanced at him.

His eyes narrowed. "All I'm saying is that too many people get married and have kids before they really get a chance to enjoy life."

"Yeah, I suppose that's true." She inwardly cursed her overreaction.

Tyler stared at her for a moment, but she avoided his gaze. "Are you married or something?"

His tone took on an edge. Did engaged fit in the or something category? But, hell, even the engagement wasn't definite anymore.

"Of course I'm not married," she answered, keeping her voice soft. "Do you think I'd be sleeping with you if I was?"

"That's a stupid question." Tyler kept staring at her. "The percentage of faithful spouses nowadays is pretty low."

"That's a pretty cynical way of thinking."

"I'm not trying to piss you off, Lena." He wrapped an arm around her shoulder. "I'm just saying that it's not easy to be in a monogamous relationship."

Wasn't that the truth? Oh, lord. Talk about making her confront her own conscience.

"And you?" She turned the tables. "Do you have trouble being faithful when you're in a relationship?"

"Sometimes I do," he admitted honestly, surprising her. "If my heart isn't in it, and it looks like I might be tempted to stray, I get out so it's never a matter of cheating."

"Wow, commendable. But it must suck for the women who fall in love with you."

Tyler gave a short laugh. "I don't think that's too much of a problem. I can't think of many women who've actually fallen in love with me."

"Are you sure about that?" Lena found that impossible to believe. How could anyone *not* fall in love with him?

Tyler turned his gaze from the window and met her stare. She regretted her question as his gaze burned into hers.

His voice dropped an octave. "Well, if they were, they never let on."

Lena's heart almost lurched into her throat. She blinked rapidly and glanced back out the window, having no idea how to respond.

She was changing with all the time they were spending together. If she'd been single, who knows what could have happened. Though with each passing day she spent with Tyler, the prospect of returning home to Keith seemed less and less appealing.

"Lena..." Tyler started to say something, but the taxi pulled to a stop beside a market.

He leaned forward and spoke to the driver in French, leaving Lena to gape at him in amazement.

When he leaned back, he turned to her with a smile. "This is the place. The apartment is upstairs from the produce shop."

"Really?" She raised her eyebrows. "And now you speak French?"

"I minored in French in college. That's why I'm the guy they send around the world." Tyler leaned across her to open the door.

She slid out of the taxi and allowed him to pay the driver. He joined her a moment later on the sidewalk.

"Okay, I'll admit. I'm impressed. I took a few semesters of French in high school but was awful at it. Foreign languages are not my forte."

"Ah, well then you'd better stay close to me while we're here." He kissed her cheek and placed a hand on the small of her back, guiding her toward the building.

Tyler took the keys Lena handed him, and they climbed the small number of stairs up to the apartment. She sure had acted funny when he'd asked if she were married. Unwanted doubt clawed in his belly. *Stop it. She told you she's not.*

They reached the door, and he inserted the key and unlocked the door, swinging it open.

Lena stepped past him and made a soft gasp of pleasure.

He followed in after her and took in the apartment. It was small but decorated with an understated sophistication. The walls were soft white, and the floors hardwood. The burgundy couches and chairs were plush and inviting, settled on an area rug that covered part of the living room.

He noted the plants in the corner and winced. Hopefully they weren't the kind that needed water. He had enough trouble remembering to feed his cat, let alone water plants.

Lena dropped her bags on the floor and rushed over to the window, pushing aside the lacey curtains to gaze at the view. He watched her stare out, her excitement so real and refreshing, and his heart ached a bit. *Keep it simple, buddy.*

"This is incredible. You need to see this."

Tyler walked up behind her, pulling open the lace curtains to expose the entire view. His arms came around her waist, and she covered his hands with her own. They gazed over the Eiffel Tower that loomed over a city pulsing with life. The sun had just gone down, and the lights of the city sent their pink flush over the evening.

"I don't remember it looking this incredible last time," he admitted, his lips moving against her hair.

Lena sighed. "I want to have this memory engraved in my heart forever."

This memory? Tyler's grip tightened around her. Did she mean more than just the view?

"Do you want to get some food?" His hands drifted over her belly.

Lena nodded. "I'm hungry. I can't think of anything I'd like to do more right now than eat."

"Are you sure?" He kissed the back of her neck.

She turned to him and lifted her mouth to his, brushing his lips is a sweet, brief kiss. "Of course there's always that. But that sandwich didn't fill me up. I need to eat first."

She stepped around him to look at the rest of the apartment, starting in the kitchen. She ran a hand over the smooth, black countertops.

He glanced around, drinking in the luxuries. "This place is nicely stocked. Check out the size of that flat screen."

"I saw it. I wondered how long it would take you to."

He wrote down the number listed on the phone and slipped it into his pocket. "Remind me to call work soon and give them this number."

"Mental note made." Lena peered into the small fridge and then into the oven. "I'm going to have to cook you an amazing dinner while we're here. This kitchen just looks like too much fun."

"And you're a good cook?" Tyler leaned against the counter. "Because I can cook a damn good Hamburger Helper, I'll have you know."

Lena smiled and leaned back against the counter. "Call me crazy, but I love that stuff. Think we can find any here in Paris? I wouldn't argue if you wanted to cook tonight. I'm a little tired—and sore—after that train ride."

He gave a soft laugh, knowing that she was deliberately trying to push his guilt button for making her sleep funny on the train.

"Are you now?" He approached her. "I do feel a little bad about giving you a stiff neck."

"You should." She gave him her cheek when he made to kiss her mouth. "You should be kissing my feet and apologizing profusely."

"I've already kissed your feet. You weren't too keen on it, remember?" He turned her face so her pouting lips were once again offered up to him.

"I never said it was that bad—"

He cut off her comment by taking the mouth that was so damn alluring. Her soft moan of surrender proved she forgave him, and his lips lingered just a moment before he again raised his head.

"So it's settled." He touched her lips. "I'll hit the store and get us stuff to make dinner with. Why don't you just relax?"

"That won't be a problem."

He kissed her forehead and headed for the door. "I'll be back soon."

Chapter Nine

Lena laughed and watched him leave the apartment, blowing him a kiss before he slipped outside. Feeling a bit giddy, she plopped herself down into the cushiony window seat and wiggled around until she found a comfortable position. She pulled a hand-stitched blanket over her body and sighed with contentment.

The view from the window entranced her. She took in every shop, landmark, and all the people still making their way around.

Her gaze moved back to a small store she'd spotted earlier, and she bit her lip. Acting on impulse, she jumped up and headed for the door. All of a sudden, the urge to make a dinner of Hamburger Helper romantic kicked in.

Lena pulled her sweatshirt back on over her head and rushed outside.

In the shop across the street, she found a variety of interesting things including candles, a lighter and a CD of various love songs. At least she assumed they were love songs because of the picture of a couple holding hands on the beach on the cover. That, and she recognized Celine Dion's name on the back.

She hesitated for just a few seconds before deciding to purchase the music selection. It could be a risky choice, but then again, imagining Tyler's reaction was pretty damn funny.

She counted out the francs to the cashier. Thankfully, they had thought to exchange their currency before getting on the train.

She made her way back to the apartment and splurged again. She stopped, trying to make conversation with a florist as she bought a colorful bouquet of flowers.

When she returned to the apartment, she kicked the door closed with her foot and stumbled to the kitchen, dropping the bag onto the counter.

She didn't just want the atmosphere to be romantic, she wanted to look the part. Hurrying to the bedroom, she searched her suitcase until she found what she sought.

Her "guaranteed to get some" dress Stephanie had helped her pick out at a shop in Amsterdam. It was simple and red, cut low and hemmed short.

She'd only dressed up those first couple of days in Amsterdam, and she gave in to the urge to look pretty for Tyler again.

She brushed her hair back into its short, flirty style and then put on some lip-gloss. A couple sprays of perfume on her wrists and cleavage and she was set.

Not bad at all, girl. She glanced in the mirror one more time before hurrying back into the living room.

Lena scooped the candles and lighter out of the bag and set them up on the little oak table. Her finger flicked over the lighter, and soon the soft glow of candlelight filled the room.

She unwrapped the CD she'd bought and slipped it into the stereo she'd spotted earlier. Sure enough, Celine's voice filled the air, and she pressed a hand against her mouth to keep from laughing.

She looked around the room and took in the scene she'd just created. Candlelight, flowers, cheesy love songs, and she'd dressed up to the max.

What would Tyler think? Doubt circled in her stomach.

They weren't even a real couple. Would this kind of romance just complicate things?

She rocked back on her heels and sighed. Maybe this had been a bad idea.

Tyler opened the door, his mouth going dry when he saw her. Or saw the back of her. She had bent over in front of the stereo. A short red dress that begged to be removed had ridden up so high that it barely covered her ass. Smooth, white thighs gleamed, and he followed the curve of her legs down to her dainty bare feet.

He cleared his throat, and she stood up, spinning in surprise.

"Hey." He adjusted the bags of food in his arms.

Her eyes widened, and her tongue darted out over her lips. Then she hurried over and took one of the bags from him.

He followed her into the kitchen and placed the bag next to hers. "Lena, you look..."

"Is it too much?" she asked, her cheeks turning pink.

"You look so damn hot in that dress." He stepped toward hers, running a hand down her bare arm. He didn't miss the shiver that ran through her body.

"You just happened to have that little dress in your bag?"

Lena smiled. "As a matter of fact, I did. You can't travel without having at least one nice outfit."

"I like it on you," he murmured. *I'd like it even better off you now.* He cleared his throat and turned his focus back to cooking dinner. "You'll never believe this, but I couldn't find Hamburger Helper."

"I thought that might be a challenge." She set the bag down on the counter and peered inside. "But it looks like you did okay."

"And I bought wine." He pulled out a bottle of Chardonnay.

"Oh, very nice. Do you want me to chill this?" She took the bottle from him and ran her fingers down the neck of the bottle.

Tyler clenched his teeth, his gaze on her hand as his blood stirred. God, he wanted her fingers stroking him like that. *Later.*

"Sure, toss it in the fridge." He turned his gaze to the dining room, and his eyes widened.

Not only had she dressed up for him, but she'd dressed up the apartment too. Candles, flowers... How had he not noticed this when he'd first returned from the store? *Because you were checking out her ass.*

"You really decorated this place."

"I thought it would be fun to make our first night in Paris..." She hesitated, her cheeks turning pinker. "Well, you know."

She couldn't say the word romantic? He lifted a brow and turned back to unload the bag of food.

"Thank you. I love what you did. Except for one thing." He glanced at her, his smile widening. "If that's Celine Dion I'm hearing, I think the music needs to go."

Lena burst into laughter, and she pressed a hand against her stomach.

"It looks great." He stepped forward, but still didn't touch her. Instead, he backed her up into the dining room against the table. She sat down onto the table and let him stand between her legs.

He reached up and cupped her face, leaning in to brush his lips over hers. Lena had a forwardness about her that pulled him in every time.

He could see her fight it, maybe not wanting to get sucked

under that tide they both got so easily lost in. But a moment later she sighed and closed her eyes, yielding to him and opening her mouth to his probing tongue.

Only then did Tyler close his eyes and move closer into the space between her legs, his hands bracketing her waist.

She pulled away and gasped, her hands unsteady as they jerked his T-shirt over his head.

"What about dinner? I thought you were starving?" he asked, cupping her breasts through the dress.

"Was I? It can wait." She dragged her nails down his chest, and he groaned. His cock hardened further. Now. He needed her now.

"Good. Because the only thing I want to do at this table right now is get you naked on it." He grabbed the hem of her dress and pulled it up and over her body.

The breath locked in his throat. She was a wet dream come to life, with a lacy red bra that lifted her breasts high and a tiny thong to match.

"Hang on." The words came out of his throat on a rasp. He grabbed the lit candles and moved them to the other end of the table. "Fire hazard."

She gave a husky laugh, her gaze following him.

He came back to her, already reaching for her breasts as his mouth crushed back down to taste hers. Her legs wrapped around his waist.

His tongue thrust deep while he slipped his fingers into the cups of her bra to tease her already taut nipples. He absorbed her guttural moan and deepened the kiss. Sliding one hand around her back, he unhooked the bra and pulled it free from her body.

He lifted his head to stare down at the breasts that were now bared. Her pink nipples puckered further beneath his gaze,

114

and he groaned.

"Lena...oh, sweetheart." Cupping both breasts in his hands, he dipped his head and drew one stiff peak into his mouth. Her flesh tasted sweet, the cry she made even sweeter. He sucked harder, his tongue rubbing against the tip while he pinched the nipple on her other breast.

"*Tyler.*"

He released her nipple and switched his mouth to the other, sucking and nibbling the tip. He squeezed his eyes shut the moment her hand grabbed his erection through his jeans. Her touch sent fire through his veins.

She worked fast, freeing him and pushing his jeans down to his knees. Her fingers were silky soft as they wrapped around his flesh. She paid special attention to the head, smoothing her thumb back and forth over the tip.

If she kept that up, he wouldn't make it much longer. He groaned, flexing his hips and pumping against her hand. He grazed his teeth against her nipple, wanting to bring her as much pleasure as she gave him.

The damp heat of her sex pressed tight against his abdomen. The smell of her arousal combined with the flowers made for a heady aphrodisiac.

"Lena, hang on, sweetheart."

"But why?" She pulled his head from her breast so he met her gaze. Her eyes sparkled with mischief and arousal. "This is so much fun."

"Yeah?" He pulled himself away from her hand and urged her back onto the table so she lay down. "You know what else is fun?"

Grasping the strings on each side of her hips, he pulled the panties down until her funny, shaved curls sprang free and the swollen lips of her sex were revealed.

She gave an unsteady laugh. "Oh, if you're doing what I think you're doing, then yes. This is good too."

Falling to his knees, he grabbed her legs and pulled them over his shoulders, bringing her cleft against his mouth. He thrust his tongue deep inside her, needing to taste her and send her out of control.

"Oh, *yes.*" Her choked words spurred him on.

His tongue delved again and again into her slick heat, tasting her and always going back for more. He brought his thumb to her swollen nub, rubbed slow circles, working her toward the point of no return.

Gripping her thighs, he dragged his tongue up to replace his fingers and licked her clit until she jerked against him.

"Oh, God, *Tyler.*"

He eased two fingers into her just as she came, penetrating her as she trembled through her climax.

When he finally stood up and gazed down at her, she whispered, "I want you inside me."

His chest tightened at the need in her voice. That same need burned in every square inch of his body.

"That's where I'm heading, sweetheart," he murmured and held her legs, pulling her to the edge of the table—which by some miracle appeared just the right height for him to penetrate her. He leaned forward just a bit, and then slid deep into her.

Lena cried out, and she reached her hands above her to grip the other side of the table.

He squeezed his eyes shut, taking a moment to savor the sensation of being inside her.

"*Please,*" she begged, clenching the walls of her sex around him. He ground his teeth together and tightened his grip on her legs. He thrust in and out of her, increasing his pace and squeezing the soft flesh of her thighs.

"Harder," she begged. "Please, Tyler."

Her words made him lose all control. He groaned and flexed his hips, pounding into her so she moved up on the table. He pulled her back down, tightening his grip as he continued the hard thrusts.

His sac tightened, and he moved one hand in to rub her magic spot again. When his orgasm exploded, she came too. Her body clenched around him again as he came inside her.

He fell forward and kissed her breast, sliding up to nuzzle her neck. His heart pounded hard. He stroked over the pulse in her neck and found it beating just as furiously.

"How are you doing, sweetheart?"

She gave a weak sigh. "Tyler, you have no idea what you do to me."

He had a pretty good idea, because she evoked the same response in him.

He stood and helped her up. "I'm going to clean up. When I get back, I'll make us dinner. Why don't you catch a nap on the couch?"

She nodded and slid off the table, but her knees buckled. Tyler gave a soft laugh and swept her into his arms, carrying her to the couch.

"And later tonight, I promise to give you the most amazing backrub. Deal?"

"Deal," she murmured and yawned.

He covered her with a nearby blanket and then headed for the bathroom.

"Lena, wake up, sweetheart."

She frowned and mumbled, "Let me just sleep for another

minute."

"You've been asleep for over an hour."

Lena blinked and sat up, rubbing her eyes to ease the sleep from them. She glanced at the clock on the wall and frowned. "Why did you let me sleep for so long?"

"You needed it." He grabbed her hand and helped her off the couch. "And while you slept, I made us a damn good-looking dinner—if I do say so myself."

She yawned again as he led her to the table. Her eyes widened as she sat down.

Each plate was laid out with a thick steak, juices oozing around it. In the middle of the table on a plate were chunks of white cheese, a loaf of bread, and two goblets filled to the brim with wine.

"This looks incredible. You're spoiling me." She glanced at him. He looked so proud, she wanted to kiss him again.

Jeez, could he be any more amazing? He'd let her sleep while he cooked them up a fabulous meal.

"I like spoiling you." He winked and sat down. "I put on a different CD though. The temptation to throw Celine out the window became too great."

Lena cocked her head and listened for a moment, then gave an approving nod. "Miles Davis. You're on a roll."

He laughed and cut into his meat.

"Do you cook a lot at home?" she asked then took a bite of her own steak. *Mmm.* She closed her eyes, savoring the taste.

"Believe it or not, yes."

"After this bite? I can believe it." She sipped the wine, swirling the golden liquid over her tongue. "Although I might have chosen a red wine with the beef."

"Snob. I told you I'm more of a beer guy." He shook his

head and drank another sip. "But on that note, we should try and stop by one of the wineries."

"Oh, could we?"

They discussed wineries and ate dinner, until the shrill of the phone cut them off.

Lena frowned as she moved to grab her phone from her purse. Seeing it was Stephanie, she answered with a flippant, "*Bonjour.*"

"Hello, darling. How's Paris?"

"Steph? We just got here. How are you?" Lena met Tyler's gaze across the room.

"Not bad." Stephanie's tone turned amused. "I take it you're having a good time?"

"I am having a *great* time." Lena laughed and looked at Tyler then gestured to her food.

Tyler rolled his eyes and picked up her plate, carrying it over to her. He fed her a piece of cheese while appearing to listen to her side of the conversation.

"That's good." Stephanie replied. "Have you checked out the hot tub on the patio?"

"Are you joking?" Lena swallowed the cheese.

Tyler raised an eyebrow. "What's going on?"

"There's a hot tub on the patio," she whispered, covering the mouthpiece before speaking into the phone again. "Stephanie, this place is amazing. I don't even know how to thank you."

Tyler had already left the room to check out the hot tub, so Lena turned her full attention to her friend on the other line.

"Are you alone, Lena? Did he go outside? Can you talk?"

"Yeah. I'm alone for a moment at least." Lena glanced at the porch and saw him fooling around with some buttons on the hot tub.

"Going to take advantage of that hot tub, huh?"

"Of course." Lena gave a soft sigh. "Tyler made us a great dinner with steak, cheese, bread and wine. It's so good. And we're already talking about going to a winery."

"Nice. I'm on a lunch break, eating a veggie burger." Stephanie's tone changed. "You sound like you're both getting along pretty well. How is he in bed?"

"Stephanie," Lena protested and then giggled, lowering her voice. "He's given me more orgasms in one night than Keith has the entire time we've been together."

"Damn, maybe I should've taken a turn with him while I was in Amsterdam."

Jealousy stabbed hard in her gut, and she almost slammed the phone down.

"I was *joking*, Lena," Stephanie said after a moment.

Lena closed her eyes and gave an inward groan. She leaned against the counter and ran a hand over her forehead. Where had that come from? The complete, uncalled for jealous rage? Toward Stephanie of all people, who she should've known was just messing with her.

"I know you were..."

"Lena, can I ask you something? How serious are things getting between you two?"

"How serious?" Lena swallowed. She'd been asking herself that question quite a bit these past days. "It's not, Steph. You know that. This trip is all about me having some fun before I—before."

The words froze in her throat, and a cold sweat broke out on the back of her neck. *Say it. Say, before I return home to Keith.*

"Are you sure about that?" Stephanie asked in a quiet voice. "Have you stopped to wonder where your heart is going throughout this whole fling thing?"

"I know where my heart is," Lena snapped, irritated by her friend's line of questioning. She didn't want to be confronted by her own doubts right now.

"Well, unless it's shrouded in ice I'd be careful," Stephanie cautioned gently. "Sometimes you don't realize you're falling in love until it's too late."

Chapter Ten

The breath left Lena's chest as if she'd been punched. Her mind reeled. Falling in love? With Tyler? No...it couldn't be possible. It could *not* be possible.

Tyler walked into the room, grinning big and wiping his hands on his pants. His smile faded when he saw her expression.

Lena turned her back to him and spoke in a low tone into the phone. "Listen, I can't talk now. Call me later, okay?"

"Lena, there's something else I have to tell—"

Lena hung up and chewed on her lip. She took a deep breath, hoping she looked composed as she turned to face Tyler.

His gaze narrowed. "Everything okay?"

"Everything's fine," she replied in a bright voice. *Nice. That wasn't obvious.*

He nodded, though she knew he wasn't convinced by her response. Fortunately he chose not to push it. "Let me know if there's anything I can do."

"I will." She nodded. "In fact, that hot tub is sounding better every minute."

"It gives a great view of the city. After dinner we should take advantage of having a soak."

"We should," she agreed and went to sit back down at the table. She broke a chunk of bread off the loaf and sank her teeth into it.

It tasted good, but her appetite had pretty much vanished after the conversation with Stephanie.

When they finished eating, he stood up and took her plate. She gave him a brief smile and let him kiss her on the cheek before excusing herself.

Once alone in the bathroom, she splashed a handful of cool water across her face.

She opened her makeup bag and pulled out her birth control compact. As she slipped the pill onto her tongue she smiled, thinking about the discussion she and Tyler had engaged in on their way to Paris. Not pleasant and certainly a little awkward, but the sex talk had been necessary.

They'd both been tested not long ago and, with a clean bill of health on each side—and with Lena on the pill—they agreed they wouldn't need condoms anymore.

She cupped some water in her hands and drank it to wash down the pill.

Afterward, she glanced at herself and sighed. Had Stephanie been *right*? Lena took a slow breath in and looked at her reflection in the mirror.

How the hell did you let your emotions get involved?

She shook her head. It just wasn't possible. She couldn't look at Tyler and think *he's just a fling.* At some point, things had changed. But did he feel the same? Or was she the only one noticing the slight shift in their relationship?

Tyler sat in the small window seat, reading a new release from a popular thriller writer. That was one thing he looked forward to on business trips. It gave him the chance to catch up on his reading.

Hearing a sound, he glanced up and saw Lena approach. She paused in front of him, looking a bit uncertain.

123

When she didn't speak, he reached out and caught her hand in his, stroking the back of hers with his thumb. Her smile was hesitant. She seemed almost nervous. What had changed?

He reached an arm around her waist and pulled her onto the seat with him. She came without protest, and he scooted over so she could curl into his body.

She pulled her legs up toward her chest and nestled her head into the curve of his shoulder. Then she gave a tiny sigh, and her body relaxed against him.

He dropped his chin to rest on the top of her head, a little unsure how he felt about the protectiveness running through him. Reaching down with his free hand, he pulled the blanket over them both. He lay for a while, listening to the soft sounds of her breath. Soon it turned deep and slow. The curve of her stomach rose in a gentle rhythm against his hand.

Out of nowhere came a vision of what it would be like to be with Lena thirty years from now. Both older, with the same chemistry between them.

He scowled. *Where had that thought come from?* He absently tightened his fingers on her stomach, and she gave a small whimper in her sleep.

Settling down with one woman or getting married had never held much appeal to him before. Why Lena? Why now? It could never work. Could it? She wasn't looking for anything serious, and pretty soon they'd go their separate ways.

His gut tightened, and a thick sadness threatened to sweep in. *Stop it. You knew the rules, just enjoy what you have for now.*

He adjusted to get more comfortable in the window seat and let out a long sigh, lifting his book to resume his reading.

Lena opened her eyes, struggling to identify her

surroundings. Light filtered in through a small window, and she was alone in the bedroom. When was the last time she'd slept so well? She didn't even remember going to bed.

She sat up, admiring the antique wooden frame of the bed she lay in. She turned and noticed the canopy corona above her, with white lace draperies tied back against the wall.

She gave a soft sigh and took in the rest of the bedroom. An antique armoire stood on another area rug, and a wooden rocker sat in the corner next to a lace-draped window.

Like the entire apartment, the room was enchanting. Whoever owned this apartment had to be crazy to ever want to leave it.

"Hey, you're awake." Tyler walked into the room, carrying a white paper bag and two steaming paper cups.

"Hi." She rubbed her eyes and yawned as he came to settle on the bed. "Did you bring me in here last night?"

"Yeah. You fell asleep in my lap while I read, and I carried you into the room around ten."

"Oh." Lena gave a small frown and sat up. "I'm sorry. What a bad sport I am. We were going to go in the hot tub, weren't we?"

He shrugged. "It's a vacation. We're here to have fun and relax. Plans don't have to be set in stone."

"Smart thinking." She sat up and accepted the coffee he handed her, crossing her legs under her bottom. "What's in the bag?"

"Croissants." He opened the bag and set out the flaky, buttery pastries, and her mouth watered.

"This is too incredible. I'm eating croissants in *Paris*. This has got to be the best day of my life." She stole one off the bag and took a generous bite. Her eyes closed at the first taste. "Have I told you how fat you're going to make me?"

"Whatever." He brushed a crumb off her lip. "Besides, I fully intend to keep you active."

"Hmm." She waggled her eyebrows. "Now that sounds like a promise."

"You bet it's a promise." Tyler took another bite of his croissant. "What are we doing today? Sightseeing? Shopping?"

"Sightseeing," she responded right away. "I want to go to Notre Dame and that cemetery, and—"

"All in one day?" He gave her an indulging smile. "We should space them out a little. Take time to enjoy each place.

"Sorry. I'm just *so* excited." Lena finished off her own pastry and then took another sip of coffee. "Ugh, I need a shower."

She grabbed clean clothes from her bag and looked at him over her shoulder. "Well, you may as well join me."

"I already showered, sorry." His look clearly indicated he was disappointed that he had. "I'll take a rain check, though."

She winked. "Okay, I'll be out soon."

They spent the day wandering through Cemetery of *Père Lachaise*. After two hours, Tyler still wanted to explore, but he gave in when Lena insisted they sit down and rest.

"I can't believe you're still going." She groaned. "I think we spent entirely too much time visiting Jim Morrison's shrine."

Tyler grinned and thought about the shrine. Probably one of the coolest things ever.

"I could've sat there all day showing my gratitude to that man," Tyler said as she slipped her hand into his. "The Doors had to be one of the greatest bands to ever grace the earth. I wish I had been alive when they were around. They set the mood to many dates in college."

"The Doors and a good amount of alcohol, I'm sure," she teased, but tried to pull her hand back.

He grasped it tighter, a soft laugh escaping him. "Does that make you jealous?"

"Of course not. Why would I be?" Her question sounded too defensive. "We're not even a couple. We're just having—"

"Sex. Right," he finished in a monotone. It had started to sound like a bad punch line to a joke that kept getting repeated. And even as she said it, he knew it wasn't true for him. But what about her? Did she still think of their time together as just great sex?

Lena cleared her throat. "Where do you want to go next?"

He took a deep breath, pushing the serious stuff out of his head.

"We still have to visit the *Arc de Triomphe*, *Musée du Louvre*, and I'm thinking we ought to grab some lunch some time."

"And what about the Eiffel Tower and Notre Dame?"

"It's only Tuesday, Lena." He smiled, relaxing again. "We have a lot of time."

"I know, but still. Let's *go*." She squealed and took off ahead of him.

Lena dropped her backpack on the floor of the apartment and sighed, stretching her arms. "I'm so glad you suggested the dinner-and-movie-in idea. I couldn't handle too much more sightseeing today."

"No kidding." He dropped the DVD and grocery bag on the table. They'd just made it through the other tourist sites before all the travel had caught up with them. They'd voted to indulge in a movie, a bottle of wine and microwave popcorn.

"Be back in a second." Lena went to the bedroom to change into her cotton nightshirt. It hit mid-thigh, somewhat sexy, but wouldn't be considered seduction-type lingerie.

Screw it. She was too tired to seduce him tonight anyway. She yawned and walked into the living room, climbing onto the couch while Tyler fiddled with the settings on the DVD player.

"There we go. Had to switch the language settings to English." The film started, and he walked back to the couch and sat down beside her, draping an arm around her shoulder.

Lena snuggled into his side and let herself get sucked into the action movie.

Most of the time, she wasn't into the blood and guts movies, but Tyler had been adamant about not getting a chick flick.

The movie wasn't half bad. She found herself enjoying the excitement and being able to clutch Tyler's arm when things got too intense.

With her head against his solid chest, she couldn't help but breathe in his cologne—faded now and mixed with just the normal smell of Tyler.

Then at times both of their hands would end up in the popcorn, and his fingers would brush against hers, sending tingles down her spine.

When the movie ended, he clicked off the television using the remote and ducked his head into her shoulder.

"You smell so good."

Lena smiled. "Like buttery popcorn?"

"Yes, but you also smell like Lena." He kissed her shoulder.

She laughed and nudged him in the stomach when he kissed the back of her neck. "Let me get this straight. You just got done watching a movie where some gangster blows a man's head off, and now you're turned on?"

"I'm a guy. And to my defense, there *was* an incredibly kinky sex scene in the movie. I've been turned on for about the last hour."

Thank God he'd said it first. Because that scene had been steamy enough to make her squeeze her legs together and bite her lip.

"Well...I suppose I could get myself into the mood." She adjusted herself so she faced him and draped her legs over his.

He slipped his fingers under her nightshirt and between her thighs, holding her gaze. "That's funny. It feels like you already are."

She caught her breath as he slipped beneath her panties to touch her.

"I umm...*oh*..." She gasped. "I guess action movies turn me on too."

"Yeah. I guess so." He lowered his head to kiss her, his fingers sinking deep.

She sighed and opened her mouth to his coaxing lips, sliding her hands over the planes of his chest.

"Speaking of kinky." She lifted her head, remembering that item she'd made him buy at the store. "I've got an idea."

"Yeah?" He tried to draw her back against him.

"Hang on." She pushed herself away from him and slid off the couch.

"Lena." He groaned. "Come on, sweetheart. Don't leave me this way."

"Jeez, a little patience."

She went to the refrigerator and pulled out the bottle of whipped cream, biting her lip as her pulse increased. Oh, the possibilities.

Heading back to the couch, she held it up in front of her.

"Oh, really?" His mouth curled, and he gave a husky laugh.

"Hey." She lifted a finger. "It's possible that you're Mr. Kinky every day of your life. But I, on other hand, am beyond vanilla. So, I'd really appreciate if you'd just let me have at it."

He leaned forward to take the bottle from her hand. "If that's your honest to God desire, than we can get a whole lot kinkier than whipped cream."

Lena saw the glint in his eyes and swallowed hard.

"Gee, that's a great offer." She snagged the bottle back. "But let's start with this for now."

"Okay. Well, then, by all means." He pulled his shirt off and leaned back, folding his arms behind his head. "Have at it, sweetheart."

Lena gaped at him and bit her lip. Hmm. Where did she even start? Of course, she had ideas what one should do with a bottle of whipped cream, but she wasn't all that confident she could do them.

"Fine." She lifted her chin, hoping she appeared a bit more confident than she felt, and straddled him. She pulled the cap off the bottle of whipped cream with her teeth and spat it on the floor. "I'm going to make you tremble, Tyler."

"That was so sexy. The way you just did that." He winked and moved his hands to her thighs. "And I have no doubt you'll make me tremble."

Lena pressed the nozzle to allow the whipped cream to come out. Nothing happened.

"You might want to shake it." He cleared his throat, and she got the impression he was trying not to laugh.

She gave him a warning look as she shook the bottle, then

pressed the nozzle again. White foam shot out like a fluffy bullet and landed all over Tyler's surprised face.

"That's not exactly where I hoped you'd put it." He grimaced and wiped away the foam.

"Oops." Lena giggled and leaned forward to lick it off his face. She thought she was doing a pretty good job at being sexy until the shaking of Tyler's stomach beneath her had her pulling away in confusion.

"What?"

"Nothing." He shook his head, but his eyes danced, and his stomach bounced with the laughter that he held in.

"What is so funny?" she demanded. "Tell me."

"Nothing. You just..." He put a hand over his face to partially hide his grin. "Okay. Don't get mad. It just feels like a dog greeting me when I come home from work or something."

Lena jerked back in shock. "You did *not* just say that. Tyler, did you just compare me to a *dog*?"

"No, of course I didn't. I shouldn't have said it that way." He tried to pull her back down to him.

Oh. Well, she'd show him. She jerked his boxers down his legs and let loose with the can between.

"Lena," he choked, his eyes widening.

She fell to her knees in front of him and braced her hands on his thighs.

"Compare this to a damn dog." She met his wide-eyed gaze before dipping her head to trail her tongue over his erection.

"Oh, God." His hands clutched her hair.

There. Now who had the upper hand? She smiled and licked more whipped cream off him. His groans intensified, and knowing she brought him so much pleasure made her even hotter. She could feel the dampness gather between her legs.

The hands in her hair held her tight against him.

She kept teasing him until every last inch of whipped cream had been removed. Only then did she open her lips over him and sink down, bringing him deep into her mouth.

"*Oh.*" He groaned loud and long, his hips bucking.

She moved up and down, taking him a little deeper.

"Please, Lena."

When he tried to push her away, she refused to move and kept tormenting him, bringing him so close to the edge. He finally pushed hard enough that she released him with a popping sound.

"Mmm." She licked her lips, her pulse racing. "I kind of liked that."

"*You* kind of liked that? You have no idea what it did to me." His voice came out hoarse. "No more, please. I need you, now."

"Then take me." She pulled off her panties and then kneeled over his thighs, lifting her nightgown up. "Now."

His response was a pained groan as she slid down onto him. She moaned, taking her own pleasure now as he filled her thick and deep. He stretched her, sinking to the hilt on the deepest of strokes. His hands gripped her hips as she moved on him.

"Tyler, *yes.*"

Then he took control, moving faster and harder up into her. Lena buried her face against the side of his neck and whimpered.

He thrust upward one more time up, just as she ground herself down onto him. His groan mingled with hers, and she squeezed her inner muscles around him as he emptied himself deep inside her.

His arms wrapped around her waist, clutching her to him. "Thank you." He kissed her forehead. "That was..."

"Pretty damn incredible." Her heart still pounded. "Yeah, I know."

He laughed and stood up, her body still wrapped around him.

"Now who's being cocky?"

"Hey, you inspire me." She laid her head on his shoulder.

She wanted so much more than a week with him. *You can't think like that. You'll drive yourself insane.*

"Bed now?"

He nodded and yawned. "Bed now."

Chapter Eleven

The next morning the streets were active with Parisians bustling through their workday.

They took a bus up to Notre Dame Cathedral. The different points of the church ominously pierced into the gray sky.

The whole building loomed over the city, displaying its magnificence and radiating its gothic aura.

"Our Lady of Paris," Tyler murmured and, when Lena cast him a sidelong glance, he nodded to the Cathedral. "That's another name for Notre Dame."

"It's amazing." She turned back to look. "I should have brought more batteries for my camera. I have a feeling I'm going to go picture happy."

Five minutes later, they were exploring the grounds in front of the Cathedral. Lena's camera clicked away, capturing all angles of the structure, while Tyler took mental notes.

"Enough." Damn, he should have brought his own camera. He'd just have to ask her for copies later. "Let's explore now."

"All right." She placed the camera back into her purse. "Show me around."

"With pleasure, sweetheart." He winked and grabbed her hand, leading her inside.

They took their time walking through the chilled hallways, and he acted as her private tour guide since he'd been there before. They climbed to the towers to look up close at the gargoyles, and then went down to the crypt beneath the

Cathedral.

They moved down the dark halls and the darkness suddenly lifted as they stood before a magnificent stained glass window. Lena gasped and stopped.

"The rose windows." He let his gaze roam over the shimmering glass. Still as impressive the second time around. "About the only stained glass window that's original in here."

Lena lifted her fingers to her lips and shook her head. "I'm not sure I've ever seen anything so beautiful."

I have. He stared at her, and his breath caught. She was lovely in the beam of filtered light coming from outside.

There he went with the sappiness again. He jerked his gaze back to the window. "You're right. The entire Cathedral is amazing, and the window just adds to its beauty."

"Do you think they sell little versions of these? Like on a key chain?" she asked, her tone hopeful. "I'd love to take this piece of Paris back with me to my house."

Tyler laughed and wrapped an arm around her. "You are the epitome of a tourist. Thank you for your efforts in reviving the world's economy."

"I do my best to help."

They walked back outside, finding the sky still overcast and a bit dreary.

Lena plopped down on a bench. "I think I'm going to sit for a moment if you don't mind."

"Go for it." He glanced back at the church. "I'm going to do another quick run through and jot down some notes."

"Notes?" Lena laughed and raised an eyebrow. "You going to build one of these yourself?"

"Maybe." He dropped a kiss on her forehead. "Stay out of trouble." Tyler wandered the grounds, exploring every crevice and flying buttress he could find. He took a ton of notes, drinking it all in.

The last time he'd been here, he hadn't been in the mindset to apply what he saw to his future career. He tapped the pen against his lips, formulating ideas on how to incorporate this ancient style of architecture into some of his more modern buildings.

"You're hard to find in here."

He'd been so deep into his own thoughts, he hadn't heard Lena's approach.

"What were you thinking about? You looked miles away."

"How amazing this all is," Tyler admitted in awe. "It makes me want to travel the world and see all kinds of buildings built in the last millennium."

"I could get you there for a good price." She nudged him and then went quiet for a moment. "Okay, just tell me. I'm too curious. What do you do?"

He paused, relief spilling through him that she really seemed to want to know.

"I'm an architect."

"Oh." Her mouth curled upward, and she squeezed his hand. "That's great, Tyler."

"Thanks, I'm pretty fond of my job." He placed an arm around her waist. "Hey, what do you say we hit the city and go shopping and get some lunch?"

"I can handle that," Lena agreed just as a plump, smiling woman approached them.

"Excuse me. Will you take a photo of my husband and me?" The woman asked in a thick Scottish accent.

"Sure, no problem." Lena took the camera from the woman and—after the couple posed—took the picture.

"Thank you, dearie. Would you like us to take your picture together?"

"Oh, no thank—"

"We'd love it."

They answered at the same time, and Tyler glanced down at her in surprise. Her cheeks turned pink, and she glanced away.

"Thank you. That would be great," he finished and smiled at the helpful woman.

"Not a problem. I'm glad to help." The woman gave a dismissive wave of her hand and took the camera from Lena who seemed hesitant to hand it over.

Tyler wrapped an arm around Lena's waist, pulling her close against him and wondered why the hell she didn't want a picture of them together.

Tension still ran through every muscle of her body a few minutes after the picture had been taken.

A picture of them together. Tangible, visible proof of their affair. Why it even worried her she couldn't be certain. Her future with Keith seemed about as solid as Jell-O right now.

What did it matter? She'd delete the picture later, and nobody would ever be the wiser.

"You know it's true. You've taken tons of pictures, but we don't really have any pictures of each other yet," Tyler said on the bus ride home.

"Hmm. You're right. I never noticed," she lied. *Change the subject.* "Maybe we should have a night out tonight, like have a nice dinner and then go to a club."

He stayed quiet for a moment. Great, was he obsessing over the picture thing? Fortunately he didn't say anything more about it.

"Good idea on the night out. Let's do it."

She sighed. "But first, I need to do some shopping. I haven't bought any souvenirs yet."

They reached the heart of the city and exited the bus, walking around the shops and exploring at random.

Lena found a chunky silver bracelet and funky purse to buy for Stephanie, and then picked up a necklace with an Eiffel Tower charm on it for Lakisha back at work.

The brief thought of getting Keith a paperweight crossed her mind, but she quickly dismissed the idea. Right now he didn't deserve the crumbs from her croissant.

Tyler had picked up numerous gifts for his sisters and parents and now hauled around a large shopping bag.

She started when he grabbed her hand and dragged her into a small shop. Then he approached a sales lady and started speaking in French and gesturing toward the mannequin in the window.

Lena frowned. What the heck was he saying? Jeez, she should have paid more attention in French class. She went to look at the mannequin in the window.

"Oh, no." She shook her head. "I could never wear this. This kind of dress looks good on tall women who are shaped like a coat rack."

Tyler raised his eyebrows as the sales lady came over and fussed around Lena. Lena scowled as she went to work figuring out her measurements.

A moment later, the lady shuffled her into a small fitting room as Lena clutched the dress.

She fought the urge to hurl it over the curtain in rebellion. With a sigh of surrender, she started to undress. When she'd finally figured out how to put the dress on, she turned to the mirror. Her jaw dropped.

The black fabric was silk. A thick strap curved over one shoulder, leaving the other bare. It clung to her curves and fell just above her calves.

"It makes my boobs look great," she murmured, running her hands over her torso. She turned, glancing over her shoulder to get a look at her backside. "Not bad on the butt either."

"Lena, are you going to come out and show me?" Tyler called from the other side of the curtain.

She started to and then paused, biting her lip. "No, I don't think I will. You picked a winner. I'll get it, but I want it to be a surprise when you see me tonight."

There was a pause from his side of the curtain. "Okay."

When Lena came out a moment later, she saw Tyler signing a receipt. Her stomach clenched, and she ran toward him.

"Oh, no. You can't buy this for me. It's *insanely* expensive." The sales lady gave her a sharp glance but didn't comment.

"Don't worry about it. And you weren't supposed to look at the price tag." He plucked the dress from her hands.

She sighed and wrapped her arms around him. "You didn't need to buy that for me."

"I know I didn't, but I did." He dropped a quick kiss on her lips and then tucked the bag under his arm.

Grabbing her hand, he steered her out the door.

"Are you going to buy yourself something?"

Tyler shrugged and eyed some of the shops they were passing. "If I see something I like."

He slipped his arm around her waist, and she leaned into him, lifting her face up for a kiss. He obliged and let his lips graze over hers. Feeling naughty, she opened her mouth to draw his lip between her teeth and gave a playful nibble on him.

He tightened his arms around her and tickled her side until she let him go with a giggle. They started to walk again when she turned to glance in a shop.

Lena jerked to a stop, seeing the familiar face of Claire—the woman from the train—staring back at her with a curious expression.

What were the chances she'd run into the other woman in the middle of Paris?

Claire gave a friendly wave as she stepped outside the shop. "Lena, no?"

"Yes. Hello again, Claire." A wave of unease ran through her. She'd told Claire she was engaged and traveling with a friend. Had she seen the kiss?

Please, don't let her bring up my engagement.

"Tyler, this is Claire, the woman I told you about from the train. And Claire, this is Tyler. My friend I'm traveling with." She could feel her face heating but kept a friendly smile plastered in place.

"Wonderful to meet you, Tyler." Claire shook his hand, her gaze warm, yet curious.

"You as well." Tyler gave Lena a broad grin. "Lena couldn't stop talking about you after she met you on the train. Apparently you made quite an impression."

Right. Lena bit back a laugh. Tyler probably didn't have a clue who Claire was or even remember her telling him about the Parisian woman. He sure played it off rather well, though.

"I'm shocked we ran into you, Claire. What are the chances?"

"My office is a block south from where we are," Claire

explained. "Are you two staying far from here?"

"Not too far."

"Lovely. And you are out shopping?"

"Yes. I still need to get some shoes to go with my dress I just bought." Lena sighed. "So it's taking us a while."

"If you would like, I can show you some of my favorite shops," Claire offered.

Lena cast a speculative glance at Tyler. "Oh, well..."

"Go for it," Tyler urged. "You go spend some time with Claire while I run some errands."

"Are you sure?"

He nodded and held her gaze for a moment, and she could see the sincerity there.

"I could really use the time to do guy stuff."

Her lips twitched. "Okay. I'll meet you back at the apartment in a couple hours."

He gave her a quick kiss on the lips and then left.

Lena stood frozen, her back to Claire. *Okay, there was no way Claire could have missed that kiss.*

She took a deep breath and turned around.

Claire stood smiling, no judgment anywhere in her expression. "Are you hungry? My favorite café is nearby. We could have lunch, or perhaps just coffee."

Lena nodded hesitantly. "Coffee sounds nice."

She fell into step beside the other woman, and before long they were seated in the wicker chairs of the café.

"And how has Paris been treating you, Lena?"

"Oh, wonderful." Lena sighed and shook her head. "I'm most enchanted by Notre Dame. It's so dark and beautiful. We don't have anything like it at home."

Claire laughed and drank a dainty sip of coffee. "America has its charms. Although it has been a while since I have visited there. The last time must have been when Monica was ten. She wanted to see the real California Disneyland."

"Ah, Disneyland." Lena grinned. "I think I went there at least five times before I got my driver's license, and then once I had it, I took road trips once a month. I didn't care if it took me a day and a half to get there. It was worth it."

Claire smiled in response and glanced down at her mug.

The silence expanded from a brief pause to a long silence. Lena's pulse sped up, and she licked her lips. *Was Claire wondering about Tyler?*

"He's my friend from New York," she blurted. "We met in Amsterdam and have been traveling together."

Friends that make out on the streets of Paris. She hoped Claire would be too polite to bring that up though.

"Tyler? He seems very nice. I assume the trip has been very enjoyable for you both?"

That was an understatement. She lowered her gaze. "Yes. Very much so."

Claire pushed her chair back and stood up, apparently not taking the conversation any further.

"Come, let me show you the side of Paris I love most."

Tyler flipped through the channels on television but stared without much interest. Loneliness bit at his gut, and he remembered how it was back in Amsterdam before he'd hooked up with Lena.

He'd sure gotten used to having her around. He clicked off the television and was debating going to take a nap when Lena stumbled into the apartment carrying two oversized bags.

Relief spread through him. "Did you leave anything for the other shoppers?"

She scowled and dropped the bags on the floor. "Shopping isn't quite as easy as it looks, you know. I just stopped that croissant from going straight to my thighs with all the walking I just did."

"Oh, I see." He winked at her. "I knew women must have an ulterior motive for shopping."

Lena kicked her shoes off and went to sit down on the other end of the couch, placing her feet on his lap. He pushed them aside before crawling forward to lean over her. She curled an arm around the back of his neck, smiling as she drew his head down to hers.

"I missed you," he murmured.

"Mmm. I missed you too."

He pulled her harder against him, slipping his tongue inside her mouth.

Her hands drifted over the muscles of his abdomen, and she pulled back a bit. "Tyler, did I ever tell you that you've got amazing abs?"

"No, you didn't." He reached down to caress a breast. "But since we're discussing body parts, I really like these."

"Do you?" She arched her back so her breast settled firmer into his hand. "How much?"

"Oh, very, very much." He slid his hand under her shirt and inched up her stomach.

"Good." She pushed him off her and rolled off the couch. "Because that'll make you appreciate them even more tonight when you get to see them again."

Tyler blinked, his mouth hanging open. "Oh, you've got to be kidding me. That's so cold."

Lena batted her eyelashes and blew him a kiss from across the room. "Trust me, it'll be worth it. I want you to be going insane for me by tonight."

Tyler groaned and thrust his hands into his pockets. He was going insane for her *now*. Tonight he'd be climbing the walls.

"Okay, sweetheart. Whatever you want."

"You know, I love it when a man says that to me."

Tyler gave her a thoughtful look. Of course, if he wanted to he could probably sway her. He crossed the room to her. "Sure I can't change your mind?"

Lena's eyes widened. "I'm sure."

He leaped toward her, and she yelped, diving in to the bathroom and slamming the door in his face.

Tyler laughed. After hearing the shower turn on, he walked into the kitchen to mix himself a gin and tonic. Drink in hand, he went to the window and stared out at the Eiffel Tower. Tomorrow they'd go there.

Opening the sliding glass door, he stepped out onto the patio and sat down in one of the wooden deck chairs. He sipped his drink, enjoyed the view, and thought about Lena.

He could still hear the shower running. And she was singing, though not very well.

A moment later, the shower turned off. His hands clenched around the glass as he imagined her toweling off her wet body.

He tipped the glass back and emptied the rest of its contents in one swallow.

Finishing off the drink, he walked back into the apartment and dropped the glass on the counter. Grabbing his book, he sat down to read.

The novel sucked him in, and he almost didn't hear her

come into the room. It wasn't until she stood in front of him did he glance up.

His chest tightened, and his blood thundered through his veins as he ran his gaze over her.

Her skin shimmered against the black dress. The exposed shoulder was so erotic he wanted to kiss every bare inch of it.

The dress itself molded over her curves and then stopped halfway down her leg, showing sexy calves and red-painted toenails that were tucked into at least four-inch stiletto heels.

She'd done her makeup darker tonight, her eyes outlined in feline fashion, and her lips were plump and painted an *I'm a sex kitten* color of red. A sweet musk scent drifted from her body.

He raised his gaze to meet hers, stunned to see her looking tentative and shy.

"Is it too much?" She fiddled with her hair, the only thing that remained the same.

Instead of answering, he grabbed her and hauled her against him. His lips crashed down on her mouth, and his tongue slid deep to rub against hers.

She gasped, holding onto him as if he'd thrown her off balance. When he let her go, she drew in a ragged breath.

"Does that answer your question?" he rasped as he stared at her swollen lips. "You'd better go put on some more lipstick."

Lena blinked at him and then ran an unsteady finger over his mouth. "And you'd better go take mine off."

He didn't respond, just wished he had time for a cold shower. With a groan, he turned and strode into the bedroom.

Chapter Twelve

Lena let out a quiet squeal the moment he left the room. His response had been more than she had even dared hope for. It was primal—something so completely foreign and new to her.

And the way she'd done her makeup made her feel like a movie star on Oscar night. To think she'd almost wiped it all off, thinking it seemed too dramatic.

Lena went to turn on the radio and then walked around the apartment. A song with a complex rhythm played, and she sauntered around to the beat, swinging her hips with her newfound confidence.

She passed a mirror and paused. Then turned around and moved back in front of it.

She took a moment to pose in front of the mirror, thrusting a foot out in front of her and pouting her lips into a seductive expression.

"Oh, yes, darling." She flexed her arms so the tiniest bulge of muscle appeared. "You are sexy. You are wanton. Purrrr."

She rolled her hips to the music and lifted her arms above her head, trying hard to imitate a belly dancer.

"You *are* sexy," Tyler murmured from the doorway.

Lena jerked upright. She spun to face him and stumbled in her stilettos, falling smack on her butt on the carpet.

"Are you okay?" Tyler hurried forward, his question offset by the laughter he obviously tried to hold back.

Her face burned with humiliation. "I'm fine, really."

He sank down on his knees beside her. "I'm sorry. It isn't funny."

"Hmm. So you weren't just laughing?"

"Well..." He cleared his throat. "Hang on a second. I have to give you something."

She turned to face him, giving him a suspicious look. "What is it?" He pulled a small box out of his pocket and flipped it open.

"These."

The small, teardrop-shaped diamond earrings glistened against the velvet lining. Lena stared at them, baffled. "You bought these for me?"

"No. They're for my sister, but I thought I'd let you borrow them tonight."

Her gaze flew up to his, and then she laughed, noting his eyes glittering with amusement.

"I'm joking, Lena."

She smiled and removed the small studs she already had in her ears, and then reached for the box.

He held onto it. "Let me put them on you."

"All right."

His strong fingers fumbled with the earrings, and then he reached up to place them in her earlobes. She watched his determined expression as he set about the task and enjoyed the pleasant sense of intimacy of the moment.

He took twice as long as she would have if she'd put them in herself, but it was worth it when he pulled away, looking so proud of himself.

"Thank you for the earrings, they're lovely." She leaned forward to kiss him on the cheek.

"No, thank you, Lena." His hand rested under her chin.

"For letting me take out the most beautiful woman in all of Paris tonight."

"Well, tell me where she is so I can kick her ass."

Tyler smiled and draped an arm over her shoulders, leading her toward the door.

"Oh, I forgot to tell you." She glanced up at him. "Claire has really taken a liking to me. She's invited us over for dinner to meet her family tomorrow night. What do you think? I said yes, but if you don't want to I can call her back."

"No, I think it sounds great." He shrugged and locked the door to the apartment.

Could he be any more supportive? Closer to perfect?

After a long, romantic dinner, they took a taxi to a club and waited in line for a few minutes to get inside. Lena chewed her lip, wishing she weren't so damn nervous.

The music pounded loud, and hundreds of people were twisting their bodies and grinding on the polished dance floor.

People wore all kinds of clothes, from barely there outfits to more sophisticated dresses like the one she had on.

"I thought I might be overdressed," Lena shouted to Tyler. "But obviously not."

"I'll say," Tyler yelled back and signaled for two beers at the counter.

The bartender handed them over a minute later, and they walked around again, looking for a table. They managed to snag a free one and sat down. Several pairs of eyes followed their progress, one woman in particular showing extra interest in Tyler.

Lena placed her hand on Tyler's shoulder and lifted an eyebrow.

That's right, he's with me.

The woman shrugged and looked away.

Lena smiled, congratulating herself on the tiny victory, and glanced at the dance floor. The heavy pounding of the Euro trance music had her almost twitching in her seat. Tyler must've picked up on it.

"You really want to dance, don't you?"

She grinned and leapt up, grabbing his hand and pulling him onto the floor.

Lena squeezed her way between people and found a spot with enough room for her to dance with Tyler. She gave a small shriek of excitement, barely heard above the music, and started to fling her body around in abandon.

"What are you doing?" Tyler yelled, standing stock still watching her.

"I'm dancing. Which is what you should start doing if you don't want to look like an idiot."

He stood still a moment longer before he threw himself into the trance music. They blended right in with the wave of movement on the floor.

A few songs passed before Tyler grabbed her hand and leaned in close to her.

"I need some water," he shouted into her ear. "You coming?"

Lena nodded and let her body slow to a standstill. Tyler dropped her hand and started to make his way toward the bar.

She went to follow when an arm snaked out and weaved around her waist, dragging her back toward the dance floor.

Lena turned to see who had grabbed her and encountered a rather large man.

He smiled at her and yelled something in French.

"I'm sorry." She shook her head and sent a furtive glance toward Tyler who hadn't noticed she'd stopped. "I don't speak French."

"Ah, you are American?" He laughed and grabbed her hands. "I tell you that you are a very beautiful woman and you must dance with me. I am Mortimer."

"That's very sweet of you, but—" She got cut off as another loud, pulsing song came on and drowned her out.

He jerked her around with the music, and she groaned, feeling a little bit like an oversized stuffed animal. How the hell had she gotten herself into this situation?

She closed her eyes for a moment and, when she opened them, Tyler's amused expression came into view. He lifted his water in a salute and went to sit down at the table.

He didn't plan on rescuing her? She made a face and kept dancing. She burned out quick and, after a moment, she couldn't bear it anymore. She pushed herself hard away from the French man and made her way back to the table. She had almost reached it when she noticed a lithe woman in a sleek pantsuit place herself next to Tyler.

Lena froze and watched for a moment to see what would happen. Jealousy stabbed deep as he smiled at the woman, then appeared to get into a quick conversation.

She watched for a moment, expecting Tyler to look for her on the dance floor, but he seemed engrossed with the woman.

Her stomach clenched, and she took an unsteady breath. The initial hurt faded, and a slow burn of annoyance replaced it.

She turned and went back to the bar, deciding to buy herself a drink.

"I can't believe this," she mumbled under her breath. "I get all dressed up and instead of him going nutty over me, he finds someone else to flirt with."

She reached the counter and smiled at the bartender. "One lager, please."

The bartender turned to get her drink with a nod.

A hand closed over hers, and her pulse jumped. She looked up, expecting to see Tyler. Her stomach sank and she bit back a sigh. Not Tyler.

The man who stared back at her was attractive and seemed very interested in her.

"Hello." The man had an English accent. "Can I buy that drink for you?"

She started to decline, but happened to catch a glance at Tyler. The woman now laughed and had placed a hand on his shoulder. Lena's teeth snapped together, and she found herself turn back to the man in front of her.

"Sure, why not? My name is Lena, and you are?"

"Absolutely in lust," he replied, running his gaze over her. "My name is Edward."

Ugh. Lena gave an inward groan. Was that supposed to be a turn on?

"Edward, thanks for the drink." She flashed him a bright smile.

Edward made a hum of interest, and she nearly rolled her eyes. Instead she turned her head away.

Her gaze connected with Tyler's. Ah, now he was looking. The steel in his gaze sent a tremble through her body. He really didn't look happy.

She raised an eyebrow and glanced at the woman beside him, then back to him. He gave a slight shake of his head, but his expression didn't change.

If he wasn't interested in the woman, than why didn't he

just walk away? Not liking the hot irritation bubbling inside her belly, she gave a hard shrug and turned away.

"Edward," she said brightly. "Would you dance with me after you have that drink?"

What the hell kind of game did she think she was playing? Tyler watched Lena parade some love-struck looking guy onto the dance floor, and his hand clenched around the beer bottle so tight it almost snapped.

The woman next to him droned on and on about a man she knew in the United States, and maybe if Tyler might know him. *Right.* Because, after all, the United States was so small.

He hadn't been able to shake her since the moment she approached. She'd been hitting on him in a not-so-subtle way, but he had done nothing to encourage her flirting. When she'd even been so bold as to reach out and stroke his shoulder, he'd shrugged off her hand and repeated that he'd come with someone else.

His gaze honed in on Lena and the other man on the dance floor. Was she jealous? Is that why she'd sought out another guy? It seemed the only plausible answer. And it didn't please him.

He had no time for women who played games. His ex-fiancée had been a master at them, and now Lena pulled the same shit.

And the longer he watched her, the more certain he became that she was setting out to make him jealous.

Unfortunately, she was doing a damn good job of it.

Why the hell had she ever thought this was a good idea?

Lena groaned as Edward dragged her body against his. She

gave him a tight smile and pressed her hands against his chest, trying to put some space between them.

He laughed but gave in and let her have her way.

A little more relieved, she glanced again toward Tyler. He still watched her with that cold gaze, but now seemed to be ignoring the woman.

Why didn't he brush her off? Tell her to get lost?

Edward leaned forward and said something in her ear. Although she still couldn't hear him, she smiled, just to give Tyler the impression she was having fun.

It worked a little too well. Tyler shook his head and stood up, striding out of the room.

Her stomach took a nosedive. *Shit, you went way too far, girl.*

She thrust away from Edward and took off after Tyler.

What on earth had she been doing? To provoke him like that? It all seemed too petty now. Especially when she watched the woman who'd been preying on him move on to another guy.

Not seeing him in the other room, she bolted out the door of the club. The frigid night air hit her lungs like a brick, and she took shallow gasps before hurrying down the sidewalks.

"Tyler?" she called out. Where had he gone? She hadn't been that far behind him.

The only response was her echo in the dim streets. She spotted a man walking fast further on down the road, and she squinted, trying to see if it could be him.

"*Lena.*"

She spun toward the voice.

Edward stepped out of the shadows and gave her a quizzical look. "Why did you run out so quick?"

God, he'd followed her? She gave an irritated sigh and

shook her head. "I have to go."

He took another step toward her and placed a hand on her arm. "Hey, what's the rush?"

"I *really* have to go." She pulled her arm back, shuddering at the sleaziness of his touch. What on earth had possessed her to flirt with him? To deliberately try and make Tyler jealous? What was she, sixteen?

"Let me get you cab or something."

Lena groaned. Maybe she should just take him up on that.

"That would be great. Thank—" She gasped as he gave her a violent shove into an alley. "Hey, what—"

Edward slammed her against the side of the brick building, and his hands closed around her throat.

Fear raced through her veins, and she gasped, reaching up to try and pry his fingers away.

Oh, God, why didn't I take that self defense class with Stephanie last year?

Edward leaned close, fumes of his alcohol breath smothering her. "You Americans sure like to tease. Coming on to a bloke and then just walking away."

"I'm sorry, please let me go." The words were hard to get out—his hand was wrapped around her neck too tight.

His other hand made a grab for her breast, and she slapped it away, bringing her knee up between his legs.

"*Fuck.*" He released her and bent over, grabbing his crotch. Lena slipped around him, her heart pounding, and ran back toward the street. She spotted the streetlamp at the end and increased her pace.

The hand on her shoulder jerked her backward, and she rolled to the ground, tearing her nylons and scraping her knee.

One moment he reached for the front of her dress, tearing

the fabric, and the next he flew backward across the alley.

Lena struggled to stand up, her body shaking. Relief spread through her when she spotted Tyler. His fist slammed into Edward's jaw, and the other man stumbled backward. He regained his footing, seemed to consider hitting Tyler back, and then spun around and ran down the alley in the opposite direction.

Tyler turned around to face her, his gaze one of concern. "Are you all right?"

Her eyes welled with tears, and she shook her head. She didn't deserve his sympathy. Not after what she'd just pulled.

"We need to find the police. Report this."

"*No.*" Her eyes filled with tears. "Please, just take me back to the apartment."

He slipped his arm around her and escorted her out of the alley.

"I'm so sorry, Tyler. For the way I acted in the club."

He didn't reply, just hailed a passing cab and helped her inside before climbing in next to her.

He kept an arm around her, comforting her, but she could tell that he was not happy with her.

When they reached the apartment, he let them in and firmly shut the door, sliding the lock into place. He urged her onto the couch and placed a blanket around her before standing up and walking into the kitchen.

He turned on the faucet and filled up a glass of water before returning and handing it to her. Never saying a word.

She accepted the glass from him, her hands still unsteady. She took a small sip and glanced out of the corner of her eye.

She took a deep breath. "Please talk to me, Tyler."

His jaw clenched, and he went to stand by the window. "Do

you even realize what could have happened to you?"

"Of course," she whispered and bit her lip to keep tears from filling her eyes again.

"Why were you even flirting with him?" His tone roughened. She stood up and went to him, placing her hands on his tense shoulders.

"I just saw you sitting so close to that woman... I think I got jealous." Shame flooded through her at her words, and she paused, closing her eyes. Then she admitted, "And I wanted to make you feel the same."

"Am I supposed to be flattered? That you'd get jealous of some random woman who attempted to hit on me?" He gave a humorless laugh. "Damn, Lena, I don't know what to think right now."

"*No.* I don't want you to be flattered. You have every right to be mad. I acted stupid, and I'm sorry." The tears did flood her eyes then. "What happened in the alley—"

Tyler spun around, dragging her against him. His arms wrapped around her in a crushing embrace, but she didn't mind. Turning her head against his chest, she let the tears fall.

Tyler groaned, his words harsh. "You have no idea the fear that went through me when I saw him attacking you."

She drew a ragged breath in. "If I hadn't flirted with him—"

"This isn't your fault. Don't try and take the blame for some asshole who should be locked up."

"That's just it. I don't know *why* I flirted with him. It's not at all like me."

Tyler grasped her chin, forcing her to look at him. "Do you want to know if I felt the same, Lena? Got jealous?"

Lena's stomach clenched and she shook her head. "No, please. Just let it go. I should never have—"

"You're *damn right* I got jealous. I wanted to pound the crap out of him, and that was *before* he attacked you."

Lena's pulse quickened. "Tyler..."

"And do you want to know what the craziest thing of all about this is?" His gaze bored into hers. "Why I should even care at all. We've known each other for less than a week. *A week.* Why the hell *do* I care so much, Lena?"

She blinked, wanting to deny it, but she felt the same.

He rubbed a hand down her neck. "From the moment I met you, everything changed. I'm playing an entirely different game this time, and I have no idea what I'm doing or if I even like it."

Lena swallowed the sudden lump in her throat. "Tyler, we shouldn't be saying these—"

"And you sit there pushing me away. Demanding I treat you like some stranger." He shook his head. "Well, I just can't do it anymore. I'm sorry."

The blood seeped from her face, and she swayed in his arms. Would he leave her in Paris? Call it off? The idea of it almost crippled her.

"I won't do it." He rubbed his thumb across her mouth. "I want to know everything about you—not just how to touch you to bring you to orgasm. I want to know everything. I want to know what your favorite movie is, what really pisses you off, your favorite color. I want to know about the cat you had to put to sleep when you were twelve." He took a deep breath in. "I want to *know you,* Lena."

Chapter Thirteen

Tyler waited for her to respond, his chest tight. Would she push him away again? Tell him they were through? Her stare seemed both surprised and hesitant. She looked down, and drew in a shaky breath.

"I didn't have a cat," she said huskily. "I had a cocker spaniel we had to put to sleep. And I was fifteen."

Hope sparked inside him. That maybe she'd absorbed some of what he said.

"Lena, do you understand what I'm saying?" He tilted her chin up again so she had to meet his gaze. "I don't know if I can look at this as a vacation fling anymore. Somewhere along the line I started to care for you." He paused, before throwing caution to the wind. "And I need to know if you feel the same."

She stared at him, her blue eyes still shiny with tears. He could sense the inner conflict raging within her. The confusion. When she didn't answer, he convinced her in the only other way he knew how. He covered her mouth with his own, brushing her lips in the softest kiss.

She clung to him, matching his strength and passion. They sank to the floor and she pulled him on top of her. His hands roamed over her body, cupping the heavy fullness of her breasts.

"Lena, hang on." Tyler pulled away for a moment. "Are you okay doing this? I don't want to rush you after what happened tonight."

"Please, don't stop. Your touch will help me forget." She

buried her face into the crook of his neck. "You consume me."

His breath hissed out in a controlled gasp. He made sure to be slow and gentle as he undressed her. He took a moment to tease the pink tips of her breasts, then brought them into his mouth and suckled until her soft cries hit fever pitch.

He slid a hand over her thigh and captured her mouth for another kiss. He slipped his tongue between her lips, and then moved his hand inward to cup her sex.

The moisture he found there signaled that she was ready for him. He slid his finger deep into her, her sigh of pleasure encouraging him onward.

He sat up and removed his clothes, then knelt again in front of her, meeting her passion-filled gaze.

"Please, Tyler." She licked her lips, and her knees fell open. He lifted her hips, cupping her bottom and pulling her forward to him.

With one thrust, he buried himself deep inside her.

They both groaned, and a tremble rocked his body. He took a moment to enjoy the sensation of being inside her, and then started a slow, steady rhythm.

Her breath came out in short bursts, and he pressed a thumb between her legs to bring her further pleasure. She gasped and pressed her hips into him, moving faster as he thrust deeper.

A moment later she clenched around him, crying out in as she found her release. He managed a few more thrusts and then groaned, his body tightening as he emptied himself inside of her.

Lena's eyes were closed, and her breasts rose and fell with her shallow gasps. She looked so sexy. So damn sexy, and yet so vulnerable. He closed his eyes for a moment, fear running through him at how lucky he'd been to get to her in time.

After a moment, he pulled out of her and stood up, then held out his hand and pulled her off the soft carpet.

She stumbled to her feet, barely able to stand. He kept an arm around her and dropped a thorough kiss on her mouth. When he pulled away, she buried her face against his chest and sighed.

"Do you mind if I take a bath?"

"I think you should." He gave her shoulder a light squeeze. "You've had a pretty intense evening, and a bath will help relax you. Are you hungry?"

Her stomach rumbled at the question.

He laughed. "I'll take that as a yes. Let me go find some place that's still open and pick us up some food."

She yelped when he swept her off the floor and into his arms. "What are you doing?"

"Taking you to your bath."

Lena wrapped her arms around his neck, a drowsy smile on her face. He was so good to her. Something she had yet to get used to. And more than once every day, she'd found herself wondering what it would be like to take this relationship beyond the week.

"You're too good to me."

He set her on the edge of the claw-foot tub and turned on the faucets.

"Can I have some bubbles?" Lena smiled up at him through her lashes.

"Bubbles?" he repeated and raised an eyebrow. "Sweetheart, I don't have any bubble bath."

"I do. They're rose scented. But they're in my bag in the bedroom."

"You really want a bubble bath?"

"Yes, please."

"All right." Tyler gave a soft laugh and then left the bathroom to grab her bubbles.

Her heart melted a little more, and she smiled, stepping into the tub.

Tyler returned a moment later, dressed and carrying a small, pink bottle. He opened the container and poured it into the tub.

Iridescent suds began to pop up, and Lena inhaled the soft, floral scent.

"All right, sweetheart, try not to have too much fun." He leaned over to drop a kiss on her lips.

Her heart skipped a beat, and she latched a hand onto his shirt. "What if I pulled you into the bath with me?"

"There's no way you're getting me into a bath that smells like roses." He pried her fingers off him. "Besides, you wanted food, didn't you?"

"Yes. So I'll let you go. This time."

He laughed and blew her a kiss before slipping out of the bathroom. A moment later, the front door shut.

Things had changed between them tonight, and for the better. Tyler calling her out on the games and rules had been the best thing to happen to her. She didn't want to hold back anymore.

She wanted the possibility of...of what? Something more.

She shook her head and sighed. Slipping under the water, she let the warmth cover her. She surfaced to the sound of her cell ringing.

"I'll bet he forgot his wallet. Or the keys." She jumped out of the tub and slipped on the floor. Righting herself, she slapped a towel around her body and caught the phone right at the tail end of its fourth ring.

"Thank you very much, Tyler. I almost fell on my butt jumping out of the bath to get the phone."

Her gut twisted when there was no reply. "Hello?"

"Who's Tyler?"

Her bubble of happiness ruptured, all giddiness sinking into her stomach. Keith. *You're technically still engaged. How easily you managed to forget that.*

"You shouldn't be calling me." Her fingers clenched around her towel.

"Lena, we've got to talk," he said urgently. "Mother contacted me to let me know what had happened. I want you to know that she means nothing to me."

His mother meant nothing to him?

"She's just a slutty little secretary at the firm. I got carried away."

Oh, not his mother. The bimbo he was fucking in Maui.

"A slutty little secretary?" Her blood pressure spiked a bit. "I'm sorry, is that supposed to make me feel better?"

"Well...no, but I just thought you should know that it meant nothing. And I'm really sorry, baby."

His apology sounded about as animated as if he'd announced he was going to get his oil changed.

"I'm really glad that you're sorry, *baby*. But I'm in Europe at the moment and not in the mood to talk about your inability to keep you dick in your pants." Lena took a slow, steadying breath. "I am on *my* vacation, and you are not going to ruin it any more than you already have."

"Hang on." His voice rose, displaying his displeasure at the unraveling conversation. "You never said who Tyler is. Tell me you're not sleeping with him."

"Actually, I am. And he's great in bed." She smiled, enjoying this a little more than she ought to. "And his dick is huge."

The line went quiet, and she frowned. Had he hung up on her? She started to disconnect the call when he spoke again.

"I need you to come home, Lena." He gentled his voice, as if he were talking to a young child. "You're not thinking rationally right now. You're obviously too upset to be on your own."

Her chest expanded with the breath she drew in to control her temper. "*What*?"

"You should buy a ticket for the next flight home—go ahead and put it on the card. Yes. Do that. I want you home as soon as possible."

"I don't give a rat's ass what you want. I'm doing what *I* want." It was amazing how controlled she kept her tone. "When—I should say *if*—I come home, we can talk then. Don't call me again, Keith."

She hung up, her body trembling. She glared at the phone, and then cursed as it rang again.

She turned off the phone completely, so he'd just get her voicemail.

Taking a deep breath, she went back into the bathroom and sat down on the toilet lid.

What an asshole. He'd just sent her back to that emotional mess stage, and this time for a whole different reason. What the hell was she supposed to do about Keith? With the wedding already set, and they owned a house together... Jeez, they'd been together for almost ten years.

And then there was Tyler. Her heart twisted a bit, a slight smile curving her lips.

Were her feelings for Tyler real or were they just an illusion? An illusion created by the romantic setting of being in Paris and having a sexy man treat her like a goddess. Maybe it *was* all an illusion. One that would disappear the moment they stepped back into America. Hell, they didn't live anywhere near each other. They were on opposite sides of the country.

"Damn." She shook her head. "I don't know what the hell to think anymore."

The thought of facing Tyler like this, emotionally confused, made her sick. She turned and ran into the bedroom, pulling on her jeans and a sweater.

Grabbing her wallet, she headed for the door. She had her hand on the handle when she paused and looked back. *You have to at least leave him a note.*

She turned back toward the kitchen to find a piece of paper.

"Hey, sweetheart, I've brought you food." Tyler let the door shut behind him.

Silence met him.

"Lena?" He searched the apartment and came up empty. His gut twisted, the fear almost paralyzed him. Then he saw the note taped to the television. He set down the bag of food and went to get it.

I have to get out. I'll be back in a couple hours. ~Lena

Crumpling the note in his hand, he sighed. "I must have scared the crap out of her with that little talk."

Walking over to the window, he cursed himself for being so confrontational with her tonight. She obviously hadn't been ready to hear that kind of declaration. And after the incident at the club, she could still be in shock.

He reviewed in his head everything they'd said earlier. What if she was wandering around the streets alone again? Hadn't she realized how unsafe it was outside? Jesus, he needed to find her.

He turned to grab his jacket and noticed her phone on the counter. It was turned off. Almost like she was avoiding all contact.

He narrowed his eyes. Maybe it wasn't her conversation with him that had made her run, but with someone else.

Removing his jacket again, he swallowed his fear and sat down on the couch. *You have to trust her.*

Lena stared out the window of the cab. Her head pounded, and all she wanted was to be stretched out in bed. *In bed with Tyler's arms around you.* Lena shoved the voice aside, willing herself to be logical right now.

The driver of the taxi glanced back at her on occasion, waiting for further instructions from his passenger other than to just drive around the city.

Coffee. Coffee would be good at this point. It would wake her up and clear her head a bit.

She leaned forward and cleared her throat. Too tired to make the effort, she didn't even attempt to speak French. "Do you know of any cafés around here that would still be open? If possible ones that have computers? Internet?"

"Yes, of course." Fortunately, he spoke English. "You would like for me to take you there?"

"Please."

A few minutes later he pulled up outside a café, the inside lit up, showing her it was still open.

Lena handed him the fare and fled the cab, eager to jump behind a computer and send an email to Stephanie.

Five minutes later, she'd secured a computer and ordered a latté. She settled herself into the small, wooden chair and logged onto her email account.

Lord, she had a lot of email. She deleted the ones that promised to increase her breast size or give her a three-day erection.

After she'd cleared out the junk, she opened a blank email and addressed it to Stephanie. She typed in everything that had happened in the past few days, pouring out her heart and holding nothing back. A half hour and another latté later, she hit send.

She rubbed her stomach, debating whether to just get up and head back to the apartment or to stay and fool around online some more.

Flipping back to her inbox, she started to read the emails. Some were from her parents—they of course went on and on about all the traveling they'd been doing, and where the best cities to party were.

She smiled and shook her head, closing out of one email and opening another from her co-worker Lakisha.

How's Europe? I'll bet you're eating pastries and drinking wine like a bum. You even going to read this, or am I going to have to chew your ass out when you get home? Thanks for leaving me to plan that honeymoon for that bitch Carolyn Monroe. She had all the papers signed, everything planned, and then comes in the next day saying her fiancé was being difficult.

Apparently, he took off for Amsterdam on work and told her not to book anything. Hey, maybe you might even run into him over there. If you do, run like hell if he's anything like Miss Stick-up-her-ass. Anyways, I gotta try and get her deposit back. Hit me back if you get the chance.

Lakisha

"Amsterdam?" Lena's brows drew together.

Something Carolyn had said floated back through her head. *My fiancé is an architect in New York.*

Tyler was an architect in New York. She shook her head. Could it even be possible?

"That would be way too much of a coincidence." Lena stood up, printed out the email, and slipped it into her purse.

She paid her bill, and then went back outside to hail another cab.

Tyler heard the door creak through the light sleep he'd fallen into. He blinked his eyes open and sat up on the couch. Lena tiptoed toward the bedroom, as if trying not to wake him.

"What's up?"

She gasped and turned his way. "I thought you were asleep."

"I was." *Tell me where you were. What's going on, sweetheart?*

Her smile seemed hesitant, and she cleared her throat. "I had to get out. I'm sorry. I hope you weren't too worried."

"Actually, I was." It seemed she wouldn't tell him without some encouragement. "You want to tell me what happened?"

She gnawed on her lip. "I'm just so tired right now."

Tyler's stomach clenched, and he looked away. "I may have been a little heavy with the earlier conversation. If that's what upset you, than I'm sorry."

"No, it's not that," she rushed to say, and her tone made him believe her. "I just need to figure out a few things. I need time to think."

"Okay. I can live with that."

"Thank you, Tyler." She yawned. "I think I'll just go to bed for now. This day has been...a little crazy."

"I know." Guilt stabbed at him. "Go get some sleep. I'll come to bed in a bit."

"All right." She turned to head for the bedroom. "Thanks again. For everything."

Lena woke up just in time to see Tyler get out of bed and go into the bathroom.

She sighed and leaned back against the pillows, tucking the sheets around her body. Lord, it had been a crazy day yesterday.

She glanced at her purse and thought about the printed email. She had to be crazy to think it, but what if Tyler was Carolyn's fiancé? The idea of Tyler being engaged to such a...raging bitch, really...kind of made her doubt the possibility.

She traced her fingers over Tyler's side of the bed, feeling the warmth from where his body had just rested. Sighing, she rolled over onto her stomach and squeezed her eyes shut.

The bed dipped again, signaling Tyler's return. He sat beside her, closing strong hands over her shoulder blades, and then began a slow knead of the tight muscles in her body.

"Mmm. That feels really nice." She shut her eyes and allowed him to massage her thoughts into oblivion.

He stopped twenty minutes later, and she rolled over, giving him an appreciative smile. It faded when she saw the quiet intensity in his gaze.

He lowered his mouth to hers in an unexpectedly tender kiss. "What are you feeling for me right now?"

She shook her head, running her tongue across her mouth. "I don't know."

"Of course you do." His mouth brushed over hers again.

"I don't," she denied, a little breathless. "It's never been like this before for me. Never."

"What are you saying?"

Her stomach flipped. "That's all I can say for now. Please don't ask me to. I can only say that...it's never been this way before."

He stayed silent for a moment. "Then that's all I need. I won't rush you. Why don't you get ready?" He kissed her forehead. "We've got big plans today. I was thinking the Eiffel Tower and some other sites. And we can't forget dinner with Claire."

"Thank you." Lena hopped off the bed and hurried to the bathroom. "I'll be out soon."

Chapter Fourteen

"How fantastic is this view?" Lena cried and slapped the edge of elevator.

"It's great," Tyler responded, pushing aside the nausea. They'd stood in line for less than fifteen minutes at the Eiffel Tower before taking the elevator to the second level. Now on the second elevator, they started to ascend to the top of the tower.

He kept his gaze directly out over the city, not looking down. How had he gotten through this the last time? Heights had never been his thing.

"Just fantastic."

Lena gave him a sharp glance, her smile fading. "What's wrong? You look like you're going to get sick."

"I'm not going to get sick," he denied, but sucked in his breath when someone bumped into him. His hands clenched at his sides.

"Tyler?" Lena's voice softened. "Are you afraid of heights?"

"No." He shook his head. "Not at all."

"Really?" Lena crowded past another person in the elevator so she could grab his hand. "Because you seem kind of nervous."

Tyler flushed as several pairs of eyes in the elevator honed in on him.

"Really, I'll be okay."

"I could understand if you were. It's a little freaky being on this elevator, rising slowly above the city." She leaned forward to glance out. "Has anybody ever gotten killed up here?"

Tyler gave her a swift warning glance, and she gave him a devilish smile.

"I mean, wow, it's a long ways down." She whistled and peered down at the ground, which was some two-hundred-fifty feet down.

Tyler closed his eyes to allow the nausea to pass, and when he opened them, the elevator doors were sliding open. He was the first one out.

"Better now?" she teased, but there was an apology in her eyes.

Tyler, still a little shaken from the elevator ride, gave her a sidelong glance and shook his head. "You're one sadistic witch."

"I can be at times." She gave him a sardonic smile and moved toward the deck so they could look out over the city. "You don't have to come to the railing if it bothers you. I don't mind going alone."

"I can handle it. Wouldn't miss this view for the world."

They moved as close against the railing as all the modern securities allowed. Her long, dreamy sigh eased his nerves a bit.

Still, he stayed behind her, content to just wrap his arms around her waist and gaze at the view from over her shoulders.

"I love Paris. It's so romantic," she murmured.

"I am feeling a bit romantic with you right now." He nuzzled her shoulder and looked out at the river. "Though my friends would give me hell if they knew I'd just admitted that."

"Romance can be manly." Lena elbowed him in the ribs lightly. "Hey, did you pack us a lunch?"

"I brought some snacks. A baguette and sausage. I have a full water bottle in my backpack. Are you hungry?"

"Not yet. But I thought we should have a picnic on that

grassy area down there." She pointed. "That spot where a few people are. Are you up for it?"

"Baby, I'm up for anything."

She stiffened. What had he said wrong?

"I'd prefer it if you didn't call me that."

"Call you what? Baby?"

"I've never liked that endearment." Her tone had grown tight. "You just always said sweetheart before, and it's just more...sweet."

"Sure." He gave her hand a reassuring squeeze and wondered if there was some kind of story behind the *baby* aversion. "Let's catch the elevator back down now. You mentioned food, and now I'm getting hungry."

A short while later they sat on small blanket, enjoying a surprisingly clear winter day.

Tyler pulled out the food and then handed her the water bottle. Lena took a sip, letting the cool water slip down her throat and then handed it back to him. They sat and ate in silence.

She sat back on the grass, supporting her body with her elbows and staring at the magnificent tower before her.

This was the life. Her gaze moved to a family that lounged a few feet away from them. The parents were cuddled close, watching their two toddlers run around in the grass. The kids' laughter was loud and sharp in the mild air.

Lena turned to look at Tyler who also watched the kids. He'd be a great father someday. She smiled. *And if he could hear your thoughts, he'd no doubt hightail it out of the country and as far away from you as possible.*

Don't mention marriage or kids to a man who's not ready. Up until recently, Keith had been a prime example of that.

"They're cute, huh?" He gestured to the kids.

Lena nodded. "Yeah, I was just thinking the same thing. That and how lucky we are to be here right now."

"Together." His gaze locked on hers.

"Together," she agreed. Had she ever been happier? "I'm in Paris, sitting under the Eiffel Towel, with a hot guy named Tyler Bentz who makes passionate love to me at night."

"It seems unfair. You do realize I don't even know your last name."

"Richards. My name is Lena Cosmo Richards."

"Cosmo?"

"Hey, I explained that my parents are pretty much ex-hippies. So don't give me crap about my middle name."

"Eh, Cosmo isn't so bad. You could've done worse." He winced. "The last woman I dated was a woman named Carolyn Monroe. Now *that's* bad."

The world tilted, and the breath locked in her chest.

"Now that's a crazy look." Tyler gave her a quizzical glance. "I said Carolyn Monroe, not Marilyn Monroe."

"Ugh, yeah. Got that." She blinked rapidly and pressed a palm against her head.

"Lena? Are you okay?" He scooted over to her and placed a gentle hand on her shoulder.

She flinched. "What? I'm sorry. I don't feel very well all of a sudden. I'm just going to run to the bathroom. I'll be right back."

Tyler opened his mouth to say something, but she pushed herself off the ground.

She hurried to the bathroom and, once inside, splashed some water on her face. She let her wrists sit under the slew of cold water.

Tyler was Carolyn's fiancé? *You saw the email last night. You knew it was possible.* She swallowed hard and shook her head. What were the chances of this happening? *Could Tyler know who I am?*

No. Carolyn hadn't even remembered Lena's name. She wouldn't have told Tyler about the silly little travel agent who'd given her information for their honeymoon.

So what did this all mean? Technically, she was sleeping with her client's fiancé—or ex-fiancé. Which was it? Either Carolyn or Tyler was lying.

You trust Tyler. She took a deep breath and left the bathroom. Tyler stood waiting for her outside the door.

"You okay?"

"I am. Sorry, just got a bit of nausea." She gave him what she hoped to be a confident smile and slipped her arm through his. "Where else did you want to go before we head out to Claire's? We have a few hours."

"Hmm?" He seemed preoccupied. "I suppose we could walk along the river and check out some of the bridges."

"That sounds good to me."

She'd bring everything up tonight after Claire's. Keith. Carolyn. All fiancés, ex or not, must come out of the closet.

Lena knocked on the door of what looked to be an upscale townhouse. Her nerves had remained rattled the entire taxi ride over, she squeezed Tyler's hand.

Tyler smiled down at her and winked. "Nervous?

"A little."

The door swung open, and she shifted her gaze forward to meet Claire's smiling face.

"Hello, hello. Please, come in."

Lena stepped through the doorway, and Tyler followed a second behind.

"How are you, Claire?" she asked as the other woman ushered them inside.

"I am wonderful. Come, I will take you to our leisure room where my family is waiting." Claire walked gracefully, leading them down the beige-carpeted hallway.

The house didn't seem large and overbearing, but intimate and decorated with pictures of the family.

Lena glanced around, curious to see the man that Claire had left her first husband for. In her mind, she envisioned a tall, handsome and distinguished looking man.

"*Mère.*" A young girl peeled out around the corner and wrapped herself around Claire's leg. "*Qui sont-elles?*"

"Remember how I told you, Antoinette. You are to practice your English tonight for our guests," Claire replied after leaning down to hug the girl.

The girl scowled and then gave Lena and Tyler a hesitant glance.

"Antoinette." Claire voice took on a firm edge.

"*Oiu, Mère,*" Antoinette replied with a sulk.

"These are Mommy's friends. Tyler and Lena. They are from America," Claire explained.

Lena smiled at the child. "Nice to meet you, Antoinette."

The girl stared. "You are not very tall."

Lena gave an abrupt laugh, not surprised to hear such a blunt comment from a child. "No, I'm not. I'm just barely taller than a child, aren't I?"

Antoinette looked at her mother in an obvious indication that she didn't understand all of Lena's words.

Tyler took over by kneeling beside the girl and speaking to her in fluent French.

Lena watched them in amazement. He charmed the girl quicker than he could have with a lollipop. Antoinette laughed and responded to him and, after a moment, she turned back to Lena.

"I am sorry," the girl said. "I speak in English as *Mère* wishes. Tyler, he is funny. Come, I show you to my family."

Lena hid a small smile, impressed at the girl's broken English. She spoke well for being so young.

As they followed her into the other room, Lena turned toward Claire.

"She's adorable. How old is she?"

"Antoinette is seven," Claire replied proudly. "My oldest daughter, Monica, is eighteen. She is the one gone to University at this time. Eric, my son, is fifteen."

They reached the sitting room decorated with several floral paintings, with floral-patterned throw pillows, and even a floral arrangement in a vase to complete the apparent theme. The woman liked floral.

Claire gestured for them to make themselves comfortable. Tyler and Lena sat down on a plush, green couch, and his hand came to rest on her knee. Her whole leg tingled at the contact, and she placed her palm on top of his hand.

Claire spoke in a soft voice to Antoinette. Lena glanced up at the other woman and had the sudden urge to confide everything about her situation with Tyler to Claire.

"Ah, Luc." Claire's voice came out on a sigh.

The entrance of a man into the room had Lena's jaw dropping a bit. The man she stared at was not at all what she had expected. He wasn't much taller than Claire, had very little hair left on his head, and had a slightly bulging stomach.

Claire's face lit up as she went to him and returned his brief kiss on the lips.

"These are my friends, Tyler and Lena. And this is my wonderful husband, Luc."

"Very nice to meet you both." Luc smiled and shook her hand. Tyler stood and gave a nod, the two shaking hands.

Luc returned to his wife's side and slipped his arm around her again, beaming down at her.

"You two are awful." The voice belonged to a lanky, teenage boy who'd just entered the room. He turned to Tyler and Lena and gave them a disarming smile. "I am Eric, the unfortunate child of these two inseparable people."

Such a teenager. Lena smiled, amused by the boy.

"You sound jealous, Eric. Your parents appear to have a beautiful relationship. Perhaps you are hoping to find the same someday?"

Eric shook his head and gave a lopsided grin. "I am only fifteen, *mademoiselle*. I cannot even begin to think about being with just one woman. There are so many who should enjoy the embrace of Eric Ames before I select just one."

While Lena gaped in shock, Tyler laughed.

"And now you have met my wonderful..." Claire paused, "...if not somewhat eccentric, family."

"What is eez sentrik?" Antoinette demanded from the floor where she played with some dolls.

"Something you will understand later in life, my darling," Luc inserted smoothly. "My wife has prepared an extraordinary amount of food for us, so perhaps we should make use of it?"

"Sounds great to me," Lena agreed. "I'm starving."

Two hours later, Antoinette had gone to sleep, Eric had left to go out with friends, and the adults lounged around in the living room, chatting.

Luc stood and stretched. "I think I will indulge in my end-of-the-evening drink and cigar. Claire does not allow me to smoke inside, so I go out onto the veranda. Would you care to join me, Tyler?"

Tyler gave a nod. "That'd be great."

Lena smothered a laugh. *Tyler was going to smoke a cigar?* "Then I will show you the game room. Do you play pool, my friend?"

Tyler nodded. "I do all right."

"Well, we must play later. What can I get you to drink?"

"Gin and tonic would be great."

Lena laughed, amused at how fast he'd switched into ultra guy mode. Before leaving, Luc opened another bottle of wine and set it down next to the women.

"Enjoy yourself, ladies." Luc winked at them and then headed out of the room.

When the men had disappeared through the double doors, Claire turned to Lena and gave a small smile. "I am so pleased we met again in Paris."

Lena returned the woman's smile. "Thank you, Claire. You've been so kind to invite us." She hesitated. "Do you often do this? Meet new people and bring them home?"

Claire laughed. "No. Not at all. I liked you. I liked you the first time we met, and I told you all about my scandalous past."

"It's not all that scandalous." Lena's thoughts briefly skipped to her own life. "And now that I see you two together, it's so obvious that you're both so very much in love."

Taking a sip of wine, Claire murmured, "I love Luc. More today than I did when I first met him."

"Amazing." Envy pricked through her. She couldn't say that about Keith, even before he'd cheated on her. Their love had been depleting slowly, like a balloon with a miniscule pinprick in it.

"If you do not mind me asking..." Claire paused. "You and Tyler seem very intimate. You say that Tyler is *not* your fiancé?"

Lena flushed, and her fingers clawed into her skirt. "No, he's not. I—"

"Where are my manners?" Claire shook her head, her face reddening. "I am so sorry. I should not have asked. It is none of my business. It is just... You two look so happy together."

"No, it's fine. Really," Lena said quickly. "I needed someone to talk to. I was hoping you could maybe give me some advice..."

"Advice?"

"Yes, I'm just so confused with everything." Lena's voice cracked. "There's so many complex things going on, and I'm going insane not being able to talk about it with another woman."

Claire gave a slow nod. "I think you are a very sweet woman, and I would love to be a confidante to you. Please, feel free to talk to me about anything you wish."

Relief weakened her muscles, and she took a deep breath before plunging in to tell Claire about everything that had happened to her in the last month. The good, the bad and the ugly.

When she finished talking, so much weight had been lifted off her shoulders. She downed the rest of her wine and sighed, leaning back into the couch.

Claire stared at her with a small, knowing smile and finally nodded her head. She looked at their now empty wineglasses and lifted the bottle to fill them again.

"First, I think we will need more wine." Claire handed her the glass back.

The wine had certainly helped to loosen her tongue. She raised the glass to her lips and took another sip.

"Truly amazing." Claire gave her a thoughtful glance. "It is like a movie, no? Lena, fate has certainly been at work in your life."

"You think that's what it is?" Lena frowned, drinking another sip. "Do you think it's fate?"

Claire continued to drink her own wine. "Of course it is fate. A coincidence as such?"

"Yeah, but it's not like a really good coincidence. It's possible he's still engaged to one of my clients." Lena tried to focus her thoughts and realized it was getting harder to do. "And she's a real bitch. Why would he ever be engaged to her in the first place?"

Claire laughed and shook her head. "I could not answer."

Lena stared at her glass of wine and frowned. How many glasses had they drunk so far? She shrugged and took another sip.

"Hey. What if he *is* still engaged, though? What if he's just sleeping with me?" She gasped, her eyes going wide. "Oh, my God, that's what I'm doing to him. *I'm* the bitch."

Chapter Fifteen

"You are not a bitch. You are a confused woman." Claire smiled and gave a tiny hiccup. "Tyler appears to care for you very much. And if I am not mistaken, you feel the same for him. Am I wrong?"

"Nope, you are not wrong." Lena shook her head, the movement making her a little dizzy. "No, Claire. I think you are very right. Very right indeed."

Claire laughed and leaned back on the couch. She stopped laughing after a moment and glanced at Lena. "I do not know why that was funny."

"Why what was funny?" Lena glanced at the wine. "Is there any more wine left?"

Claire leaned forward and reached for the bottle. It tilted, but she righted it before it could spill.

"Good job. Close call there." Lena gave a serious nod.

Claire laughed and poured them each a half glass of wine more to finish off the bottle.

Lena sighed and ran her finger around the rim of her glass. What was Tyler doing right now? Was he thinking of her? The wine moved through her body, warming her. She closed her eyes and thought about how good it felt to have his lips on her body.

"What are you thinking about?" Claire asked.

Lena opened her eyes. "How good the sex is."

Claire eyes widened in shock, and then her body shook

with silent laughter. "I suppose that helps."

"I mean, the sex is *really* good," Lena repeated, more firm this time. "And I *like* having good sex."

"You were having bad sex with the fiancé?"

"Terrible sex. Anti-sex."

"Such a shame." Claire clucked her tongue and stood up, glancing around the corner as if to see if anyone might be listening. She hurried back to the couch. "Luc and I have amazing sex. Even after twenty years."

"That's great." *Go Claire.* "I'll probably end up with cobwebs and a *do not enter* sign in twenty years."

Claire burst into laughter and wagged her finger at her. "Ah, but not with Tyler around."

"Tyler." Lena's heart skipped. "Tyler could make a nun leave the convent."

Clair laughed louder, and Lena joined in. When they finally calmed down again, Claire curled her legs under her bottom and turned to face Lena.

"How do you feel about Keith now?" Claire pulled the clasp out of her hair, and her restrained twist fell in waves down her shoulder.

How did she feel? Lena frowned. Now if that wasn't the question of the month.

"Well, he's an okay guy. Most of the time. When he's not banging some chick in Maui or refusing to have sex, or being a neurotic health nut, or telling me that my job isn't good enough, or—"

"Do you listen to what you say? He is a, how do you say it, a jackass." Claire gave a soft snort. "Sorry, I am the last person who should judge someone else. But perhaps it is a sign?"

"A sign? What, that I'm too boring for him? I just don't

know. I thought I loved him, but then I met Tyler. And nothing's the same. *Nothing.*"

"Perhaps—" Claire leaned forward and gave a sage nod, "—you are being given a glance at what life *could* be like. If you choose to stay with Tyler."

"I don't know. We made such a big deal of how this is just a vacation fling. And now it's all changing. Everything is changing."

"You will only know if you ask him. But you must tell him about Keith and ask him about this Marilyn lady."

"Carolyn." Lena's nose wrinkled.

"Of course. I apologize." Claire paused. "Unless you intend to return home and forget about Tyler. You will simply marry Keith as planned?"

"Ugh." Lena gagged, a shudder ripping through her.

"Ugh?" Claire stood up and turned on the radio. "Is that no? It sounded like no."

"Keith just seems like...cheese in a can. While Tyler is the real deal."

"They have such a thing? Cheese in a can?"

"Hell, everything comes in a can nowadays." Lena closed her eyes. Had the room started to spin?

When she opened them again, she stared at Claire, who appeared to be doing some kind of interpretive dance. She blinked, to see if the image would clear, but Claire kept dancing.

"Claire?"

"Mmm?" The other woman didn't even break in her movements.

"How much wine did we drink?"

Claire hesitated, looking a little surprised. "I am not sure.

But I think it is safe to say we may have overindulged a bit."

"Just a bit." Lena tried to make an inch sign with her fingers, but they slipped past one another.

"Come and dance with me, Lena. This is an old song. I feel like a teenager again." Claire cried.

Lena sighed and stood up. "Oh, why the hell not?"

"A combo, with the five ball in the corner pocket." Tyler lined up his shot and then took it, proving right his prediction.

"You are quite the player." Luc gave him an approving nod. "Do you play much?"

"I go out after work sometimes to shoot some stick. You're not bad yourself." Tyler leaned in to take out the eight ball after calling the shot.

"I love to play," Luc admitted, picking up his stick when the eight ball skimmed off the side, rolling past the hole.

Luc gestured with his stick to call the shot, and then banked the eight ball.

"Nice game." Tyler shook Luc's hand and then picked up his drink. "You as well."

Luc sipped from his own glass. "How long have you and Lena been dating?"

Tyler hesitated. What could he say to the other guy? *We're not dating, just fucking. Though I'm trying to convince her to be more.*

"Not very long. We just started, actually."

"That is the truth?" The other man looked surprised as he shook his head. "That is all? You have the ease of a long-married couple."

Tyler gave a brief smile. "We're not quite to that stage yet."

"You have plenty of time. You are both young. Would you

like another drink or cigar?"

"I'll take another drink."

Tyler followed the other man back into the sitting room and froze when they reached the doorway.

Music blared, and Lena and Claire were tossing their bodies around as if they were at a rave.

"Well," Luc murmured with amusement. "I probably should not have left the full bottle of wine."

Tyler raised an eyebrow, staring at Lena, who seemed oblivious to his presence.

Claire turned her head and spotted her husband. "Oh, my wonderful Luc."

She launched herself at Luc, almost knocking him over as she rained his face with kisses and babbled away in French.

Tyler gave a soft laugh and then looked at Lena. She kept dancing, though her gaze locked on him.

He walked across the floor, not breaking eye contact. He reached her side and slipped a hand around her waist. "Are you enjoying yourself, sweetheart?"

"Totally." She hiccupped. "We had a little wine."

"So I see."

Lena lowered her lashes, her expression turning seductive. "Tell me, Tyler. Do you think I'm sexy?"

Tyler's head swiveled to see if the other couple had heard her. Seeing they were busily wrapped up in each other, he turned back to Lena and traced a finger across her collarbone.

"You know that I think you are *damn* sexy, Lena."

"Good." She wrapped her arms around his neck and swayed to the music. Her nose crinkled. "You smell like cigars."

"I should. I smoked one." Hell yeah, she looked sexy. Even wasted off her ass, she was still adorable.

"That's nice. I think I'd like to smoke a cigar." She grinned. "And maybe have some more wine."

"You know, I don't really think you need any more."

"Look, aren't they cute?" Lena flung her head in a gesture toward Claire and Luc who were slow dancing to an upbeat song.

"They're adorable." The *cute* couple would likely want to be alone soon. "Time to go, sweetheart."

"Aw, so soon?"

"Yeah, it's getting late. Maybe we can even stop at a shop and grab some chocolate to bring home." He hoped chocolate would tempt her into leaving.

"Oh...chocolate." Lena grinned. "I like that idea." They went to say good-bye to the other couple.

"You two are leaving?" Claire sighed.

"Yes, we're going to go have some chocolate," Lena replied, all too solemn.

"Oh, is that what it is called now?" Claire winked at her and gave a sly smile.

While the two women hugged and whispered something to each other, Tyler shook Luc's hand again and thanked him for inviting them over.

After another few minutes of good-byes, Tyler managed to steer her out the door.

"Where are we going to get chocolate?" Lena asked, leaning against him for support. "These streets are awful. I can barely walk."

"They're terrible," he agreed in amusement, though he managed with no difficulties. "Why don't we just stop at the nearest café that's still open?"

"Okay, café is good. Café is a French word, isn't it?"

"I believe it is."

They found a café and went inside to sit down. Tyler ordered two coffees and a rich-looking chocolate confection.

"Mmm." Lena narrowed her eyes and stared at the morsel before her. She picked up her fork and took a bite, then closed her eyes with a near orgasmic expression. "Oh, yeah."

Tyler took a sip of his coffee and leaned back in his chair, watching her with amusement.

"Tyler?" She ran her finger over the half empty plate.

"Hmm?"

"Do you believe in fate?"

He paused. "Do I believe in fate?"

"Yeah, fate."

"Sure, why not?"

"Hmm." She frowned, looking not entirely satisfied by his response. She looked down at her plate for a bit and then groaned.

"What?" His gaze sharpened on her. Oh, shit, that color of green on her face could only mean one thing.

Lena smacked a hand over her mouth and jumped up, making a beeline for the bathroom.

I should have seen that coming. Tyler groaned and followed her toward the door. He heard the sound of retching and grimaced.

Why the hell had he taken her out to get chocolate?

He gave gentle knock on the door and her answer came in the form of a groan.

"Lena? Are you okay?"

Her only response was another pitiful groan.

Tyler glanced at the few occupants of the café, relieved to

see no one was watching them.

"Lena?" he repeated softly. "Do you want some water?"

"Yes, please." Her voice came weak through the door. "And my head is killing me, can you get me some aspirin out of my purse? I have a bottle in there."

"Poor girl." Tyler strode back to the table to find her purse.

He slipped his hand inside to search for the bottle and then swore, pulling his hand back out and staring at the paper cut just starting to well with blood.

"Damn it." He reached back in to find the aspirin and, as he did, a drop of blood splattered onto the paper, now wedged half out of her purse.

Tyler grabbed the bottle of pills, and then a napkin off the table. He blotted his finger and then reached for the paper to wipe off the blood.

He folded it back up to put away, when his gaze picked up a name on the paper.

"What the fuck?" His heart started to pound. He sat back down to read.

Sun. Too much sun. Lena groaned and pressed a hand over her eyes, rolling over in the bed. She opened one eye and looked around. Tyler lay asleep beside her, though in his sleep he scowled.

Hmm. Must be a crappy dream.

A wave of tenderness swept through her. He'd been so patient with her last night. She could barely remember the taxi ride home from the café. She leaned over and kissed his forehead.

Lying back against the pillow, she went over the conversation she'd had with Claire after dinner. There was no way she could marry Keith now. Not with how much Tyler had come to mean to her—how much happiness he represented.

Her head still throbbed as she climbed out of the bed to go get some water in the kitchen. She paused to use the bathroom, brush her teeth, and rinse with mouthwash. When she returned, Tyler lay on his side, his back to her.

She climbed back into bed with him and wrapped her arms around his chest. She felt him stiffen. He was awake?

"Tyler?"

"Hmm?"

"Are you mad about last night?" She pressed her cheek against his back. "I'm sorry. That was pretty crappy of me to drink so much and make you deal with it."

He didn't answer for a moment. She bit her lip. Crap, maybe he was pretty annoyed.

Tyler rolled over a moment later and met her gaze. His intense stare sent a ripple of unease through her. Finally, he closed his eyes and sighed.

"No, I'm not mad that you drank. It was almost cute, in a way."

"Yeah, real cute. Which part did you like better?" She grimaced. "The part where I danced like a hooker at Claire's, or when I puked at the café?"

"Both were kind of great, actually."

"Nice. Exploit my weak moment." She nudged him in the ribs.

Lena..." He paused, appearing to lose his train of thought as his eyes roamed over her again. "You're enchanting."

"And you're way too diplomatic if you're calling a hung-over chick enchanting." She flushed and ducked her head against his chest.

He smoothed a hand down her back. "What's going to happen in a few days?"

Oh God. Was this going to be a serious talk? "What do you mean?"

"With us? Are we just going to say good-bye and leave it at that?"

The blood drained from her head, and the nausea she'd experienced when she first awoke returned.

Say good-bye? Did he...was that what he wanted? Because she was beginning to realize that wasn't what she wanted.

"I'm just curious if I'm going to be a diary entry after Sunday."

A diary entry? "What makes you think you're just a diary entry to me? You know that's ridiculous."

"Is it? Look, I just want us to be honest with each other."

Honest with each other. It sounded way too easy. But honesty right now—explaining Keith—would mean a big, big mess. She closed her eyes.

"Why did you come to Amsterdam?"

She blinked and lifted her head. "Stephanie and I were taking a vacation together. You know that."

"I know. It just...the timing."

"The timing?" she repeated, a bit uneasy now. She'd been thinking that same thing yesterday after she'd read the email.

"I just get the feeling you're not telling me everything, Lena."

I'm not. But I will. Let me end things with Keith, then I'll tell you everything.

His fingers gripped her chin and lifted her head until their gazes locked. "I found that email in your purse.

Lena blanched and struggled to breathe.

His eyes narrowed. "You know who Carolyn is, don't you?"

"Yes." The words were a whisper. "She's your fiancée."

"No. She was never my fiancée. We were just dating, and I broke it off before I left." He paused, his glance scouring her face. "I realize Carolyn can be a bit of a bitch. Did you realize who I was and then decide to sleep with me to get back at her?"

"What? *No*. That makes no sense." She licked her lips. "I just found out myself. Look at the date on the email, Tyler. I printed it out the night before last."

His nostrils flared. "You've known for two days and never thought to say anything?"

"I know this looks bad, and I thought about it." She pulled away and sat up. "I just freaked out. I mean, you can't argue that it's a crazy coincidence."

"No, I can't exactly **argue** that." But he still didn't sound convinced.

She had doubts of her own. "Is it really over between you two? She seemed pretty convincing."

"So do sociopaths. The woman is nuts, Lena. It's over." He sighed and shook his head. "Besides, I wouldn't be in bed with you right now if I were engaged."

Lena felt the blood leach from her face and looked away before he could see her reaction to his words. Thank God she hadn't told him about her situation. It sounded like he wouldn't exactly be understanding.

She'd get a moment alone today and call Keith. She'd break off the engagement and *then* tell Tyler everything. How would he react though? Would he still be angry that she hadn't told him about Keith in the first place?

Of course he will.

"Is there anything else you're not telling me, Lena?"

The urge to blurt out the truth was right on her tongue. But the fear overpowered it. The fear of his expression when she told him—what he'd potentially do. Walk away. The idea made everything inside her shrivel up with fear. She had to end things first with Keith. Make it a non-issue when she told Tyler.

"No. There's nothing else." Her stomach revolted at the blatant lie.

He climbed out of bed and slipped his arms around her from behind.

"Thank you." He brushed a kiss over the back of her neck. "You know, my company also has an office in Seattle. I've been thinking about relocating out there. That's not too far from Portland, is it?"

Was this some kind of long-term reference? Her pulse quickened. "Just a few hours' drive."

"I love the west coast. It's beautiful."

The urge to call Keith—now—roared up inside her. Lena pulled away, wanting to get out of the apartment and call him as soon as possible. End it all immediately so she could be honest with Tyler, beg him to forgive her for lying to him in the first place. She should've done this long ago. Like the minute she'd found about Keith's infidelity. Or especially before she'd gone to bed with Tyler.

"I need coffee."

"Sweetheart, you don't feel well. Go back to bed and I'll grab it for you."

"No." She shook her head. "I need fresh air. I'll grab it. I'll just go to that corner shop. Would you like some?"

"Sure, if you don't mind." He yawned and stretched his arms above his head. "I'll grab a shower while you're gone."

"Okay." She rushed to pull on her jeans and a sweatshirt, then pressed a quick kiss against his lips.

He caught the front of her sweatshirt, pulling her closer, and brushed his lips over hers again.

"Don't be gone long."

"Oh trust me. I intend to make this quick."

"Good." He kissed her again. "Hey, grab some croissants too."

"Deal. I'll be back in fifteen minutes tops." She walked out the door, ready to close the door on one part of her life and open another.

Tyler had just turned on the shower, when a loud pounding came on the door. He turned the shower off again and wrapped a towel around his waist. Maybe Lena forgot her purse.

He opened the door and then blinked.

A man stood outside. Tall and groomed, he looked as if he'd just stepped out off the cover of *GQ*.

"Can I help you?"

The man gave him a once-over and made to step through the doorway.

Tyler slammed his hand against the other man's shoulder to stop his advance. "I don't think so, buddy." His voice took on the slightest edge. "What can I help you with?"

The man gave his head a shake of disgust. "I think you'd better let me in so we can talk. It's Tyler, right?"

How the hell did the man know his name?

"Maybe," Tyler replied with deceptive calm. "But you have me at a disadvantage. Why don't you introduce yourself, GQ?"

"The name's Keith," the man replied with a humorless smile. "And I'm here to find out why you're fucking my fiancée."

Chapter Sixteen

Shit.

Lena entered the apartment, stressed to the max. Keith hadn't answered his phone. Where the hell was he? He was making this ridiculously difficult.

Her cell shrilled to life. Lena set the coffee and croissants on the counter and answered her phone.

"Hello?"

"*Lena*," Stephanie said urgently. "Oh my God, has he shown up yet?"

"Steph? Hey, what's going on?" She frowned. "Wait, has who showed up?"

"Hello, baby."

She spun around and her heart dropped. "What are you doing here?"

"Oh God. He's already there."

"I'll call you back, Steph," she muttered, almost numb.

"I tried all last night to warn you, but you never answered the phone—"

Lena ended the call and stared at Keith. "You didn't answer my question. What are you doing here?"

His eyes narrowed. "Bringing you back to your senses. You're having a total breakdown."

"I'm not having a breakdown." Wait, why was the apartment so quiet? Her stomach clenched. "Where's Tyler?"

Keith didn't reply, and she pushed past him toward the

bedroom. It was empty. His suitcase gone.

Her heart slammed in her chest as she spun back to face Keith. "What did you do to him?"

"What did I *do*? Don't be so dramatic. I didn't do anything to him. He left about ten minutes ago." Keith looked pleased to break the news to her.

"He what?" She had to grab onto the counter as her knees threatened to buckle. "No, he wouldn't."

"Of course he did."

"What did you say to him?"

"Nothing I shouldn't have." He shrugged. "I told him that you were my fiancée, and that he was a revenge fuck after you learned I'd been cheating on you."

"You told him that?" she choked. "Oh, God. And he believed you."

She stumbled to the window and sat down in the seat, pressing her head between her knees. Of course he believed Keith. She had just lied to him less than an hour ago, and the living proof had shown up on the doorstep.

"You're a bastard." Lena shook her head, her body trembling. "You had no right."

"He *is* a revenge fuck, Lena. I get it. And so does he now."

She stood up, her fists clenched at her side. "You have no *idea* what he is to me."

"You don't mean that." Keith softened his tone. "Baby, I know I screwed up, but you got even. I'm not real happy about it, but I'll move past it in time. Besides, you wouldn't turn your back on this life we've built together, would you?"

Lena clutched her stomach, nauseated. "Yeah, I think I will. I don't love you anymore and, to be honest, I don't know if I ever did."

"Nonsense." He didn't look the slightest bit convinced. "You don't mean that. You're just confused."

She gave a humorless laugh. "I swear you're denser than a brick. Why am I arguing this with you?"

Tyler was gone. He'd left her life as quickly as he'd entered it. She swallowed against the thickness in her throat.

"I packed your bags, Lena. Our flight leaves in two hours. Unless you plan on staying in France alone?"

She glanced around the apartment, and her eyes flooded with tears. What could be accomplished by staying here? She would have to straighten things out when she got back to the States. She would get a hold of Tyler and explain things.

How? How would she contact Tyler? They hadn't exchanged phone numbers. *Maybe I could just call Carolyn and ask for his number.* She pushed back a hysterical laugh.

"I need to use the bathroom." She stood up and walked into the bathroom, knowing she was going to get sick.

"I'm sorry, ma'am." The voice came back on the line. "That number is unlisted."

"No, there's got to be some mistake." Lena clenched the phone as desperation clawed at her stomach. "Can you look again? The name is Tyler Bentz."

"Ma'am, I've checked twice now for you. I'm sorry, you'll have to find another means of contact. Thank you and have a good day."

"No, don't—damn it." She slammed the phone down after the woman hung up on her.

She glanced around the living room of her parents' house and groaned.

She'd only been back in the States for a few hours, and jet

lag pummeled her body without mercy. Thankfully she'd had enough sense to insist that Keith drop her off here. She had no intention of stepping back into that house as long as Keith lived there.

Sighing, she pressed a hand against her forehead. There had to be another way to find him. Maybe she could Google him and find the company he worked for. He might have his name on a website somewhere.

Her cell phone rang, and she dug frantically in her purse for it. Her heart sank a bit. Stephanie.

What, you expected Tyler?

She flipped it open. "Hey."

"What happened? I need details, and I need them now."

"I can't." Lena fell back onto the sofa and swiped at the tears that had gathered in her eyes. "I screwed up so bad, Steph. And now he's gone."

"Who, Keith?"

"No. I can't get *rid* of *him*. Tyler," she choked. "God, I'm such an idiot. I should have told him, and I kept putting it off. And then it all came back to bite me in the ass. I had him...and then I lost him."

She couldn't hear any words Stephanie might have said in response, because she was crying so loud.

Stephanie's firm voice cut through her tears. "Hello-oooo. Leeeena...blow your nose, honey. Blow your nose and listen to me."

Lena grabbed a tissue off the coffee table and blew her nose.

"Have you called him?" Stephanie asked.

"I don't have his number. I tried information, I tried looking him up online, I—"

"I have his business card—"

"Tried to locate his—you what?"

"He gave it to me outside the coffee shop the first day we met him, remember?"

"I love you. *I love you.* Give me his number." She leapt off the couch, knocking the used tissue onto the floor as she scavenged for a pen and paper.

"Hold on, let me get my purse." There was a brief silence and then the sound of the phone being picked up again. "Okay, got a pen? Here goes."

Lena jotted down the number and took a deep breath "It's going to be all right now. It has to be. I'll call him, explain everything, and then let you know how it goes."

"You'd better. I'll be waiting by the phone."

She hung up and stared at the number. The thought of calling him terrified her so much, her fingers shook as she dialed the phone.

It started to ring. Once. God, what if the number was wrong? Twice. What if he didn't answer? Three—

"Tyler Bentz."

Her fingers clenched around the phone, and she closed her eyes. The sound of his voice brought tears to her eyes and made her stomach flip.

"Hello, can I help you?" His tone sharpened.

"It's Lena."

Silence met her announcement.

Oh God, this was not going to be easy. "I...um...know what you must be thinking. But it was all just a big mistake. Give me a chance to—"

"Exactly, it was a mistake. This is my work number. Please don't call it again. Actually, I'm going to ask that you don't make any more efforts to contact me."

"But if you'd only—"

"Look, Lena." His voice turned harsh. "I don't want to hear it. You wanted a fling, well, you got it. Now let it go."

A fling. Her stomach clenched as if he'd hit her.

"Tyler..." But she spoke to dead air. He'd already hung up.

Her body numb, she set the phone down, but missed the charger and it fell to the floor.

She sank down to pick it up, and crumpled into a ball on the rug. Choking on a sob, she pressed her fist against her mouth.

It was too late. She'd already blown it. He wanted nothing to do with her.

Tyler stared at the phone, his mouth drawn taut.

The blood pounded in his veins and his throat had gone dry. *She called me.* He hadn't been back at work for more than an hour, and she'd called.

He hadn't expected to hear from her again—hadn't wanted to. Not after the shit she'd pulled. Engaged. Their entire time in Europe they'd been living life as a happy couple falling in love, and she'd just been using him for sex.

Which is what she told you was all she wanted from the beginning.

His chest tightened, and he dragged in a ragged breath. Damn, she'd played him for the biggest fool. And apparently he'd only been all too willing.

That phone call though... That phone call had just shattered any progress he'd made on moving on. Not that he'd moved on. Jesus, it hadn't even been twenty-four hours.

Maybe he hadn't handled her too well on the phone. But

yesterday morning he'd been ready to declare his love for her. His lips twisted in a bitter travesty of a smile.

And yet, call it morbid curiosity, but he *wanted* to know what explanation she could possibly offer. If there was an explanation, it probably would have just been a half-assed apology loaded with weeping, and "poor me" excuses, but it all came down to the same thing. He'd just been the pawn in her game of revenge.

He stood up from his desk and turned to glance over the city. She'd made him look like an idiot. It went far beyond wounded pride. He'd fallen hard for her, had been willing to give up his life in New York for her.

Unfortunately, he'd made the mistake of assuming she felt the same.

"Don't hang up the phone again. Please, won't you just have lunch with me?"

Lena groaned and stretched out on a couch at her parents' house. She pressed her fingertips to her temple. "No, Keith."

She wanted to hate him for everything he'd done. He'd cheated on her and then screwed up any chance she'd had at making a life with the man she'd fallen in love with. Her throat tightened at the thought of Tyler, and she blinked back tears.

Yes, she wanted to hate him, but couldn't. That emotion would take too much energy. If anything, she was just indifferent.

"Please, just hear me out."

Lena sighed. This had to be getting embarrassing for him. This unwavering persistence at getting her back.

"There would be no point. It's over. If just talking to you pisses me off, how on earth could you think I'd still want to marry you?"

"I'm not saying we need to get engaged again, baby," Keith coaxed. "But if we could sit down and have lunch...talk about things. All your stuff is still at the house. Even if you are determined not to listen and consider working things out, we need to at least discuss what to do about the house and all that's in it."

He had a point, Lena thought. She'd been staying at her parents' house for a month now. They were, once again, traveling. She missed having her own space though.

Yes, the lavender-painted room of her childhood offered a certain security. With all her awards and trophies, she knew this to be a loving environment. But she was a grown woman.

And the more she thought about it, the more she leaned toward buying her own place.

Maybe if she met with Keith she could convince him to sell the house, or at least buy out her share.

"All right, Keith. Are you free Friday?"

"You look beautiful."

Ok, he's going to make this awkward. Lena took a deep breath.

"Thanks, Keith. Look—"

"I can't tell you how much I've missed you, Lena." He reached across the table to grab her hands, which she promptly pulled back into her lap. His expression darkened, but he continued. "You've changed. You know that?"

"Well, I did get my nails done." Lena cleared her throat. "Listen, about the house. I think we should—"

"Oh, hold on." Keith snapped his fingers in the air to flag down a waiter. "Could you get us a bottle of champagne?"

"Certainly, sir." The waiter gave him a brief smile. "And

your preference?"

"Whatever's cheap." Keith turned his focus back to Lena. "Yes, about the house. I think we should sell it."

Relief washed through her. "Me too. I'm so glad that you—"

"It's much too small. We'll need a bigger one for the kids."

"Kids?" She gaped at him. "Keith, hold on, if you're back on the marriage highway, then you better get off at the next exit. Let it go. It's not going to happen. Here's what I was going to say. I want to sell the house and split the profit."

"Lena." He looked pained. "I can't imagine not spending my life with you. Please, don't be so quick to throw away everything we have."

"And what did we have?" she asked quietly after a moment. "Was it really that special? So special that you had to go and sleep with someone else?"

"I know I made a stupid choice. I won't lie and deny it." He nodded, looking properly chastised. "I swear I haven't touched her since. In fact, I'm trying to transfer her to another office."

"Oh, how gallant of you." Lena smiled without humor. Why couldn't he accept that things were over? Even if she'd believed him, which she didn't, she wouldn't go back to him. Her heart belonged to someone else.

"Here we are." The waiter arrived at the table with a smirk. "One bottle of our cheapest champagne."

"I've gone about this wrong," Keith stated as the waiter filled their glasses. "I won't pressure you any more today. I just wish you wouldn't be so hasty in kicking me out of your life. We have too much history, Lena, baby."

Lena took a sip of the champagne and winced. She set the glass back down with no intention of ever picking it up again. "Keith—"

"Promise me you'll just think about things for a while."

"I've had a month to think about things." She sighed, knowing her feelings would never change. Jeez, he was like a dog with a bone.

"I love you, Lena." This time he succeeded in grabbing her hand, his intent gaze focused on her. "Just give it a while to think it over. I'll wait for you."

She met his gaze with skepticism. "You'll wait for me?"

"There's no one else for me," he insisted. "I'd do anything for you. Promise me? Just *think* about it?"

I ought to tell him to shove his cheap champagne up his tight ass.

Another idea hit her.

"I'll think about it, Keith. For one week. But if I decide that it's just not going to work, I want you to agree that you'll sell the house."

His lips tightened, an indication he wasn't happy with her terms. But then he nodded. "I know that won't be an issue, but I agree."

Chapter Seventeen

"I am so damn hungry," Stephanie complained as she slid her mirrored sunglasses back over her eyes.

Lena settled herself in the car and prayed her hair would stay somewhat in place with the roof down on the convertible. She sighed and looked out the window. This weekend away in Seattle with Stephanie would be a nice little break.

"Can we stop and get some food somewhere?" Stephanie asked. "Before we head up to Seattle? I don't think I can make the drive without getting something to eat."

"Yeah, that's fine with me." Lena tucked her backpack under her feet. "There's a Mexican restaurant right down the road. Great place."

"Works for me. Hey, don't let me forget to tell you about this amazingly built guy I met in the Bahamas. We're still in touch." Stephanie grinned. "We're talking an ass like granite."

Lena laughed and turned to look at her friend. "I've missed you. We have got to stop going three months without seeing each other. It's just not healthy."

"Damn right." Stephanie glanced over. "Your hair's growing out. Are you going long again?"

"I'm thinking about it. Besides, I got sick of looking like a guy."

"Do you actually think anyone could mistake you for a guy with your curves?" Stephanie grimaced. "I'd kill to have your body."

"*My* body?" Lena burst into laughter. "Do you have any idea how much I envy *you*? You're gorgeous."

Stephanie snorted. "I'm nothing exciting. Excuse me while I yawn, but tall and skinny is dull. You're cute. Men want to protect you. To take you home and cuddle with you."

Lena snorted. "Yeah, I'm a cocker spaniel with breasts, gotcha. There's the restaurant."

Stephanie whipped the car into the parking lot, and they climbed out and made their way inside.

They ordered food and got drinks, then Stephanie gave her a pensive look.

"What?" Lena shifted. "Do I have something in my teeth?"

Stephanie shook her head. "So how are things going?"

"Things? Things are great, I guess." *Liar. Everything has been shit for the last three months.* How bad was it that she couldn't even admit that to her best friend?

Stephanie accepted her margarita from the waiter, and then flicked her tongue over the glass to lick off the salt.

"Are you still thinking about taking Keith back?"

"Not really. I just need to tell him. It's been a week."

"Hmm. Do you ever talk to Tyler?"

Lena choked on the beer she'd just sipped. Her hand shook as she tried to sound casual. "Tyler? Why would I? That's been over for months now."

Stephanie's mouth tightened, and she glanced away. "This whole situation is just ridiculous."

"What situation? We had a fling, and it ended." She forced the words out.

"I don't understand you." Stephanie turned back to her, her gaze accusing. "Don't you have any idea what you and Tyler had together? I don't know why either of you won't even acknowledge it."

"Because there is nothing to acknowl—what do you mean *either of us?*" Lena's heart pounded, her palms grew damp.

Stephanie didn't reply right away, and Lena leaned forward, gripping her friend's hand.

"Have you spoken to him, Steph?"

Stephanie pulled away and eyed her. "Yes, I spoke to Tyler. I had to find out what happened after you got back to the States, because you sure weren't telling me." She took another sip of her drink. "I was in New York for a couple of days, and I still had his business card, so I figured I'd appease my curiosity."

"You actually went and saw him? Tell me you aren't serious?" Her voice shook. "*Steph.*"

Stephanie lifted an eyebrow and then shrugged. "Hey, if you're so over him, then why are you freaking out?"

Lena ignored her question. "What was he like when you saw him?"

"Does it matter?"

"Answer the damn question."

Stephanie paused and looked away. "He was hurting. I could see it in the way he looked at me. I was an obvious reminder of you. He wouldn't even let me stay, kicked me out after two minutes."

Lena's breath caught, and hope bloomed the tiniest bit in her heart. She quickly pushed the threatening emotion away and took a sip of her beer. "Well, he acted like a jerk when I called him. So maybe it serves him right."

The words were complete crap, and just speaking them sent regret through her. Apparently, Stephanie wasn't too thrilled either by the way her eyes narrowed.

"Okay. You *both* suck. You're acting like teenagers."

"Look, Tyler was a fling. It just hit me a little hard coming home." Lena shrugged, pushing back the ache in her heart that had become second nature by now.

Their food arrived, saving them from further discussion. When they had finished eating and were waiting at the register to pay, there was a sudden commotion toward the back of the restaurant.

Hearing a woman's voice raised in obvious hysteria, Lena turned to investigate.

The water hit her smack in the face. She sputtered, raising the sleeve of her shirt to wipe away the water.

"Oh, she did *not* just do that." Stephanie lurched toward Lena's attacker, but Lena grasped her arm, holding her back from the woman in front of them.

Although the term woman seemed almost inappropriate. The girl may have been twenty at the most. She was pale, with blonde hair and a waif-like body. She stood trembling in front of them, clutching the now-empty glass of water.

The girl's friend stood to her right, looking mortified as she tried to pull the girl away from Stephanie and Lena.

"Do you know where Keith was last night?" the girl asked, her blue eyes full of tears and blatant hatred. "Do you even know who I am?"

Lena blinked in dismay. *Ugh, I have a pretty good idea.*

"He was with me. He came back to me, *again.*" The girl's voice rose. "Do you realize I have to look at your picture on his desk every day? I go to bed with him at night, knowing he's sleeping with me but trying to get you back."

Lena blinked. Should she pity this girl or want to smack her? Pity won out in the end.

"Look, kid, you can have him. I don't want him," she replied with a terse smile. "And, please, give him that message for me."

"You might want to stop sleeping with other women's men," Stephanie advised and slapped down the bills on the counter to cover their check. "But don't worry. I'm sure Keith would never cheat on *you*."

Leaving the girl staring at them in shock, Stephanie grasped Lena's arm and steered her out of the restaurant.

Lena glanced over her shoulder to see the girl's friend usher her toward the bathroom.

"Stephanie, that was just mean."

"She's a little tramp. Stop being so nice." Stephanie glared at the restaurant and started the car.

"She's just a kid," Lena protested. "I bet she's barely in college."

"I don't give a rat's ass if she's twelve. She knows right from wrong." Stephanie swerved into traffic. "Stop being so damn nice."

"You know what's really funny?" Lena asked. "Keith said he would wait for me. He said he wouldn't be with anyone else until I gave in and came back to him. He is such a dick."

"I'm glad you're not marrying him. I couldn't believe you were even giving him hope."

"I already told you I wasn't going to marry him." Lena glanced out the window, thinking about the younger woman.

Now that had been a girl in love. A girl who'd been in such anguish, she hadn't known what to do with herself.

Kind of like how she was with Tyler. Her stomach flipped and an idea took root in her head.

"Did he really seem unhappy, Steph?"

Stephanie glanced at her and lifted an eyebrow. "Are we

talking about Tyler again? Yes. He did."

Lena took a deep breath. It was time she took a risk. Time to try and get Tyler back. Why keep denying how she felt for him? By the end of their time in Europe, she had been completely and hopelessly in love with him. The feeling hadn't faded with time.

She calculated the amount of sick days she still had left and then bit her lip.

"Stephanie, I think I'm going to search for a cheap flight from Seattle to New York."

Lena zipped up her backpack and then glared at the ringing phone. The entire weekend she'd stayed at Stephanie's apartment, the phone had rung at least once an hour.

"I'm so sorry, Steph."

Stephanie sat on the bed watching television, channel surfing with the remote.

"Stop apologizing for the fact that your ex is an asshole." Her friend shook her head.

"I don't think it quite sunk in when I told him I would hire a lawyer if he didn't agree to sell the house. He told me to call him when my PMS went away."

"Pathetic." Stephanie shook her head. "I'm so glad you're going to New York."

"Me too." Lena pulled off her shirt and grabbed the dress that hung over a chair. She pulled it on and looked in the mirror. It had cost her a pretty penny, but it had been worth it. It was a sleeveless, pale blue dress that flared out at the knees. The square neckline hinted at her cleavage, and a darker blue belt accented her waist.

"Good thing this fabric doesn't wrinkle easily. I'm going to nap on the plane." She took a deep breath in. "Will you zip me?"

Stephanie came over to pull the zipper up. "This is cute. It's a great color on you, and very spring. I don't think I could pull it off. Too cutesy. But you do it justice."

Lena frowned. "Cutesy?"

"You know, I can't see Tyler turning you away. That man was hooked on you, from what I could see. Besides the fact that there was enough chemistry between you both to blow up China."

Lena gave a nervous laugh and smoothed a hand over the dress. "Well, hopefully the fuse is still lit. You didn't hear how angry he was when I called him."

Stephanie rolled her eyes. "That's just his pride. I'm sure he'll melt when he sees you face to face."

"Lord, I hope so."

"So. Are you going to be okay?" Stephanie bit her lip and gave her a probing look. "Going out to New York all by yourself to confront him alone?"

"It's a roundtrip ticket." Lena shrugged, wishing she were just a little more confident. "Worst case scenario I'm on a plane home tonight after I see him."

"That won't happen. Think positive. And you'd better call me the minute you get back."

"You know I will." Lena glanced one last time in the mirror. *You can do this.* "Okay, let's go."

Lena sat on the stool at the bar, staring down into the clear liquid. Vodka. Liquid courage. She swished the tiny glass around, eyeing it as if it were the devil's brew.

Damn, I hate vodka. But it would work fast.

"Why did you order a shot if you're just going to stare at it, lady?" The bartender leaned over the bar, watching her with open curiosity. The bar was near empty, being still early in the day.

She glanced back up at him and grimaced. "It's not something I normally drink, but today I'm feeling the need to make an exception."

"Yeah?" He wiped a glass dry with his towel. "So where are you from?"

"Oregon." She took a deep breath and slammed the shot down. The liquid burned her throat and had her eyes burning with tears. She coughed and pressed her hand against her chest.

"So, whatcha doing in New York? You come to see the Yanks?"

"Yanks?" Lena asked as she pulled her hair back into two small ponytails to keep them out of her face. With how fast it had grown, she wasn't used to having it flowing around her face. "Is that basketball?"

The man's bushy eyebrows drew together.

Apparently not. "Sorry, I don't follow sports. I'm more of a ballet girl. Besides, I'm just here on business."

The bartender grunted. "The ballet, huh? You look like the type."

"The type?" Lena frowned. "And what type is that?"

"Oh, you know, you've just got that look. Little naïve. Cutesy. Yuppyish?"

"Okay, I'm just going to focus on the cute part and ignore the naïve and yuppy."

"It's just the dress, I'm sure." He winked. "What business brought you to New York?"

"Well..." She paused, still a little annoyed he'd called her a yuppie. "I have to make a business proposition to an old friend."

"You a stockbroker?"

Lena gave him a thoughtful glance. Did she look like a stockbroker? "No, I'm not a stockbroker. Hey, what time is it?"

"Ah, let me check." He glanced at his watch. "About four thirty."

"Oh no." she squeaked and leapt off the chair. Time difference—she'd almost forgotten the time difference. She'd planned on slipping into Tyler's office just before he left for the day.

"I've got to go."

"Well, good luck, lady. I hope your deal goes through all right."

Me too, she thought, and rushed out the door into the streets of New York. The sun was hot, the air humid, but the city thrived despite the heat. Taxi horns blared and throngs of people strode down the street after a long workday.

Lena adjusted her purse over her shoulder and set off down the street, using her hand to shade the glare from her eyes. After a few moments, she found herself standing at the base of a skyscraper.

She clutched the tiny piece of paper in her hand, then gave another nervous glance at the double glass mirrored doors. *Shit, I should have had two shots.*

She was crazy. She had to be insane to be here. Lena cursed to herself as she stepped into the building and went to the directory on the wall.

"Tyler Bentz." Her heart slammed against her chest as she fingered the gold lettering. Making her way to the elevator, she quickly pressed the button that would take her to the forty-eighth floor.

A few moments later, the door slid open. She took a step out of the elevator, and then hesitated.

No. You've come this far. Walk your stupid butt into that office and see what happens, you pansy.

She took a deep breath and approached the door, gripping the handle tight before swinging it open.

Her gaze landed on a tall, lanky man, dressed in a very expensive-looking suit, behind a reception desk. His expression turned curious as he watched her enter.

"Hello there." The man smiled, his gaze ran over her dress, and she could have sworn she saw amusement in his eyes.

"Hi." She swallowed hard. "I'm here to see..."

"Yes? Who are you here to see?"

"Uh..." Tyler. Who could step on her heart as if it were a bug and leave her an emotional wreck. *I can't do this.* "No one. I think I have the wrong office actually."

The man frowned. "Why don't you tell me who you're looking for, and maybe I can help."

"T—" *You're a pansy. Just say Tyler's name.* "Ty—omas."

"Thomas?" The man gave her a puzzled look. "You know, you look a little pale. Why don't you sit down a moment, and I'll get you a glass of water."

Lena shook her head and backed toward the door. "No, really. I have the wrong office. Thank you for your help."

She turned to flee and slammed into something hard. Her hands reached out to keep herself from falling. She stared at the crisp blue shirt and felt the ridges under it—familiar ridges. She jerked her eyes up to meet Tyler's stunned gaze.

Her heart thudded in her chest. *Shit.* Why had she ever thought this a good idea?

"Lena?" Tyler's expression became guarded. "What are you

doing in New York?"

"New York?" She gave a weak laugh. "Is that where I am, New York?"

"You're a long ways from Kansas, Dorothy," the receptionist muttered not quite under his breath.

She shot him an irritated glance and then glanced back at Tyler, licking her lips. "I shouldn't he here. I think I'd better go."

"Hold on." Tyler grasped her arm as she made to move past him. Tingles spread through her entire body at his touch, and she bit back a gasp.

"Are you sure this isn't the Thomas you were looking for?" The receptionist asked innocently.

What the hell kind of receptionist was he? Lena shot him a vicious look.

"Why don't you come into my office for a second?" Tyler's grip on her arm tightened, and he urged her into a corner office.

Lena licked her lips again, took a deep breath, and then went inside.

Tyler watched Lena step into his office and then followed her in, shutting the door behind him. God, she was actually here.

The roar of blood in his veins sounded in his head, and his gaze devoured her from head to toe. She was just as beautiful now as she had been in Europe. It was apparent, even in those silly little ponytails, that her hair had grown out some, and it looked as if she'd lost weight.

After their conversation on the phone, he never thought he'd see her again. Didn't think she'd have the guts to show her face.

And yet here she was. *Lena had come to New York.* His

chest tightened, and he clenched his fists so he wouldn't drag her into his arms. He watched as she walked to the window and glanced out over the city.

"You have a beautiful view."

"Thank you." He didn't want to talk about the fucking view. "Can I get you some coffee?"

"Sure." She glanced back, wringing her hands. She appeared a bit skittish. "Thank you."

Tyler picked up his phone and pressed a few buttons. "Could you please bring us two coffees, Danny? Thanks."

He replaced the receiver and stared at her. Their gazes locked, and the air almost crackled with tension. She took a ragged breath in and then jerked her gaze away.

"What are you doing in New York?" he asked, keeping his tone neutral.

"Visiting." She turned to look out the window again.

The urge to cross the room and touch her hit strong, but he forced himself to keep his distance. "I didn't realize you knew anyone in New York. Who are you visiting?"

She didn't answer right away, and then her voice came out in a whisper. "You."

The door opened and Danny swept in carrying a tray with two steaming mugs of coffee.

"Here you go." He handed Tyler one. "Black with one sugar. And how do you take yours, Miss?"

"No sugar and just a little cream," Tyler answered for her. Danny looked at him in surprise and then to her for confirmation.

Her cheeks grew pink, and she nodded.

Danny fixed her drink and then handed her a mug. He winked and then left the room again, shutting the door behind him.

"Why don't you have a seat?" Tyler gestured to the small couch that sat in the corner.

She walked slowly over to it and sat, the leather crunching as she made herself comfortable.

"This is a very nice office."

"Thank you." His jaw clenched as she crossed her legs, and the dress inched up, exposing more of her thighs.

She must have seen him looking, because her eyes widened, and she quickly uncrossed her legs and smoothed the dress back down.

She needs to leave. Get her on the next plane home before you do something stupid. Being ruthless would be the only way to survive this.

"So, Lena...why would you come to New York when I told you never to contact me again?"

Chapter Eighteen

She flinched and lowered her gaze. "What if I said I didn't know?"

"I'd call your bluff."

She closed her eyes, and his jaw clenched as he awaited her response. When she opened her eyes, she met his gaze directly.

"I came to see you, Tyler. I want to explain why I acted the way I did."

An explanation. Not a declaration of love or an announcement that she'd called off her wedding. Hell, she might already be married by now. The realization had his gut clenching.

"I know why you acted the way you did." He made sure to show no reaction. Instead, he walked to the window and stared out over the city.

"You left me without even saying good-bye," she whispered. "And I tried to contact you, to explain, but you wouldn't even talk to me. If you would have only listened—"

"What was that?" Tyler's jaw clenched. Anger stirred a bitter brew in his stomach, and he took a deep breath in. "Were you just trying to throw this back in my face? I was never anything but honest with you. You were the one living a lie the entire time."

"I—I never meant..." She groaned. "I was going to tell you."

He gave a harsh laugh. "I doubt that."

"You've got to hear me out."

"You were engaged. Engaged and having a good old-fashioned revenge fuck." He turned around and narrowed his eyes. "I hope you got everything you needed."

"I *hate* that term. I wish everybody would stop using it. You weren't a..." She broke off, and he could see the guilt flicker in her gaze. "Okay. Initially, maybe. But—"

"Forget it. It's in the past," Tyler interrupted, his voice cold. "If you came here to apologize, then you could have done it on my voice mail."

"I didn't come here just to apologize," she cried, her expression pleading. "I'm here because...because there was something there in Europe. Between us."

"Yeah, there was. It's called sex," he replied brutally. "Aren't you getting married soon? What is it you want?"

His stomach lurched. The thought of Lena marrying someone else made him sick. Suddenly, it hit him. Why she'd come here if not to apologize.

She'd certainly used him before, why would she hesitate to do so again? And despite how she'd thrown his heart into a blender, God help him, he still wanted her. Wanted her like he'd never wanted another woman before in his life.

"I see." He nodded, and his gaze moved over her body, taking her in before raising his eyes back to hers.

"No." Lena shook her head. "Tyler, you've got the wrong idea."

"Do I?" He shrugged. "Maybe Keith's just not doing it for you, and you came to me for a *fix* because you know I can get you off."

Her jaw fell open, and anger flickered in her gaze. "Of course not. Jeez, what do you take me for?"

"You don't really want me to answer that, do you?"

Her mouth tightened, and she gave a slight shake of her head. "No. I probably don't."

She stood up, placing her cup on the mirrored coffee table. Her hands trembled so much that the brown liquid sloshed out of the cup onto surface.

He'd upset her. Obviously, he'd hit a nerve.

His control broke. The desire to touch her, hold her in his arms, overrode any sense of reason. He stepped close to her, sliding his hands around her waist and down to the soft curves of her hips.

"Tyler..." She pressed her hands against his chest and turned her head away.

He brushed his lips against the side of neck, inhaling the floral perfume he remembered so well. Damn, he was weak.

He kissed the other side of neck, closing his lips over the pulse that beat hard and fast there.

"Tyler," she gasped. "This isn't what I came for."

"No?" He lifted his head and traced the outline of her lips with the pad of his thumb.

Her lips parted a bit, and he eased his thumb past the softness of her lips, to stroke the moist interior.

Lena groaned and closed her eyes. A second later, her teeth clamped down on his thumb, and he jerked back in surprise. She scurried across the room to his desk.

"We should talk," she insisted, sounding breathless.

"Why?" Tyler followed after her. "Is this a game to you?"

"I don't play games."

"You do. Remember at the club in Paris?" He closed his hands over the soft skin of her forearms, trapping her against the desk. "When you tried to make me jealous?"

A tremble ran through her body, and he gave an inward curse. She was probably thinking about the attack afterwards, not the time in the club.

"I shouldn't have come here today." Her words were almost inaudible. "Please, just let me go, Tyler."

Let her go. Damn, if it were only that easy. He'd been trying to let her go for the last three months. Had finally begun to sleep at night and not have her haunt his dreams. And now she had come to New York to see him. Letting her go was the last thing he wanted to do.

He reached a hand up to caress the side of her face and lowered his mouth just a fraction above hers. "You don't even want a kiss?"

"No," she whispered.

"Liar." His gaze narrowed, before he slammed his mouth down on hers, needing to kiss her, to taste her again.

She gasped and clutched at the lapels of his jacket. Her soft lips brushed against his, and he pressed his tongue past them to taste the sweet interior of her mouth. He rubbed his tongue over hers, and she tentatively touched him back. Almost as if she were innocent and not just a woman out for a quick screw.

The thought had his chest tightening, and all thoughts of making it romantic or gentle evaporated. He lifted her onto the desk, and her dress hiked up her thighs. He stepped between her legs and slid his hands up to the top of her thighs.

His mouth left hers to trail down the curve of her neck. She groaned, and her head fell back, giving him access to the fast-beating pulse.

He closed his hand over the swell of her breast, and she arched into him with a sharp cry.

Through the fabric, he stroked her already tight nipple. He

jerked the straps of her dress down, then the soft cups of her lacy bra. Her breasts, so sexy and familiar, filled his hands. He dipped his head and caught one stiff peak between his teeth, rubbing his tongue over the tip.

She groaned. "Tyler..."

His name, husky on her lips, cleared his head. The blood pounded through his veins as reality set in.

He was about to give her exactly what she'd come here for. More meaningless sex. When she could already possibly be married. What the *hell* was wrong with him?

He closed his eyes and his chest tightened. It was time to end this. Once and for all. He needed to make sure she didn't fly across the country every time she got the itch for a good screw.

"This can't happen."

Her lashes fluttered up, the dazed arousal in her gaze was like a kick in the stomach. God, he wanted her.

"Tyler, I'm not—"

"We had good sex in Europe, Lena. And I'll admit that I mistook tapping a nice piece of ass for being in love," he lied, trying to be as much of an asshole as possible to kill any hope she had. "But I'm home now and have moved on. And you should too. You can start by letting Keith be the one to get you off."

The confession that she wasn't marrying Keith died on her lips. He couldn't have hurt her more if it had been his fist connecting with her stomach.

Tapping a nice piece of ass. That's what he'd reduced their time together in Europe to?

She turned away from him and strode to the window,

unwilling to let him see the tears that flooded her eyes.

Out of all the mistakes she'd made in her life, flying to New York took the top spot. How could she have been so stupid as to think this had been anything more than a fling to him?

"Look, I don't mean to be a dick or anything. But I kind of have plans to meet someone in an hour."

The blood rushed to her head, and she dragged a ragged breath in. He had plans to go out and meet a woman? After he'd almost screwed her on his desk?

Oh, God. She was going to be sick. Spinning around, she grabbed her purse off his desk and hurried for the door.

"Do you want me to call you a cab?" he called after her.

She didn't bother to answer, just bolted to the elevator before he could see the tears running down her cheeks.

Tyler stared down at the busy street from his window. His heart pounded, and his stomach clenched with disgust. Disgust at himself for what he'd said to Lena.

He saw a flash of blue, and a woman climbed into a taxi outside the building. A second later it disappeared. He closed his eyes, the ache in his chest tightening.

The door to his office banged open.

"Tyler, who was she?" Danny demanded, hurrying into the office. "The farmer's daughter? Oh, my goodness, she was just too *cute*."

The cab pulled away from the curb and merged into traffic. Tyler dragged in a breath and turned around, schooling his expression into one of indifference.

"Lena." Tyler turned away from the window.

"Okay..." Danny shook his head and blinked. "Are you going to tell me how you know her?"

Danny had been his secretary for the past two years, and Tyler had more than gotten used to the guy's flamboyancy.

"She's the girl I met while I was in Europe."

"*That's* the Europe girl?" Danny gaped and shook his head. "Well, where in the hell is she going?"

"Home. Oregon." Tyler thrust his hands in his pocket. "Back to her fiancé or husband, or whatever he is to her now."

"She's with someone else? Are you sure? She seemed all a-twitter to see you."

Tyler shook his head and gripped the back of a chair. "They've been together for almost ten years. She might have a little lust for me, but he's the one she loves."

Danny raised an eyebrow. "Well, why did she come here then?"

"One last fuck," he said to be crude, not adding that he'd almost given it to her.

He closed his eyes, remembering what it had felt like to see her again, hear her sweet voice. To briefly hold her and kiss her. The smell of her perfume still lingered in the office.

"Something's off." Danny sounded unconvinced. "You think she flew all the way to New York for a *quickie*? That seems a little a bizarre to me. Not to mention pricey—plane fare is *ridiculous* nowadays."

"Look, I'd rather not talk about it anymore."

"Not to mention the poor girl looked ready to burst into tears when she ran out of here."

Tyler ground his teeth together and scooped up the papers he'd shoved on the floor.

"What happened in Europe?" Danny asked.

"None of your damn business."

"Mmm hmm." Danny sighed and headed toward the door.

"Well, I'm going to get an iced mocha, you want one?"

"No, I'm fine. Thanks." Tyler waited until Danny had left and then sat down behind his desk.

It was better this way. Everything. He would be better off without her in his life.

"I'll be just fine."

Lena grunted and dropped the cardboard box onto the hardwood floor. Straightening, she wiped her hands on her jeans and glanced around her new apartment.

"I really think I'm going to like it here." She glanced at Lakisha, who was looking around.

"I can't believe you moved to Seattle." Her friend shook her head. "Who am I going to gossip with at the office?"

"Anyone who will listen," Lena teased and dragged another box in from the hallway.

Lakisha reached to lift a box off the ground. "Any word back from that job you applied for?"

"Yes." Lena pushed the box into the corner and stood up, smiling. "I got the job."

"Girl, and you didn't tell me? That's great."

"I only just found out this morning." She grimaced. "Sorry, I've been preoccupied with unpacking and settling in. Thanks, by the way, for coming up here to help me."

"No problem. You're buying me lunch anyway." Lakisha winked. "Is there any other reason you moved to Seattle? A new man in your life or something?"

"No. There's no new man." A familiar ache stabbed low in her gut, and she swallowed hard.

She'd never confided in Lakisha about what had happened in Europe. About meeting Tyler and his connection to their client. Two months had passed since she'd gone to New York. Five since she'd given her heart away to a Tyler in the midst of a Parisian winter. The idea of dating anyone made her sick.

"That's okay. You'll meet someone." Lakisha patted her shoulder and went to grab another box.

"How's the rent 'round here? Affordable?"

"Jeez, barely. It's affordable because the building is so old, or how Stephanie terms it, retro. Of course, she's renting out a two-bedroom, compared to my studio." Lena glanced out the window at the view of the Space Needle and Puget Sound beyond it. "But the view is what makes this place amazing."

"Why don't you take one of Stephanie's rooms?"

"She did offer me one," Lena admitted with a shrug. "But I wanted to do this on my own. I've never really done that. Besides, I have a little bit of money saved until the house in Portland sells."

Lakisha scowled. "Lazy ass man. Should've agreed to sell it months ago."

"Yes, he should have."

Lakisha stood up and stretched. "When do you start the new job?"

"Two weeks. I want to get the apartment settled this week, and maybe take the week after to relax." Lena sat down on top of one of the more solidly packed boxes. "Stephanie has a cabin I'm going to ask to borrow for a few days. It's this great little place buried up in the Cascades. No phone, no television, no one for miles around."

"Ooh, girl, if I didn't have to work I'd make you take me with you."

"Hey, someday, right?"

"Right." Lakisha tilted her head and smiled. "I'm going to

miss you like hell, Lena Richards. But I'm proud of you for what you're doing."

Lena stood up and gave her friend a hug. "Thanks, hon. It means a lot. And I'll email you almost every day. I promise."

"You'd better." Lakisha pulled away. "Now I'm hungry. Didn't you say something about you taking me out to lunch? I want a big meal before I spend three hours driving my ass home."

Chapter Nineteen

"Your place looks great." Stephanie kicked her feet up on the couch and looked around. "I'm surprised how fast you got everything set up."

Lena sorted through a pile of books. "I had some help from Lakisha."

"Good deal. I always liked that girl." Stephanie glanced at her nails. "Have you heard from Tyler?"

The book in her hand slid to the floor, and she gave Stephanie a sharp look. "Why would I hear from Tyler? I told you what happened."

"Yeah, but I still don't get it. It doesn't make any sense. He just told you he wasn't interested and sent you on your way?"

Well, after nearly screwing me in his office. Lena's mouth drew tight. "That's about the gist of it."

"Hmm."

"I was way off track when I flew to New York. Europe happened ages ago, and I'd rather just put Tyler and that whole experience behind me."

"Oh, come on. Who are you kidding?" Stephanie shook her head and sighed. "I think maybe if you just talked to him again and explained things—"

"*No.* Look, Steph, I tried all that. He just wasn't interested. Now please, for my sake, let it go."

Nice job losing your cool. She so knows you're nowhere near being over him.

Lena stood up, needing some kind of distraction. "Do you want to give each other pedicures?"

"I'll do you. I just got one done yesterday."

"Sounds good." Lena went to the kitchen, relieved Stephanie had let her change the subject. She grabbed the bucket full of various nail polish and polish remover out of the cupboard, then went back into the living room, handed it to Stephanie, and then sat down on the couch next to her.

Stephanie took the bucket and peered at the various shades. "Okay. What color are you thinking?"

"Something pinkish."

Stephanie pulled a small bottle and read the label. "Bridesmaid pink."

"Ouch, maybe you should pick a new color," Lena teased.

Stephanie scowled. "Absolutely not. It could be an omen."

"For whom? You?"

"I think not."

"Well, not me," Lena protested. "Keith is out of the picture."

"I wasn't thinking of Keith."

"*Steph.*" Lena groaned.

Stephanie laughed and shook her head. "All right. Okay. Just give me your toes, woman. I'm about to make them cute."

"They already are cute," Lena scoffed, but obediently slid her feet onto Stephanie's lap.

Stephanie went to work, painting each toenail with near perfect precision.

"Hey, I meant to ask you," Lena murmured. "Do you think it would be possible to borrow your cabin next week?"

"Shouldn't be a problem." Stephanie used her nail to scrape away a bit of polish from Lena's skin. "Let me just check with my brother and make sure he's not using it."

"That would be wonderful."

"Done." Stephanie stood up and stretched, reaching down to pick up the bucket of polish. "Where do you keep this?"

"Oh, second cupboard in the kitchen. It's full of all kinds of junk."

Lena waved her feet in the air to help them dry.

Stephanie opened the cupboard and put the bucket back inside. Then she pulled out an envelope and raised an eyebrow.

"Europe pics?"

"*Wait.*" Lena jumped up in an attempt to reach her before she could open it, but Stephanie had already pulled out the pictures inside.

"Oh, wow, look at this picture of you two." Stephanie turned the photo to face Lena. It was the one of her and Tyler in front of Notre Dame. "I'm surprised you still have this, seeing as you want to put it all behind you."

Lena ignored her light tone, unable to look away from the photo. Tears pricked at the backs of her eyes, and she blinked rapidly. "I just haven't gotten around to throwing that one away."

Stephanie nodded and then walked over to the garbage can. She lifted the lid and dropped the picture inside, watching Lena the entire time.

The breath locked in Lena's throat, and she wanted to run and retrieve the picture. She hadn't been able to resist having the image of them together printed. Or resisting looking at it at least once a day.

Her smile numb, she murmured, "Thanks."

"Sure." Stephanie seemed to be waiting for her to grab it out of the garbage, so she deliberately turned her back and walked away.

Lena needed to get out of the apartment for a minute. Try and compose herself a bit again.

"Steph, I'm going to drop off a check at the landlord's. I'll be back in a few minutes."

"All right. I'll be waiting for you."

Lena grabbed the check off her television and walked out the door. Soon as Stephanie left later tonight, she'd get that picture out of the garbage, wipe it off, and put it in a safe hiding place.

She went to drop off the payment, desperately needing the few minutes alone. It gave her time to rid the ghost of Tyler from her mind again.

When she returned to the apartment, Stephanie was speaking on her cell phone.

"It'll work, Danny. Trust me on this." Stephanie glanced up and saw Lena. Her smile brightened, and she wiggled her fingers in a wave.

"Listen, I've got to go. My friend just came back, and we're going to grab some grub. I'll call you later."

"Who was that?" Lena glanced at the garbage can, relieved to see the picture sitting unharmed on an old fast food bag.

"Just an actor friend." She waved her head in dismissal. "You want to go get a pizza?"

Lena nodded. "Yeah, as long as it's Pagliacci's."

"As if I'd go anywhere else." Stephanie pulled on her sweater and headed for the door.

"Well, it'd better work."

Tyler walked into the reception area and caught Danny muttering into the phone. Danny spotted him, and his eyes widened.

"Me too. 'Bye." He replaced the receiver and stood up. "Gee, it's almost five. Another day, another dollar. Everything should be done, all calls returned, all files put away...oh, and don't forget that conference in Seattle next week."

Tyler nodded and then glanced up sharply. "Wait. What conference in Seattle? I've got plans to see my parents. When did this come up?"

"Ugh, you don't remember? I brought it up last week and left the itinerary on your desk." Danny gave a nervous laugh. "I swear it had to be maintenance. They're always coming in and throwing away things."

Tyler exhaled in a deliberate move of control.

"Oh, dear. You're pissed. I'm so sorry. I can see if we can get you out of it. I mean, it'll be really hard, and we've already made arrangements—"

"Easy, Danny." Tyler sighed. God, what he wouldn't pay for one thing—just one damn thing—to go right lately. The stress had just snowballed. He'd been irritable—everyone in the office tiptoed around him.

"There's not much we can do about it now. How long is this conference?"

"Just a couple days. Um, I think you're booked at the Westin, and you're getting picked up by...a driver at the airport. I'll get you a copy of the, err, itinerary ASAP."

"And you'll be calling my parents to explain the situation?"

Danny's eyes widened in horror. "You want me to call your parents, whom I have never even met?"

Tyler cracked a smiled and adjusted the file in his hands. "Sarcasm. You, more than anyone else, should have caught on to that. So is George or Frank going to this conference?"

Danny's smile froze and he shrugged. "Uh, no. Well, Frank's kid is getting christened next weekend. And they only

231

requested that one of you guys from the New York office come. George and Frank both got kids, so I thought you'd be more up for it."

"Lucky me."

Of course, he'd be the one who got sent everywhere. The single guy, no kids, nothing to tie him down.

"Get me that itinerary as soon as you can." Tyler went back into his office and shut the door.

Seattle was only a few hours from Portland. He crossed the room and glanced out over the city. He could always rent a car and drive down to see Lena. Then apologize for being a complete asshole and beg her to leave Keith.

You're a fucking idiot. He took a deep breath to ease the tightness in his chest. Picking up the phone, he dialed his parents' number to call off the visit.

By the time the sun started to rise on Monday morning, Lena had already packed and loaded up her car.

She slammed the trunk of her Volkswagen and ran over to Stephanie, who stood watching her from the sidewalk.

"Thanks for lending me the cabin. A week away is going to be wonderful."

"I'd tell you to call me..." Stephanie grimaced. "...but there's no phone, and you won't have cell service anywhere near the cabin. So be careful, because it's a long drive, and you're going to be out there all by yourself."

"I'll be just fine. Besides, there'll be a forest ranger somewhere if I get really desperate."

"Oh, yeah, that's just what you need." Stephanie rolled her eyes. "Go jump the forest ranger."

"I'll do that. Thank you again." She gave her friend another tight hug.

"You're welcome. I hope you have a great time and get everything you're looking for."

"Everything I'm looking for? That's a steep order to fill. I love you, Steph. See you soon."

"Love you too, sweetie. 'Bye now."

Lena jumped into the Bug and gunned the motor. She hit the gas and didn't look back.

The road to Stephanie's cabin was narrow. It wound through tall, rugged peaks, which, in winter, would be capped with snow. Oftentimes during heavy snow, the roads far up into the mountains would be closed for weeks at a time.

Her car sped down the isolated road, and Lena sighed, feeling almost content for the first time in months.

She rolled down the window and allowed her arm to drape out, the summer sun tickling her skin and promising more freckles.

Pulling her hair down from its short ponytail, she tossed her head and inhaled the clean mountain air. The sun stabbed through the huge evergreen trees, creating a dancing light show on the curvy road.

After flipping through her CD case, she slipped her favorite jazz album into the stereo.

The smooth sound of a walking bass, paired with the husky throaty vocals of Nina Simone filled the car.

She passed a sign welcoming her to the last town for nearly eighty miles, and stopped to fill up her gas tank and buy groceries for the cabin.

Back in the car a half hour later, Lena glanced at the receipt and gave a soft whistle. What was it about the cost of living when you were in the middle of nowhere? She could have bought almost twice the amount of food back in the city for the same price.

She stuffed the receipt back into the paper sack and shrugged it off. It was worth it for the week she would be having.

Just relaxing and not thinking about Tyler. Damn it. She winced. She'd just broken her own rule by thinking about not thinking about him.

Someday he'd be a distant memory. Someday. Slipping on her sunglasses, she pulled out onto the deserted road and made for the cabin.

Tyler glanced around the baggage area, scanning the crowd for someone who would be holding up a sign with his name on it. He saw parents waiting for kids, husbands waiting for wives, and then his gaze landed on the figure before him.

"You've got to be kidding me," he muttered under his breath.

"Tyler Bentz, how the hell are you?" Stephanie's slender body rushed toward him. She threw her arms around his neck and gave him a big kiss on the cheek. "Wow, it's been a while."

"Is this some kind of joke?" Tyler demanded. "Is Lena waiting in the car or something?"

Stephanie's teeth flashed in a big grin, and she gave a tinkling laugh. "Lena? Of course not. She has no idea you're here and probably wouldn't care to know."

She waved a hand in dismissal. "Anyway, I heard you were coming into town for a conference and volunteered to pick you up."

"You just happened to hear I was in town?" he repeated

and gave her an incredulous look. "I'm not sure how stupid you think I am. Where's my driver? Did you pay him off?"

He adjusted his carry-on bag and turned away from her, walking toward the exit.

"Tyler, stop." Stephanie called after him. "Come on. Let me give you a ride into the city. Your only other option is a taxi."

"Which is beginning to sound better by the moment." He glanced at her, irritated as all hell that he had to deal with this shit after a long-ass flight.

"Tyler, we're friends. At least I'd like to think so," Stephanie encouraged. "So, please, let me drive you to your hotel."

"How did you know I'd be here? Indulge me." He stopped abruptly, folding his arms over his chest.

Stephanie sighed and then shrugged. "Fine, I got chummy with your assistant when I dropped by your office a while ago. I asked him to let me know if you ever came to Seattle."

"Danny?" Tyler's eyebrows raised, and his temper flared. "Are you insane? Is *he* insane? I'm going to see that his ass gets fired—"

"Calm down. Why don't we get in the car and have a little talk?" His mouth tightened, and he looked away. He'd bet his next paycheck that Lena would be waiting in the car.

"Please," she pleaded. "I'll take you straight to your hotel and, if at anytime I make you uncomfortable, you can get out of the car. Please, Tyler. We got along great in Amsterdam. Just give me an hour. That's all I'm asking."

"This is ridiculous." He shook his head.

"You'll be at the hotel in no time, *and* you won't have to pay for a taxi."

"Fine. Where's your car?"

"In short-term parking." She gave him a triumphant smile.

"Do you have any more luggage?"

"No, I always bring just a carry-on if it's business."

"Oh, aren't you a good boy." She smiled, and they made their way through the crowded airport.

Irritation pricked in his gut, and he scowled, following her. He still wasn't convinced Stephanie and Lena hadn't concocted some joke to play on him. As much as he hated to admit it, the thought of seeing Lena wasn't altogether unappealing.

"What is it you wanted to talk about?"

"This and that," she replied breezily as they reached her car. "I'm dying for something to drink though. I think I'm going to stop at a coffee shop, is that okay with you?"

Unless Lena hid in the trunk, she wasn't here. He swallowed hard against the disappointment.

"Do I have a choice?" Tyler settled himself into the car.

"No. But I'll treat you to a mocha."

"I haven't had my morning coffee yet. I guess I could handle that."

"Shit, and you're on New York time?" Stephanie clucked her tongue and started the car. "Maybe some java will help your mood."

Lena straightened from putting the groceries away and glanced around the cabin. God, she loved this place.

The rustic cabin was made with logs, and had been built at the turn of the century. The furniture inside wasn't flashy, but conventional and cozy.

She'd come up here many summers with Stephanie growing up. She knew the cabin and woods around it inside and out.

Walking outside onto the porch, Lena glanced down the

several mile long dirt path she'd just driven up in order to reach her retreat. She stepped off the porch and headed toward the back of the cabin to where a river ran beside the property.

She knelt down and allowed her hand to trail through the cool water. With her body already overheated from the drive, it felt wonderful. Later, she would come back and swim. A wicked little smile curved her lips. And seeing as her nearest neighbor was miles away, she could even do it naked.

But not now. She shook the water off her hand and headed back to the cabin.

Tyler stepped out of the coffee shop, squinting at how bright it was outside. Damn, who'd have thought there'd be so much sun in Seattle?

"How you doing, buddy?" Stephanie gave him a slap on the back and nudged him toward the car.

He scowled, sinking down into the bucket seat. Once seated, his body went lax against the comfortable seat. He shook his head, realizing he was more tired after the mocha then he had been before.

And talk about a shitty mocha. He should have never agreed to stop for coffee. Hell, agreeing to drive with her at all seemed to be a bad decision.

His thoughts were compounded when Stephanie hit the gas and spun out of the parking lot, leaving Tyler to clutch at the door handle to stay seated.

"You're a terrible driver," Tyler mumbled, his head feeling a little thick. "Which, I'm sure you've been told before."

Stephanie laughed. "Never. Why? Does my driving scare you?"

"No. I ride in New York taxis all the time." He closed his eyes.

"How long until we get to my hotel?"

"Not too long."

He blinked his eyes open, and everything blurred before the road came back into focus. "Man, I'm tired."

"Good."

Good? Why was that good?

"Do you think about Lena very much?"

"Do I think about Lena?" He closed his eyes again, the image of Lena now in his head.

Sweet, sexy Lena... What the hell was wrong with him? Why did he feel so damn sluggish?

"Stephanie, why do I feel so weird right now?"

"You feel weird, hmm?" Stephanie glanced at him. "Like you just want to go to sleep for a few hours?"

She sounded amused. As if she wanted him to sleep—oh, God. The mocha had tasted strange. Was it possible that she...? He tried to straighten up, but the effort was enormous.

"Stephanie. What was in that mocha?"

"Oh, the usual. Coffee, milk, chocolate," she gave a casual shrug. "Prescription strength sleeping pills."

"You put...sleeping pills...coffee?" He made an effort to sit up again, but the seatbelt strained, and he fell back. Panic spread through his weakened muscles. The thickness in his head made it almost impossible to form a sentence. "Crazy bitch."

"Yes, I am." Stephanie sighed. "I just think you and Lena should spend some time together."

Lena? Lena was behind this, too? "You can't play God..."

He fumbled with his seatbelt but didn't even have the energy to unbutton it. It felt as if there were a ten-pound weight on each eyelid. Groaning, he gave in and let his eyes drift shut again.

"When I wake up...I'm going to kill you," he mumbled and then sank into the drugged sleep.

Chapter Twenty

Lena jumped when the teakettle came to life, whistling through the solitude of the cabin.

She pressed a hand against her chest and went to pull the kettle off the stove. She made herself a cup of tea and then went back to the small living room to sit down on the couch.

Not that she needed television, but when there wasn't one in the cabin it just made it that much quieter. Too bad she'd forgotten to grab a book.

Maybe Stephanie had something on the bookshelf. She glanced over the various titles and scowled. Horror or romance. Hmm. Scary books tended to be...well, a little too scary.

"Let's try a romance." Lena grabbed a random romance novel off the shelf and went back to the couch.

She curled up, settling the book against her knees, and then opened it. Twenty minutes later she was one-hundred-percent sucked in.

She read until the light outside had faded and she had to stand up to turn on the lights. The only sound she heard was the insanely loud crickets.

Lena settled back down on the couch, picking her book up again. She became so wrapped up in it, a moment passed before she realized a sound came from outside.

She frowned, trying to place the source of the noise. She blinked as fear made her stomach lurch. A car. Someone was driving up the dirt road. The store clerk's warning came back to her to be careful. What, was there some serial killer running amuck up here?

Lena stood up fast, now more than a little alarmed. Who could be driving down the road this time of night? Or at all, for that matter? It was a small, dirt road, barely visible from the highway, and the cabin was the one home on it.

She hurried to the window and lifted the curtain, glancing outside. The beam of headlights bounced along the road, bringing the car closer.

She dropped the curtain back into place and swallowed hard, her heart racing. Darting into the kitchen, she grabbed a steak knife and clutched it, then went back to the window.

Again she lifted the curtain, just an inch this time, so she could peek out. The car had reached the driveway, and it stopped out front. The motor clicked off, and the headlights blinked out.

Lena frowned and dropped the knife. She hurried to switch on the outside light, then threw open the door and ran onto the porch.

"Steph? What are you doing here? You scared the crap out of me."

"Yeah? Well, I'm exhausted." Stephanie placed her hands on her hips and glared. "I've been driving for three hours. Here, come help me unload something."

Lena stepped off the porch into the cool night air and went to the car where Stephanie tried to lift something out.

"Oh, my God." Lena jumped back. "That's not a something. That's a *someone.*"

"Yes." Stephanie grunted as she hooked her arms under the armpits of the limp person.

"Is he...dead?" Her stomach twisted and all kinds of images filled her head. Stephanie hitting some guy on the road, dragging his body up here to bury him. And this was why she didn't read horror novels.

"No, he's not dead, you moron. He's asleep." Stephanie grunted and pulled the body halfway out of the car. "Could I get a little help here?"

"Who is he?" There was something familiar about the hair, the shape of the body. "Stephanie... Is that *Tyler*?"

"Yes," Stephanie groaned in exasperation. "Will you please come here and grab his legs?"

"What's Tyler doing in Washington? Oh my God and passed out in your car?" Lena rushed forward to help carry him before Stephanie dropped him.

"Shit. He's heavier than he looks. What does this man eat?" Stephanie demanded as they dumped him on the couch.

"He's actually pretty toned. I'm sure it's just muscle," Lena said absently, running her gaze over him. Jeez, he was completely out. Not even a twitch. "You need to talk to me, Steph. What is Tyler doing here?"

"Where are your keys?" Stephanie ignored the question by asking one of her own. "I need to grab something out of your car."

"They're on the table." Lena turned back to Tyler.

His mouth hung open a little, a bit of drool trailing out of his mouth. She walked over, knelt beside him and used the corner of his shirt to wipe down his cheek.

She straightened up as the motor of Stephanie's car gunned to life.

Lena looked toward the door, unease clawing at her stomach now. No. She wouldn't have... Groaning, she ran outside and down the porch.

"Stephanie."

Stephanie tossed an envelope and a black bag out the car

window, and they landed on the driveway. Dirt spit into the air as the tires spun, and then the car shot off down the road, the red glare of the taillights eventually fading.

What the hell had just happened? Remembering the envelope and bag, she went back to retrieve it.

Going to the porch swing, she sat down and opened the envelope first, skimming the page.

My dearest, best friend, Lena,

You are a complete idiot. You're both obviously in love and refuse to work things out. And so that is why Danny (Tyler's secretary) and I have decided to force you both to spend seven days together. I want you to explore your feelings for each other and whatever else may need exploring. Along those lines, I've placed a box of condoms in Tyler's jacket. I will return to pick you both up in seven days. Please don't be mad. You'll thank me later.

Love you, Steph

Thank her? She planned on *killing* her. Lena dropped the letter, her blood pounding and her jaw clenched.

She stared down the darkened road and then back into the cabin. Of all the nerve. What had Stephanie been thinking? This was *her* life. There was no way—absolutely *no way*—she intended to stay here with him all week.

She grabbed the black bag and stormed back into the cabin, tossing it by Tyler on the couch, then went to pack her things up. She grabbed her purse and then froze.

Stephanie had her keys.

I gave that bitch my keys. God, how could I have been so stupid?

"Oh, no. This isn't happening." Lena slid down the inside door of the cabin to the floor and groaned. "I can't stay here with him, I *can't*."

She buried her face in her hands, fighting off the wave of anxiety threatening to overtake her. She took in deep breaths until her heart rate slowed.

When she again looked up, she had regained control.

She eyed the couch curiously, wondering how long Tyler had been out and how much longer he would be.

She stood up on her knees and scooted across the floor until she knelt beside him.

He looked so harmless in sleep. Her eyes narrowed. How deceptive.

The tension eased from her body a bit, and she sighed. Even if he was an asshole, it was good to see him. Even after so many months away, and their last meeting having been just a painful mess, the urge to touch him became too strong.

She lifted her hand to push away a tendril of hair that curled onto his forehead. He groaned and shifted a bit.

Lena jerked her hand back to her side, her heart beating like mad. Would he wake soon? How would he react when he did? And what the hell made him sleep so soundly?

Could he just be really drunk? Or had Stephanie drugged him? She cringed and then brought her face close to his and grasped his chin and upper lip. She pried his mouth open and hesitated just for a moment, then sniffed the cavern of his mouth. Nothing too bad, maybe a little Doritos from lunch or something, but no overwhelming smell of alcohol.

She slid her fingers through his hair, searching for some kind of wound or bump that would indicate Stephanie had struck him to knock him out. The soft strands distracted her, and she groaned, trying to remember her purpose. Nope. No bumps. Not as if she'd expected one. Stephanie might be a bit crazy, but not enough so to actually hit someone over the head.

Which meant she must've drugged him. Lena grabbed his wrist and checked his pulse. She found it, relieved it was strong.

Rocking back on her heels, she stared at him. This was real. Tyler was here and asleep in the cabin.

Damn, tomorrow would be awkward. Although, awkward might be a bit of an understatement. If she were smart, she'd grab her backpack, hike her butt out to the road, and take a risk hitchhiking. Anything would be better than facing him when he awoke.

She stood up and sighed. There wasn't a whole lot she could do now. Going to the linen closet, she pulled out a woven blanket. Twisting the thick blanket in her hands, she made her way back to Tyler before draping it over his still body.

After another lingering glance at him, she went to bed. All she could do now was sleep. Sleep and wait.

The crash woke her. Then came the sound of breaking glass. Lena's eyes snapped open, and her body froze after she'd jerked the blankets up to her chin.

It all came rushing back. Tyler was in the cabin.

Daylight had not yet broken, but she could hear the twitter of birds and the faintest light that suggested dawn fast approached.

She held her breath and stared at the closed door of the bedroom. Tyler was most definitely awake. His curses and footsteps filled the cabin.

"Where the hell am I?" His yell resonated.

Lena flinched, wishing that there were a lock on the bedroom door. Why hadn't she barricaded herself in? Or put the dresser in front of the door as a way to slow him down?

"Where are the damn lights?" He let out a yelp of pain. "Damn it."

Great, he must have stubbed his toe or something. Oh, yes, he was awake and as ornery as a bear.

"There's gotta be a light around here," he muttered. "Wherever here is."

Light appeared through the crack of the doorway, signaling he'd found the switch for the living room. His footsteps echoed in the hallway.

Lena watched the doorknob twist and gave a silent prayer, tugging the blanket all the way up to her nose. *Maybe he'll be too out of it to see me.*

The door swung open, and she bit her lip to keep from groaning. Tyler poked his head in and glanced around. It was silent for a moment, and then he shut the door.

Lena blinked and lowered the blanket and then sat up. He hadn't noticed—

The door burst back open, and she screamed, scrambling to get out off the bed.

Tyler bolted across the room and jumped on the bed, sending her bouncing across to the other side of the mattress.

He grabbed her leg before she could fall off. His hands jerked her back onto the bed as he pinned her down flat on her back, her arms held above her head.

"I'm going to kill you, Stephanie," he growled and then went still. "Lena."

"Umm...yeah. Surprise." She attempted a light laugh. Oh, Lord. He was lying on top of her. She couldn't think with him on top of her. "You're kind of heavy. Would you mind getting off me, please?"

Tyler paused a moment before lifting his body from hers. He swung his legs off the bed and groaned.

"Tyler—"

"I don't even want to know right now," he mumbled. "Don't try to explain, and don't tell me anything. I just really need something for this headache."

"Headache?" Maybe he had been drinking last night. "Are you hung over?"

His head turned and the look he gave her could have frozen boiling water.

Her eyes widened, and she scurried off the bed. "Right. Let me go see if I can find something for you."

She hurried into the bathroom and came back a minute later with two aspirin and a paper cup of water. She sat down on the edge of the bed and handed them to him.

"Thanks." He swallowed the pills and water. Pulling his legs back up on the bed, he stretched his body out and pulled a blanket over himself.

Her breath caught. No way. There was no way she would sleep in the same bed with him.

"Umm, Tyler, this is actually my bed. If you could—" He opened one eye to stare at her, and she broke off.

"Lena, I feel like I got hit by a train. This is a double bed that can fit two, so I'm not moving. If you've got a problem, you go sleep on the stupid couch."

"But—"

He reached up and closed a hand over her mouth. "We will talk in the morning. Now be quiet."

Annoyance sparked in her belly, and she thrust his hand

aside. She glared at him, hoping it would inspire him to change his mind. But he'd already shut his eyes and seemed oblivious to her telepathically yelling at him to get the hell out of her bed.

Her gaze drifted toward the living room and her second option, the couch. The idea of padding across the cool floor and sleeping on the couch with just an afghan held little appeal.

She sighed and lay down next to him, scooting as close to the edge of the bed as possible so their bodies wouldn't touch.

Squeezing her eyes shut, she focused on the image of what she'd say to Stephanie when she came back to pick them up.

The birds were being obnoxious, singing aria after aria outside the window. Lena groaned and tried to block out the noise. To stay submerged in the most delicious dream she was having.

She turned her head back into her pillow and curled her body closer to the warmth. Her hands reached for the fleece blanket, but she encountered a firm barrier. The remainder of sleepiness ebbed out of her body.

Her eyes snapped open, and she stared straight at the crisp, white shirt on Tyler's chest. Her lips parted, and she tried to jerk out of his arms, but he held onto her as if he were a child and she his teddy bear.

Her face burned hot. Thank God he still slept so he would have no recollection of her groping him in the wee hours of the morning. She somehow doubted that had been part of her dream.

She clenched her teeth and once again tried to dislodge his arm without waking him. He moaned and tightened his grip. His other hand slid down to cup her bottom.

Lena exhaled heavily, and her body jackknifed against him. The sharp motion woke Tyler up, and she found herself under heavy surveillance from those incredible brown eyes.

"Good morning." She gave a tight smile. "Would you kindly remove your hand from my butt?"

His gaze lingered on her face for a moment, and then his lips twitched. "I like your butt."

"*Tyler*," she gasped when he squeezed the flesh.

He trailed his other hand through her hair. "Your hair grows fast, you know."

If he didn't stop grabbing her ass, she would do something really stupid. Like sleep with him again. And that could *not* happen.

"Tyler, I am so close to kicking you in a place that would ensure you never have children."

He grimaced and let her go. "Good to see you too, sweetheart."

Sweetheart. The pet name sent all kinds of memories of Europe through her. Bittersweetness tugged at her heart, and she sighed, rolling out of bed.

"So how do I get out of here?" Tyler asked. "Could you drive me to the nearest town so I can take a bus or something?"

Lena closed her eyes for a few seconds and then opened them to meet his gaze. "No. I can't drive you anywhere. Stephanie took my keys."

He stared at her for a moment and then shook his head in disbelief. "Fine. Then I'll walk."

"Probably not such a good idea. We're miles off the main road, and then it's about a forty minute drive to the nearest town."

His nostrils flared. "Are you serious?"

"Unfortunately, yes." She folded her arms across her chest. "Look, I'm no more excited about this situation than you are."

"Do you have any idea how crazy Stephanie is?" Tyler demanded. "She drugged me and dropped me off in the damn wilderness with you. You, the last person I would *ever* want to be alone with."

Ouch. God, that had hurt like hell. Lena forced a smile, so proud that she hadn't winced. "The feeling is beyond mutual." But for different reasons. It was torture being around the man she loved. Especially when the only emotion he had for her was loathing. "How the hell did she get you to take sleeping pills?"

"Drink," he corrected. "She put them in my mocha."

"And you didn't notice? Like, hmm, my mocha kind of tastes like ass."

His eyes narrowed. "I figured you just had shitty mochas out here."

"This is Seattle. Think about what you're saying." Lena bit her lip and shook her head. "The bottom line is, we're stuck here."

"For how long?"

She bit her lip, preparing for the explosion. "A week."

"A week?" he yelled. "Where's the phone?"

"No phone."

"Fine. I'll use my cell and have a taxi pick me up. It would be worth paying four hundred dollars to get the hell out of here."

Lena opened up her mouth to warn him his cell wouldn't work either. No. Maybe just let him figure it out on his own.

A moment later he exclaimed, "Son of a *bitch.* What do you mean, no service?"

He turned and stomped out of the bedroom, then she heard the door to the cabin open and slam shut.

Chapter Twenty-One

Lena showered and had breakfast cooked by the time Tyler returned an hour later. She had just finished her own meal when he calmly walked in through the door.

She had almost convinced herself that he'd hiked to the nearest road and was surprised—and dare she say relieved—when he reappeared.

The situation they were in sucked, but in the shower she'd made up her mind to attempt to be civil. Apparently, Tyler had too, she realized as he sat down at the table without hurling accusations again.

She set a plate of eggs and sausage in front of him. Tyler nodded, the closest to a thank you she would get, apparently.

She watched him pick up a fork and lay into the food before going to pour him a cup of coffee. She set it down next to his plate and took a seat across the table.

"When was the last time you ate?"

"I think I had some chips on the plane."

That would explain the Doritos breath from last night.

"Other than that, yesterday morning." He looked up at her as he picked up the coffee and took a sip.

"Hmm." Lena stood up and went to wash up the dishes in the sink. She listened to his chair scrape back a few minutes later, and then he appeared beside her, setting his plate in the sink.

The hairs on her body lifted, and a tremble moved through

her body.

"Thank you for making breakfast," he said, his breath all too close to her ear.

She licked her lips and almost groaned in disappointment when he stepped away. "You're welcome."

He leaned back against the counter next to her and gave her a thoughtful look. "So I went for a walk this morning and did some thinking."

"Oh, yeah?" Her stomach did that little lurching thing, and she bit down on the inside of her lip to get herself under control.

"Yeah. And I think that since neither of us is going anywhere, let's just agree to call a truce until we figure out a way out of here."

"Okay." *A truce.* Not the words she wanted hear, but better than nothing. "I'm going to go and gather some wood for a fire. At night it can get pretty cold up here in the mountains."

"All right." He glanced around the kitchen. "Do you want some help?"

Lena's fingers fumbled over one of the buttons on her jacket. "Thanks, but no. I wouldn't mind a quick walk alone myself."

She took a deep breath and rushed outside, wanting to put as much distance between her and Mr. Temptation as possible.

Tyler stared at the closed door for a moment and then went to sit down on the couch.

Talk about a nightmare. Spending the next week locked up with the one woman who still haunted his dreams. A woman he still fantasized about at least once a day.

It may have been months, but he hadn't forgotten the smell

of her. The feel of her. The taste of her. The entire damn problem was he just hadn't forgotten.

And now, having her so near to him, knowing she was married and off limits, drove him crazy. If she hadn't been married, maybe even if she'd still been engaged...well, this might have been his breaking point.

He would have bagged all his good intentions and turned all his fantasies into reality to make her understand how made for each other they were.

Stop it. You're doing it again. Tyler cursed and stood up to distract the train of thoughts. If he were going to get through the week, he'd have to get this under control.

The bottom line was that he needed to keep his hands off. Lena belonged to someone else now, and he'd just have to deal with that reality. Like it or not.

In no hurry to get back, Lena spent a couple hours walking alongside the river. Her thoughts lingered on Tyler, despite her intention to put him out of her head.

It was probably for the best that they didn't get involved again. He'd made it clear he didn't love her, and that it had just been sex for him. Besides, a guy like Tyler must have moved on to his next girlfriend by now. Men like him didn't stay single.

After they got through the week, Tyler would leave her again, and she'd be stuck with the same heartache she'd had when she returned from Europe.

She'd come so far. She'd been almost convinced she was on the road to recovery from Tyler. Almost. And then Stephanie pulled this kind of idiotic stunt.

Damn, if Steph were here she would give her a piece of her mind—if not beat her senseless.

But she wasn't here. And Tyler was. Lord, she'd missed

seeing his face. Hearing his voice. This week would be a blessing and a curse. But more so a curse. It was like having the excitement of looking at fat slice of chocolate cake, but knowing she couldn't touch it.

She headed back toward the cabin and grabbed as much wood as she could carry before trudging back to where Tyler waited.

Through the window, Tyler watched Lena ascend the steps of the cabin. Her foot caught on the last step, and she went flying, dropping her armful of logs all over the porch.

He hurried to open the door and found her scurrying around to retrieve them.

She lifted her gaze, running it slowly up his body. And then she burst into laughter.

"Where on earth did you get those clothes?" She covered her mouth, obviously to stifle the giggles.

Tyler frowned. True, he'd replaced his suit with a plaid flannel shirt and jeans that hung too loose on his body, but he didn't look *that* bad.

"You look like a lumberjack."

Tyler raised an eyebrow and leaned over to help her up. "Do you like the clothes? I found them in the closet in the bedroom. I mean, come on, the only damn thing I packed were suits."

"No, I don't suppose you could wear those all week. I think those are Barry's clothes." She wiped her hands on her jeans.

"Barry?" His blood quickened, and his fingers tightened around the stack of logs he'd picked up. Had she taken a new lover on top of being married?

"Yeah. Stephanie's brother."

"Stephanie's brother comes up to your cabin with you?"

Fuck, he sounded like a jealous husband.

"No," Lena gave him a close look. "Barry comes to *his* cabin whenever he wants."

"His cabin." Great, now he just took the idiot of the year award. "Then this is Stephanie's cabin?"

"Stephanie's and Barry's. Their parents left it to them in their inheritance."

"Stephanie has an inheritance?"

"Yes, they both do." She opened the door to the cabin and stepped inside. "That's how she was able to foot the bill to Europe."

"Lucky you."

Lena dumped her load in front of the fireplace and turned around, hands on hips.

"She's a good friend."

"Except when she's leaving you stranded in B.F.E. with some guy you can't stand."

"Except that." Her lips twitched. "And I never said I couldn't stand you."

The expression on her face shifted, became more vulnerable, before she jerked her gaze away.

His pulse kicked up a notch, and his jaw tightened. *Keep it platonic or you'll never get through this week.* Which meant if he didn't get out of this cabin again for a bit, he'd be all over her.

He set down his own stack of logs next to hers. "I think I'm going to take another walk down the river."

"Oh. All right." She lowered her gaze and nodded.

Interesting. She'd almost looked disappointed that he was leaving.

"I'll be back in time for dinner." He headed out the door.

Lena sighed and watched him go. So apparently, the only

way they were going to maintain this truce was just to avoid each other.

She stood and wandered around the cabin, looking for something to do. Why the hell couldn't there be a television in here? Her previous love of the rustic cabin had now turned into a mild irritation. Tyler had her on edge again.

She went in search of the romance novel she'd been reading. That should work to entertain her—she'd left off in a rather entertaining spot in the book.

After fluffing the pillows on the couch and lying back, she flipped open the novel and engrossed herself in a land where orgasms were multiple and happy endings were mandatory.

Twenty minutes later, the main characters were done screaming in ecstasy, the windows had ceased their rattling, and the characters were now falling asleep on one another.

She yawned. Sleep sounded pretty good, actually. With the whole Tyler drama of last night, she hadn't gotten much.

Her eyelids drifted shut, and she took a couple of deep breaths. She didn't realize she'd fallen asleep until something brushed across her stomach and woke her.

"Well, what have we got here?"

Lena jerked upright and reached for the book that had been on her stomach, and then realized Tyler held it in his hand. He stared at the cover of the book, a smirk on his face.

"Will you check out the pecs on that guy? His chest is ten times bigger than the girl's."

"Give me the book back." Lena could feel her cheeks burning up. "And how did he even get her in that position? Bent over a horse of all things—"

"Tyler, my *book*." She reached out to grab it back, but he twisted effortlessly and held it above her head.

"That can't be comfortable, being at that angle. I mean, look at her back. Oh, wait a minute, is that what I think it is?" He squinted and glanced closer at the cover of the book in amazement. "I'll be damned. It sure is. We've got nipple action coming through the dress."

She launched herself off the couch and ripped the book away from him. She glared at him and clutched the book protectively to her side.

"Do you mind?" she demanded. "I'd appreciate a little privacy with my things."

"And I'd appreciate you letting me get a look at what's on the inside of that book." He whistled. "Judging by the cover, that's some hot stuff."

"Didn't you say something about cooking dinner?" she reminded him to change the subject.

"Sure. I can do that." He grinned and turned to walk into the kitchen. "I can see why people love it here. It's beautiful. And I don't think I've breathed such clear air...ever."

"Yeah, I love coming here." Lena stuffed the novel between the cushions of the couch to hide it from him.

She sat for a moment, her pulse beating a little too fast. She enjoyed this. Having him here and being able to have that easygoing nature again. Even if it was only because of a truce.

"Do you want tomato soup or chicken noodle?"

Lena sighed. "Tomato will be fine, thank you."

"Good choice."

Her stomach growled when he returned ten minutes later with the simple meal. Steaming soup, along with a sandwich cut neatly into two triangles, sat on a tray.

"I was going to eat outside on the porch. Did you want to come?"

She took the tray and nodded. "Sure, I'll meet you out there."

Tyler joined her a moment later on the porch swing, sitting down beside her.

His thigh brushed against hers, and the breath locked in her throat.

Truce. We're just friends now.

Drawing in an unsteady breath, she picked up one of the sandwich halves and glanced inside. "Peanut butter and jelly?"

"Yes. I hope that's okay." He took a bite of his half, taking out a good part of it.

"I like peanut butter and jelly. It's good old comfort food. It brings me back to childhood."

"Not mine." He paused to lick a glob of sticky jam that had ended up on his pinkie. "My mom never got off on the whole peanut butter thing. It was either tuna or turkey."

Lena's gaze focused on his pinkie and his tongue, and heat spread through her. "I'm sorry to hear that. Every kid should have peanut butter and jelly."

"Agreed." He finished his sandwich and moved on to the soup. Something tickled her foot, and she glanced down in time to see a squirrel running across the porch.

She shrieked and jumped up. The tray went flying, and her bowl of soup tipped over on her tank top.

"*Hot.*" She jerked the fabric over her head, wiping tomato soup out of her cleavage.

"Lena." Tyler's voice came out on a choke.

She froze. Oh, crap. Had she just stripped down to her bra in front of him? Was she a complete idiot?

"I'm going to shower." She dashed back inside before he could accuse her of doing it on purpose. Of trying to seduce him again.

Her stomach twisted, and she sighed. Why had Stephanie done this to her? They would never last a week.

Tyler stared out at the darkened forest and groaned. He shifted on the swing and adjusted his jeans. Great. He now had the vision of Lena's sweet breasts in his head, and a massive hard-on.

You cannot touch her. She's off limits.

He focused on the sound of the river rushing by the property, tempted to jump in and cool off.

Right now, she was inside taking a shower. Naked and wet. And naked. Wonderfully naked.

He cursed and stood up, picking up both their trays and taking them into the kitchen. He did up the dishes, yawning the entire time.

He must be more tired than he thought. He glanced at the couch and scowled. That thing was too damn short. He couldn't even stretch out.

Lena came out of the bathroom, a robe around her body and a towel over her hair. He could smell the floral shampoo, or soap, or whatever she used.

"I think I'm going to go to bed early," she told him, averting her gaze.

"I was thinking the same thing."

She lifted her head and looked at him, her eyes wide. Something passed between them in that look, and more blood went to his crotch.

She licked her lips and glanced at the couch. "I know that's not comfortable. Maybe we could...put pillows between us and share the bed."

The pillows would be gone by morning. He'd bet his life on it. "Okay." He nodded and cleared his throat. "I'll go brush my teeth. I'll be there in a bit."

He took longer than he needed in the bathroom, hoping she'd be asleep by the time he got in the bedroom.

He stared at himself in the mirror. *You can't touch her. You'll never respect yourself again if you do. The woman is married.*

Setting his toothbrush back into his travel bag—thank God he'd had some necessities—he headed back into the bedroom. Apparently Lena had the same concerns about behaving.

The lights were out, and there were three pillows in a line down the middle of the bed. She had rolled onto her side, facing the other wall, and appeared to be asleep.

Disappointment stabbed in his gut, but he refused to acknowledge it. He climbed into his side of the bed and closed his eyes, willing sleep to come.

Lena groaned, blinking her eyes open in confusion just as her hips jerked. *What the heck?*

Tyler's hand squeezed her ass again, and she bit back a gasp. He had to be awake. Her gaze lifted to his face, but his eyes were still closed, his breathing heavy.

She glanced around and spotted the pillows on the floor. Damn, what a useless plan that had been.

It appeared to be early morning. The room had just the faintest hint of sunrise.

His hand slipped into her panties to squeeze the bare cheek. She groaned and closed her eyes as moisture pooled between her thighs.

Oh, God, she missed this with him. The way his slightest

touch could set her body on fire.

The heat between her legs increased, and suddenly she didn't care if he was awake or not. Sleepy morning sex sounded all too good right now.

You'll regret it thirty seconds after your orgasm. Lena pushed the annoying voice aside and kicked one leg over Tyler's, giving him access to between her legs.

Right away he slid his fingers downward and rubbed against the folds of her sex.

Lena gasped and raised her gaze to his face again. He was very much awake and watching her.

Still holding her gaze, he slid his fingers inside her. Her nipples tightened, and she groaned, digging her nails into his shoulders.

He brought one finger up to rub her clit, spreading the slick moisture over the swollen nub.

She lifted her hips and gasped. "Tyler...please."

His eyes darkened, flickering with some kind of emotion. It almost looked like anger. But then the heat returned, and he rolled her onto her back and straddled her.

He cupped her breasts, molding them in his hands and pinching her nipples.

"Lena. Lord, what you do to me." He lowered his head and covered her mouth with his, thrusting his tongue deep inside.

He stroked her nipples rougher and deepened the kiss, catching her cry of pleasure.

He pulled his mouth away and closed his lips around one nipple, sucking hard.

"Oh, God." She lifted her hips, her sex clenching with the need to have him inside her.

Pushing up her nightgown, he lowered his head to kiss her

stomach. He adjusted his position so that he knelt between her legs.

Lowering his head, he traced the slit of her sex through her panties with his tongue. She closed her eyes and sighed, threading her fingers into his hair.

He continued to rub his tongue against the silk, stroking her clit. Pleasure built inside her, and she squirmed against him, her panties growing damp from more than his mouth.

He tugged her panties to the side, and then his tongue was on her, licking and circling, driving her toward that cliff of ultimate pleasure.

He slid a finger inside her, and she broke. Her stomach clenched, and she closed her eyes, gasping through the waves of sensation that rolled through her.

The warmth of his body over her lifted, and she cried out, opening her eyes in time to see Tyler pushing off his pants and boxers.

He returned to her, threading his fingers through hers and holding them above her head. His erection probed at her entrance before he flexed his hips and sank inside.

They moaned together, and Lena tightened her fingers around his. Lord, it felt so good to have him inside her again. She lifted her hips, meeting his thrusts.

"Lena..." He increased his pace, slammed harder into her, and she wrapped her legs around his waist.

He released one of her hands and reached between them to rub her clit.

"*Tyler.*" She tightened her muscles around him as the second orgasm hit. The room tilted and everything turned fuzzy.

He cried out, and she could feel him empty himself inside her while he kept making small thrusts.

She smoothed her hands up and down his back, tightening her ankles around the middle of his back.

"I love you, Lena." He groaned, pushing deep into her and staying.

She froze. Her hands stopped moving. Had he just...? He loved her?

Hope flared in her heart. Could it be possible? She opened her mouth, but no words came out. She was almost afraid to break the moment.

Fuck. Tyler blinked, slid out of Lena's tight body, and rolled onto his side away from her. What the hell had made him confess his love to her? She was a married woman. *A married woman you just fucked.*

Guilt and depression warred in his gut, and he climbed off the bed and reached for his jeans. He had to get out of this cabin. Now.

"Tyler?"

Her soft voice compounded his guilt, and his jaw tightened. "How far are we from the main road?"

He didn't miss the small choked sound she made, but he kept his gaze averted.

"You're leaving?" The question came out on a tremble.

"I can't do this," he ground out. "Yes. I'm leaving."

Please don't bring up the fact that I said I love you.

"The highway is three miles down the road outside the door." Her voice was flat now.

He turned to look at her but found her rolled on her side facing the opposite wall. The curve of her naked back jerked and then jerked again. Was she crying?

Doubt flickered in his gut, but he shoved it aside. *She's just upset that her plans aren't going well.*

He grabbed his bag and left the bedroom.

Almost to the door, he turned and looked back. *Go. You need to just go or you'll never get over her.*

Turning, he opened the door to the cabin and left her.

Chapter Twenty-Two

Tyler adjusted his bag over his shoulder and shook his head. His feet were starting to ache from walking down the damn dirt road, but the pain didn't compare to the ache in his heart. Damn, how could he have been so stupid? Both of them?

His chest tightened, making it a struggle to even breathe. Once he reached the road he'd have to hitch a ride and ask to be dropped off at the nearest store. Maybe he could get a cab out here. Even if it cost him hundreds of dollars, it would be worth it to get the hell back to New York.

A new thought hit him, and he reached into his back pocket for his wallet. What if Stephanie had taken his credit cards so he'd be truly stuck? He pulled out his wallet and a piece of paper fluttered out with it.

What the hell?

Frowning, he leaned down to pick it up. It was a note. He unfolded it, unease sudden in his gut.

Tyler,

Look, I don't know what happened between you and Lena, but I have no doubt that you guys belong together. I've known Lena my entire life, and I've never seen her so loopy over a guy. So completely and utterly in love. You belong together, and that's why I arranged for you guys to be alone for the week. So whatever it is, an argument, a misunderstanding, I hope you guys can clear it up. You're the reason she didn't marry Keith.

*(And, by the way, I owe you the biggest freaking thanks for that.)
So make things right and don't hurt her. Or I WILL have to kick
your ass.*

   ~ Stephanie

Tyler's heart pounded. His mouth went dry. *No.* Was it
true? Had he just made the biggest fucking mistake of his life?

He turned and glanced back down the tiny road he'd just
spent the last half hour walking.

Lena wasn't married? But he'd...she'd never actually said
she was married. His mind flashed back to their lovemaking
this morning, and how their fingers had been intertwined. *No
ring on her finger.*

"Oh, my God." He tightened his grip on his bag and
sprinted back up the road.

Lena rolled onto her back and gasped in another breath,
unable to stop the sobs that rocked her body. She'd given
herself to him again. Again, when she promised herself she'd
never let it happen.

And now he'd just ripped open the wound over her heart,
the one she'd tried so hard to heal, and this time she was
positive she wouldn't recover.

She swung her legs out of bed and stumbled to the
bathroom. Turning on the shower, she put the spray on the far
end of cold, wanting to jolt any remaining tenderness for him
from her body.

She stepped under the stream and cried out, shivering as
the icy water hit her skin. She ground her teeth together and let
it run over her, taking it as somewhat of a punishment for being
so stupid.

"Never again." She shook her head, sending droplets of water flying.

Goosebumps covered every inch of her skin, and her teeth chattered. The hot tears that spilled down her cheeks were a contrast to the water. Her knees went weak, and she fell to the floor in the shower.

Her body grew numb under the cold water. She pulled her knees up to her chest and wrapped her arms around them, tucking her head down as she sobbed.

The bathroom door smashed open, and the shower curtain drew back.

"Oh, God, Lena." Tyler kneeled down and slid his arms around her, pulling her out of the shower. "What are you doing? Why is the water so cold?"

Tyler was here? He'd returned? Her mind tried to process the information, but her teeth chattered too hard. Her body shook against him as he carried her into the bedroom.

He slipped her bathrobe on her and belted it around her waist. Urging her to the bed, he pushed her beneath the blankets and then slid in next to her.

She blinked, confusion swirling in her head as she stared at him. Already warmth seeped back into her muscles.

"Why are you here?" She tried to compute what was going on. "You left me. You said you never wanted—"

"Why didn't you tell me you weren't married?" He ran a hand down the side of her face.

"Married?" she repeated. He'd thought her married? "I didn't marry Keith. I broke off the engagement the day Keith showed up in Paris."

His eyes closed. The anguish on his face puzzled her.

"Tyler? Why did you come back?"

"I'm so sorry, Lena." He shook his head. "I'm the world's biggest asshole. I thought when you came to New York you were just looking for another fling. And that you were married—"

"But I told you I wasn't looking for a fling," she reminded him, her heart pinching at the reminder of New York. "And the things you said..."

"Self-preservation. I didn't mean a word of it." He cupped both her cheeks now and brushed his mouth across hers, sending more tingling heat through her body. "The only thing real was when I told you I loved you an hour ago."

Her pulse jumped. *He did love her?* "Tyler—"

"I'm sorry, Lena. I'm so sorry." He kissed her again, sliding his tongue between her lips to stroke against hers.

She pulled away. "Tyler, I lied, too. I should have told you about Keith while we were in Europe. And at times I came so close—"

"It doesn't matter, sweetheart."

"Yes, it does. I was in love with you. I was just so convinced you'd think me despicable and I would lose you." Her eyes filled with tears again. "And, in the end, I did."

He stilled and desperation flickered in his gaze. "You love me?"

Lena sighed and wrapped her arms around his waist. "Of course I love you, Tyler. I came to New York to tell you that."

His breath came out ragged against the top of her head. "Damn. I am such an asshole."

"Maybe a little bit." She smiled and gave a soft laugh. "But I wasn't much better."

"You know," he murmured, running a hand down her back. "I think we'd better send Danny and Stephanie a big box of chocolates along with a thank you card. Because I don't think we'd have had a chance in hell without their interference."

"Give that man a raise," she murmured, her pulse quickening. "You know, it's going to be awfully hard. You commuting from New York to Seattle to see me."

"Well. I'm hoping you have a big apartment." He pressed a kiss against her forehead. "Because I'm transferring to the Seattle office as soon as possible and moving in until I can convince you to marry me."

"It's tiny, but I've got a big bed." Warmth moved through her body, and her heart skipped a beat. "And I won't need much convincing."

"That's too bad. I was kind of looking forward to it." His hand slipped low on the neckline of her robe.

"Well, since you put it that way. Convince away..." She smiled and pulled his head down to hers.

About the Author

Shelli is a New York Times Bestselling Author who read her first romance novel when she snatched it off her mother's bookshelf at the age of eleven. One taste and she was forever hooked. It wasn't until many years later that she decided to pursue writing stories of her own. By then she acknowledged the voices in her head didn't make her crazy, they made her a writer.

Shelli currently lives in the Pacific Northwest with her daughter. She writes various genres of romance, is a compulsive volunteer, and has been known to spontaneously burst into song. You can visit her at www.shellistevens.com and join her newsletter at www.shellistevens.com/contact.

SAMHAIN
PUBLISHING

It's all about the story...

Romance

HORROR

Retro
ROMANCE

www.samhainpublishing.com

CPSIA information can be obtained at www.ICGtesting.com
Printed in the USA
BVOW07s1437250713

326956BV00007B/402/P